"There's no love like the first." - Nicholas Sparks

KISS ME First

ANNA B. DOE

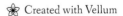 Created with Vellum

BLURB

I fell for Katherine Adams the moment she moved to my small town.

My life has always revolved around three F's – family, friends and football. But when she showed up, I had to think about expanding my list.

Seeing her for the first time was like getting hit in the head by a football. I'd know because that's exactly what happened. The moment I laid eyes on her, I knew she was mine.

Unfortunately, my feelings are one-sided, and Katherine is doing everything in her power to avoid me.

But I'm not a quitter. When I want something, I fight for it. And if I have to fight to make Katherine a part of my life, that's exactly what I'll do.

The rules are simple - I'll do everything I can to show her how good we could be together, but she has to make the first move. She has to kiss me first. But once she does, all bets are off.

Prologue

EMMETT

It's barely seven in the morning but Bluebonnet Creek, Texas, didn't get the memo that summer is almost over and fall is on its way, with school starting in less than a week.

Sweat is dripping off my face, and there is no solace in the light breeze, which is so hot that it makes it ten times worse.

Looking up, I blink the sweat away.

That's when I see her.

I stop in my tracks, completely stupefied. I'm not really sure who she is, which is saying something since Bluebonnet Creek is so tiny you have to know where to look on the zoomed-in map to actually be able to find it, but something about her demands my attention. Dressed in a simple white tee, a pair of jean shorts showing her tanned legs, and red chucks, she passes by the football field with determination a sergeant would be proud of, her thick, dark ponytail swaying from side to side with every step she takes.

"Yo, Emmett," Miguel, my best friend, calls out to me, but I'm too stunned to answer him, my mind still reeling with thoughts of her.

Who the hell is that?

But before I can ask, or go after her to find out, something smacks me over the head. Hard. *Fucking hard.* A zap of pain spreads through my scalp, my hand flying up to cover my throbbing head, but even that doesn't prevent me from following her with my gaze.

Who is that girl?

"You listening?"

I don't bother answering. Instead, I tip my chin in the direction the girl disappeared, asking the question that really interests me. "Who is that?"

Miguel looks up, but the girl's already too far away for him to see her face clearly.

"No idea." He tilts his head to the side. "But she has a nice ass."

This time it's me who's smacking him over the head.

"Hey!" Miguel moans in protest. He rubs the back of his head and turns to glare at me. "What was that for?"

"Watch your tongue, asshole," I hiss at him.

It's irrational. This surge of anger I feel because my best friend is watching a girl I don't even know. A girl I have never met. I never minded it before, but something about this girl...

I shake my head, trying to clear my mind.

"What, you know her?"

I want to roll my eyes at him, but instead, I turn around, watching the little dot that was a girl disappear out of view. "No, but I plan to find out."

"Santiago! Fernandez!" Coach turns and glares in our direction. "You two better start moving your asses, or I'll make you run drills until you puke your guts out."

Chapter 1

EMMETT

"So I told her, I'll decide whenever the hell I feel like I'm ready to decide, you know?" Miguel grumbles as we walk through the busy school hallways on the first day of school.

"Mm-hmm..." I mutter, hoping I sound like I'm at least attempting to listen. In reality, I'm scanning the space in hopes of finding the mystery girl from last week.

I hadn't seen her since that morning when I caught a glimpse of her during practice. Not for lack of trying, either. Every time my family needed something from town, either for the house or the ranch, I volunteered to go and get it so that I could peruse the streets and stores for my mystery girl.

"You're not even listening to me," Miguel grumbles, elbowing me in the gut.

People greet us as we go to our lockers. I nod at some, fist-bump the others, making sure never to linger too long in one place.

She has to be here somewhere.

Why the hell would she come by the school that day if she's not going to Bluebonnet? It just makes no sense.

"Sorry, I'm just—"

"Emmett!" A sugary sweet voice interrupts me before I get to finish. Miguel coughs pointedly but tries to cover it with his hand. Just then, one of our teammates calls out his name, and Miguel joins him, leaving me all on my own.

Asshat.

I turn around just in time to see Rose Hathaway stride toward me in all her charming southern glory. Her dress sways around her long legs as she walks toward me, a big smile on her pink lips. She wraps her fingers around my biceps, plastering herself to my side. "That was some party last weekend."

"Yeah, it was okay," I mutter, not really paying her much attention. My whole focus is on spotting that brown ponytail somewhere in the hallway.

Like most of the people in our class, I've known Rose since we were in kindergarten. She's one of the prettiest and most popular girls in our school, and that's saying something since we're only juniors—but it's not her that has my attention.

Seriously, can somebody get lost in this crowd?

I didn't think it was possible since our school has less than six hundred students. It shouldn't be so hard to find somebody.

"I mean, it's so cool of your family to let us use the pond on your ranch so we can have these parties," Rose continues excitedly, not noticing my distraction. "If they were anyone else's parents, they'd probably freak out or lurk around all the time, but not your parents."

"They're cool," I agree absentmindedly.

Rose chats away, and I listen to her with half an ear, not in the least interested in what she's talking about as we walk down the hallway to our lockers.

Juniors and seniors have their lockers in the west wing, while freshmen and sophomores are in the east. Calling it a "wing" always cracks me up. It's basically just left or right hallway from the entrance, but somebody thought they'd make us sound more sophisticated if we used "wing" instead.

I obviously don't hide the fact that I'm not paying attention very well because the next thing I know, Rose's fingers dig into my skin as she pulls me to a halt. She turns, so she's facing me, placing her palms on my chest.

"Are you even listening to me?" Rose giggles, but the sound comes out forced and unnatural. She's trying to pretend everything's okay, and she's all cheery when in reality, she's quietly freaking out.

Before I can answer her, a movement catches my attention.

The swing of a ponytail.

I suck in a breath. My heart speeds up in excitement, but when I look closer, I realize it's not the new girl but somebody else.

Rose traces her fingers over my jaw, forcing me to turn my head and look at her. "Are you okay, Emmett? You seem completely out of it."

"I'm fine." I sigh and look down at her.

Those big brown eyes watch me expectantly. They're filled with hope and adoration, making me want to run in the other direction.

Fuck, this is about to get ugly.

"You seem distracted. Was it practice?"

I run my fingers through my hair and take a step back. "Practice was okay."

"Then what is it?" The cheery, giggling girl is gone. Instead, her eyes narrow at me, hard and calculating.

"You're a nice girl, Rose. You know that, right?"

My words sound condescending even to my own ears. There is nothing more cliché than the whole *it's not you, it's me* explanation, but there isn't another way to do it. It *is* me.

Her throat bobs as she swallows, and I hate myself for doing this.

Shit, I should never have gone down that road in the first place. I should have known Rose would get the wrong idea, thinking this is more than it could ever be. Becky, one of my best friends, has been telling me for years that Rose has a thing for me, but did I listen? Of course not. Add one too many beers, and having those dark eyes shining brightly in the light of the bonfire one night earlier this summer made me think it'd be a good idea to kiss her.

A little kiss never hurt no one.

Well, wrong.

"Is this the part where you tell me I'm too good for you?"

Of course, she'd think that; after all, she's Rose Hathaway. The mayor's daughter, a cheerleader, and the prettiest girl in town. Any other guy would kick me in the balls just to have her on his arm. But I'm not that guy.

"Something like that." I scratch at the nape of my neck. "I really am sorry, Rose. It was never my plan to hurt you."

Rose sniffles softly, then nods. She tries to smile, but it falls flat. "I guess I should have realized this would happen when you spent the last few weeks ignoring me. But I kept telling myself you were busy with the ranch and then the start of practice."

"You deserve a better guy than me, Rose."

She shoves me away lightly, lifting her chin up. "Damn right, I do. Now, if you'll excuse me, I'm going to the ladies' room. See you later?"

"Later," I whisper as I watch her walk away. I feel like shit for hurting her feelings, but I know it isn't right to lead her on any more than I already did.

In a hurry, she almost crashes into Becky and Miguel, who're turning the corner.

"Hey, watch out!" Becky yells, glaring after her.

Nobody would guess that those two used to be best friends when we were younger. I'm not sure what happened, but one day they just stopped hanging out.

"What the hell's her problem?" Sighing, Becky turns to me. "Did you break her heart or something?"

I bite the inside of my cheek to stop myself from making a face, but of course, she sees it because this is Becky we're talking about. She and Miguel are the siblings I never had. I think she can sniff me bluffing from miles away.

"Oh my God! You did!" She punches me in the bicep. "What the hell did you tell her?" Without waiting for an answer, she turns to Miguel, who's typing something on his phone. "Didn't I tell you? I knew something like this would happen when I saw them hooking up at that party. Rose is so clingy, bless her heart. You kissed her, and she probably saw wedd—"

"Can you slow down?" I shake my head at her. "Seriously, Becs, *breathe*. And no more talking about Rose. You know I don't gossip."

Sighing, I turn around, and both my best friends fall right into step behind me.

"Oh please, you like to think that, but you guys are bigger gossips than all of us girls combined. It's a proven fact."

Maybe if I ignore her, she'll get the memo? Yeah, right. Fat chance of that happening. Still, it's worth a try.

"Proven by who?" Miguel asks from the other side.

"One really smart woman, I'm sure."

I pretend to listen to her as she tells us all the things that guys do wrong as we go down the hallway. I need to grab my books before homeroom starts, but as I'm scanning the lockers to find mine, somebody crashes into me, knocking the air out of my lungs.

I try to reach for them, but it's too late; they're already on the floor.

I open my mouth to apologize, but when I look down, I'm left breathless.

She is here.

Chapter 2

KATHERINE

"Here's your schedule, my dear. And here's the map of the school grounds."

Mrs. Burke, that's how she introduced herself, slides both across the counter toward me. She's an older lady, probably in her late fifties or early sixties. With her short, almost fluffy gray hair, a bright pink suit, and a row of pearls around her neck, she gives me Betty White vibes.

"Junior lockers are in the west wing."

My brows shoot up, but I keep quiet as she indicates the place that I guess is supposed to be said wing to me. When I was walking up to the school, it seemed pretty tiny compared to some of the schools I went to in California, but what the hell do I know?

"Your locker number and combination are in the folder."

"Thank you, Mrs. Burke," I say as I grab the folder off the counter and put it on top of the books I've been carrying.

I need to get my ass to the west wing; otherwise, I'll have to drag all these things around for the rest of the day, and that's not an option. My shoulders already ache from all the extra weight.

"If that's it, I'll go and get myself situated."

"Well..." Mrs. Burke looks toward the door and then back at me. "There was supposed to be a student from our welcome committee to show you around, but I guess she's late."

First west wing and now welcome committee?

Are these people for real? As if I don't draw enough attention all on my own. Why don't we just write "new kid" across my forehead and be done with it?

"That's okay." I force out a smile. "I'm sure I'll manage."

After all, this isn't my first rodeo.

When we got to Bluebonnet Creek, Texas, the welcome sign read a little over ten thousand inhabitants. Seriously, how big of a school can this be?

She blinks, looking a little bit lost. "Are you? I'm sure she'll be here..."

"No, it's fine really. I need to get these to my locker." I lift my hands in the air so she can see the stack of books I'm carrying. "I don't want to be late to class on my first day."

Mrs. Burke pushes a strand of hair behind her ear. "I guess you're right. Well, have a great day, my dear."

"Thank you, Mrs. Burke, you too."

With another smile I don't actually feel, I turn around and go for the door.

The hallway is buzzing with activity, animated chatter and laughter echoing against the tiles as friends reunite after the summer.

Maybe that would have been me in another lifetime, but as it is, we moved so much in the last few years, I got used to packing my things and starting over—not that it actually got easier.

West wing. West wing.

I look left and then right.

Why do people insist on using east and west? Wouldn't left

or right be easier? It's not like I have a compass, for God's sake! Do they even make those things any longer?

Huffing, I turn left.

How hard could it be?

"Oh, damn it."

Shifting my books to my left hand, I flip open the folder on top of it and try to pull out the map Mrs. Burke put inside, but of course, the dang thing gets stuck.

I tug harder.

"Gimme a bre—"

I don't get to finish because I connect with a wall.

No, not a wall.

A living, breathing...

I try to defy gravity, but the backpack full of books that's hanging off my shoulder is stronger than me. It pulls me back, making me fall to the floor. The books I've been carrying in my hands fall down, some landing on the floor while others fall over me, knocking the air out of my lungs.

"I'm so sorry," a deep voice says from above.

Ouch. I blink, sucking in some much-needed air. *That fucking hurt.*

The guy winces, making me realize that I must have said it out loud. "I really am so sorry. Here, let me."

He squats down to my level and starts picking up books and stacking them together.

"It's okay, I was a bit d—" I try to grab one of the books, but his hand is already there. We reach for it at the same time, our fingers brushing together.

Warmth shoots up my arm at the touch, burning my skin. I suck in a gulp of air, my head snapping up. Our eyes lock, his dark irises widening slightly.

Pulling my hand back quickly, I tuck a strand of hair behind my ear. "Distracted."

The guy shakes his head. His light brown hair is cut short, barely peeking out from under the black baseball hat that's turned backward on his head. "I should have watched where I was going."

Grabbing the stack of books, he jumps to his feet easily and extends his free hand down. He's tall even for a guy, probably over six feet. He flashes me a mischievous grin, and I swear his eyes sparkle in amusement. "I promise I'm not going to let you fall."

My heart skips a beat at the sound of his deep voice, my palms turning sweaty.

What the hell is up with that?

As inconspicuously as possible—as if that's even plausible at this point—I dry my hands against the side of my leg before placing one in his.

His fingers clasp around mine, strong and secure. Like the rest of him, his palm is big, enveloping mine completely. A jolt of electricity spreads from his hand and into mine, making my heart beat faster. He helps hoist me up but doesn't let go instantly. Instead, his fingers linger, brushing against the inside of my wrist.

A shiver runs through my whole body, and my blood starts to race. I can feel a warmth spreading through my body and making my cheeks flush.

He looks at me more closely. "Are you okay?"

Nope, not at all.

I pull my hand out of his, stuttering, "S-sure."

Get outta here, a little voice inside my head screams in warning, so that's exactly what I do. I take my books from his hands, making sure not to touch him again, and clench them tightly to my chest.

"Thank you so much for your help," I say, forcing out a smile.

"No problem. Why don't you let me..."

I shake my head, already pulling back. "I'm good, but thanks, seriously."

With one final nod of my head, I rush away, not once turning back, but I swear I can feel his gaze boring into my back all the way down the hallway.

"You're Katherine Adams, right?"

I look up just in time to see a girl slide into the open seat next to mine.

My brows shoot up as I return her curious gaze with one of my own. "Should I be freaked out that you know my name when I'm pretty sure we've never met?"

After living most of my life in California where nobody gives a damn who you are if you aren't some kind of big celebrity worth their while, it's hard to get used to the little looks and whispers behind your back. Something that has happened on more than one occasion since we got here a few weeks back.

The girl throws her head back, her reddish-brown hair swaying as she laughs like my question genuinely amuses her. "What would worry me more is if folks didn't find out about you by now." She turns in her seat, offering me her hand. "Becky Williams." I shake her hand. "And just for reference? This isn't our first time meeting."

"No?"

I try to remember where I could have met her, but I haven't left the house much since moving here, which means I don't really know anybody.

"Nope, I was there when you and Emmett collided this morning."

A mischievous grin and kind, teasing eyes flash in my mind.

"Oh, right."

I'd be a liar if I said he hasn't been on my mind since this morning. He has. It's like I've been secretly looking around just to catch a glimpse of him between all the unfamiliar faces of Bluebonnet Creek High's hallways.

When I look up, I find Becky observing me carefully.

"Right," Becky drawls slowly, which only makes her accent thicken. A smile plays on her lips. "I guess you guys were in your own little world when it happened."

"Something like that, probably," I agree readily, happy to have an excuse for my lack of attention.

"He can be such a klutz sometimes," Becky tsks, shaking her head. "I swear, I have no idea how he ended up on the football team. Out of all of us, he was usually the one who ended up bruised and scraped more often than not."

I hum noncommittally, not sure how to actually respond. Do all the people in small towns like to share information like this? It seems like something that only happens in movies. "You know him well?"

Becky gives me a funny look, one I'm not sure how to interpret. "Girl, we all know each other around here since we were in diapers. Anyway, where are you from?"

"Gossip squad hasn't learned that tidbit of information?" I ask, feigning shock.

Last weekend I went to the store with my aunt, where she stumbled into one of the church ladies, and she interrogated me so thoroughly you'd think I was being questioned by the FBI. Hell, the FBI has nothing on those ladies.

Becky chuckles. "We're so obvious, aren't we?"

"It's okay." I shrug. "Being here will definitely take some getting used to, though."

"Not used to small-town life, are you?"

I remember the ten-story building in a shitty part of Hollywood and the sound of traffic outside of my window.

"Not really," I admit. "Mom was always more interested in the blinding city lights."

"Did your momma move here with y'all?"

Her question throws me off guard for a moment. Mom didn't like the idea of us moving here at all. She didn't even want to come here. Like ever. In my seventeen years, we've never stepped foot into her hometown. I'm not sure what happened to make her dislike this place so much. It didn't even matter. All I knew was that I had to get out of Cali, and this was as good a place as any to be. Not that Mom agreed. We had a huge fight over it, but it was one thing I wasn't backing down on, so she had to give in.

"No." I shake my head. "No, she's busy with a... project. It's just my sister and me."

That gets her attention, and I swear silently. "Is she going to school here too?"

"No, she's in middle school."

"Oh, then maybe she knows my brother, Matthew. He's in middle school too. What grade is she in?"

I open my mouth, but before I can answer, the bell rings, and our teacher strides inside. Thankful for the interruption, I give Becky an apologetic smile while at the same time thanking God for giving me an out.

"Settle down, kids, and let's get to work."

I pull my book out, grateful that this guy doesn't seem the least bit interested in me like the last few teachers did, asking me to stand up and introduce myself. I figured we were done with it, nobody in my previous few schools cared enough, and I rarely bothered since I knew I wouldn't be staying for long anyway.

The teacher starts writing on the whiteboard, but the

marker falls out of his hand. I look around as some laugh quietly while others stare at me, giving me curious glances.

Becky turns to me and rolls her eyes.

I'm not sure what to make of Becky Williams. She seems friendly enough. At least she's talking to me instead of about me, so there's that.

Do I really want to do this, though? There is a reason why I keep to myself, and Becky doesn't seem like the kind of person who'd be okay with me keeping her at arm's length. Plus, there is also her friend.

Emmett.

Just thinking about his name has a shiver running down my spine.

Get a grip, Kate. You're here for your sister, not for cute guys with mischievous grins and shiny eyes.

Chapter 3

EMMETT

I'm good, but thanks, seriously.

What the hell's with that shit?

I watch as Katherine exits the food line, only to stop for a moment and look around for a free table. When she doesn't find one, the frown between her brows deepens.

Since this morning, a few strands of hair have slipped from her ponytail, curling around her face. One slipped into her face, but when she tries to puff it out of the way, it only falls right back.

It looks cute.

She looks cute, all flustered like that.

Yes, I've found out her name. It wasn't even that hard. She's the only thing people have been talking about. Who is she? Where does she come from? Why is she here? What's her deal? There have been dozens of different stories going around, but so far, she has been quiet, mostly keeping to herself. Even now, while she looks around for a place to eat lunch, she does it in such a way as to avoid eye contact with anybody.

I'm good, but thanks, seriously.

An elbow connects to my ribs. "What the hell are you growling about?"

I turn around to glare at Nico, the running back on the football team. "I'm not growling."

He takes a huge bite of his sandwich and mumbles as he chews, "Sure sounds like it."

There are more grunts of agreement coming from around the table as the guys keep stuffing their faces with food. My stomach growls, reminding me that I've been ignoring my own lunch while I was waiting for the infamous Katherine Adams to show up. So far, we haven't had any classes together, and I haven't seen her in the hallway since this morning, but I knew she had to show up eventually.

"That's bullshit. The only thing growling is my stomach," I mutter. To make a point, I lift my cheeseburger and take a huge bite, chewing extra loudly, not that they care about it.

"He's just pissed off that the new girl ignored him," Miguel says, making me choke on my food.

What the hell?

"No shit?" Nico's eyes bug out as he glances at me and then turns his attention to Miguel, who's still talking. Why is Miguel still talking?

"Shit. It all played out right before homeroom when the hallway was full of people. Everybody's been talking about it," Miguel says—always useful, that one. He looks at me and frowns. "Dude, are you okay?"

No, I'm definitely not okay, but I can't say that since the food is still stuck in my throat.

I pat at my chest a few times until I can finally inhale properly.

"She didn't ignore me," I protest, glaring at him. No way I want them to talk shit like that behind my back. "She just walked away to get to her class on time, that's it."

And she didn't even bother to turn back, a little voice reminds me.

"Umm, yes she did, dude." Miguel throws a fry into the air and catches it with his mouth. "Becky and I were there the whole time."

"Emmett Santiago looks after the new girl like she just stole his puppy," John mocks, and I want to smash my fist in his face to shut him up. The guy's been getting more and more on my nerves lately. He's always been irritating, but he's grown intolerable since Coach didn't put him in the starting lineup along with Nico, Miguel, and me, making him the only junior who isn't a starter. Hell, even one sophomore made it.

"Will you keep it quiet?" I hiss, glaring at him across the table.

"Why? I think it's funny."

"Funny?" I repeat slowly, my eyes narrowing at John. "You think it's funny?"

"Well yeah, you always get any girl you want. The hot ones. The ugly ones. Hell, even..."

"I think you better shut up, John," Becky says sweetly, smacking him over the head. "Because Emmett seems like he's ready to jump across the table and bite your head off, not that anybody would blame him."

"Yeah, John, you better listen." I hold his gaze for a moment longer before lifting my eyes to Becky, only she's not alone.

"Scoot over," Becky says, nudging Nico with her hip. "We have company. And for God's sake, can you act like human beings and not animals?" She looks over her shoulder at Katherine, who's standing a few steps behind, looking unsure and out of place. Not that I can blame her, we're a big, loud bunch. "They're not so bad when you get to know them, really. C'mon, Kate, sit down. There's an open chair next to Emmett."

"I can—" Katherine tries to protest, but Becky pushes her toward me, determination written all over her face.

"Nonsense, sit." Becky pulls the chair out and forces Katherine into it. "Emmett will take good care of you. Out of all the guys, he has the best manners. Not that it means much, but hey, they're cute."

"Umm, thanks?" I say, trying to figure out what the hell she's doing, but Becky just winks at me. She straightens and looks across the table, where John is shoveling food in his mouth once again. A frown appears between her brows. "At least some of them. For others, there's no hope."

The guys burst into laughter while John's cheeks turn beet red. Becky shakes her head and goes around the table to her seat between Miguel and John.

Katherine shifts in her seat, nervously pushing the runaway strands of hair behind her ears. Transfixed, I watch how different shades of brown shimmer in the light until she catches me staring.

"Hi."

"Hey, again," I croak nervously, my voice more high-pitched than usual. It's like I went back in time and turned into the pimpled thirteen-year-old kid who barely opened his mouth because he was afraid what sound would come out if he spoke.

Get a grip, dude. She's just a girl, for fuck's sake.

One breathtakingly beautiful girl.

A frown appears between her brows before recognition flashes in her eyes. "Oh, you're the guy from earlier."

I flinch back as if she punched me.

She doesn't even remember me?

Somebody whistles loudly. I'm pretty sure it's Miguel, but I don't bother to turn around to glare at him. No, my whole focus is on the girl sitting next to me.

"Yup, the guy from earlier." I do my best to play it cool. Like it doesn't bother me that she found me so unmemorable while I couldn't stop thinking about her for the past week, looking for her in every dark-haired girl I saw. "You know, the one who you tried to run over?"

"Run over?" Kate's lips fall open in surprise, forming a perfect little O. She turns in her chair to face me. "Wait a minute now. I was the one who ended up with my butt on the floor and things scattered around if I remember correctly."

"So you do remember me," I say, and there is no stopping the self-satisfied grin that spreads over my lips as I lean back.

Miguel, who still doesn't seem to get it, punches me in the side. "I told you she ignored you."

I'm going to kill him. I swear to God, I'm going to strangle him.

Katherine opens her mouth as if to say something, but nothing comes out. Realizing that she's been caught, she presses her lips in a tight line.

"Of course she remembers you! You almost gave her a concussion," Becky chimes in helpfully—seriously, what's with these people today and their "helpfulness"?—and winks conspicuously at Katherine.

I turn to glare at Becs across the table. "Whose friend are you, again?"

She taps the back of her fork against her chin as if deep in thought. "I guess it depends on who's asking."

"I figured as much." I roll my eyes at her. Seriously, I need new friends.

"What? Don't be like that." Becky kicks me under the table. "Us girls gotta stick together. You know I always have your best interest at heart."

"When it suits you."

"That's better than nothing, right?" Becky smiles extra-wide, batting her eyelashes. "Besides, Kate's right. This morning was totally your fault."

Maybe, but there is no way I'll apologize for that. Not when it landed Katherine right at my feet. Quite literally.

"Traitor."

"Stubborn," Becky throws right back. "Anyhow... Kate, these are the guys, guys, this is Katherine, as you all probably already know."

Everybody mumbles hellos, their eyes glued to us like we're some kind of sitcom. That's because we probably are.

"You obviously already know Emmett. The guy next to him that desperately needs a haircut is Miguel."

"Hey!" Miguel protests, running his hand over his curly hair defensively. "What's wrong with my hair?"

"You look like you're in a gang." Becky throws a carrot in her mouth, chews, and then continues. "Then there are Nico and John. And as you can probably guess, since hello varsity jackets, they're all on the football team."

Kate looks around the table, her eyes wide. "All of you?"

I nod my head. "And then some."

My stomach growls loudly, so I pick up my burger and continue to eat.

"This is Texas, babe." John grins, and the need to punch him in the face returns in full force. "Here we live and breathe football. What brings you to Texas, Kate?" There's a low *thump*. "*Ouch!* What was that for?"

"Keep eating, John, will ya?" Becky asks sweetly.

"What? I'm just curious. We don't often get new folk around here."

Becky and Katherine exchange a silent glance. It's kind of freaky, given the fact that they just met.

"See what I was talking about?" Becky sighs loudly.

"It's okay," Kate tells Becky, chuckling softly before returning her attention to John. "We move a lot," she explains and looks down at her plate, stabbing a piece of chicken and salad on her fork. "Currently, we're staying with my aunt for a while."

"Oh, so you're here temporarily?" This comes from Nico.

"What is this? Twenty questions? Give the girl some space to breathe, you busybodies." Becky rolls her eyes. "And they say girls are nosy. Just ignore them."

"It's fine, really."

"It's not, but you better get used to it. It's a small town thing. Everybody around here thinks just because they knew your great-great-grandmother, they have the right to put their nose into your business."

Miguel balls up a napkin and throws it at Becky. "Don't you go pretending you're any different, Becs. You like good gossip as much as everybody else."

Becky pokes her tongue out at him. "At least I don't pester people with stupid nonsense."

Kate looks around the table, her lips twitching as if she's trying to decide whether to laugh or not. For an outsider, I guess it must be entertaining to follow the group dynamics and all the bickering.

I lean down and whisper, "Just ignore them. They've always been like this. I think their rivalry goes back all the way to pre-K. Sometimes when Miguel pisses her off, Becs reminds him of the days when he pulled her pigtails."

"Pester?" Miguel huffs. "The only person who pesters is you with all your nagging."

"Nagging?"

Kate bites into her lip as Becky's voice rises.

"Yes, nagging. Which is exactly what you're doing right now."

"Oh, please, if you had any manners I wouldn't have to nag. But sure, be a dick. After all, that's what you're best at!"

"Whatever." Miguel pushes away from the table and gets up. "I'm out."

"Is this normal?" Kate whispers as we watch him stroll away, tugging angrily at his bandana in the process.

"Oh, yes. They're always like that. Like cat and dog, these two."

Kate hums, taking a bite of her lunch. Becky puffs out a breath and pushes her hair behind her ears as she tries to compose herself. Her cheeks are red, lips pressed in a tight line.

I gently nudge her foot with mine under the table. "You okay, Becs?"

"Sure." She forces out a smile, but it doesn't fool me. She's putting on a brave face, something she always does after one of her fights with Miguel. They've always been at each other's throats, but lately, it seems like they get irritated at each other even easier than before.

Instead of facing whatever just happened, Becky pushes it back, turning her attention to Katherine. "So, how much of Bluebonnet Creek did you see so far, Kate?"

And I'm not the only one who notices. Kate opens her mouth as if to say something but changes her mind. "Not much really. We just got here a few weeks ago."

I pick up my lunch, listening to them talk for the next fifteen minutes. The guys switch to football, and I join in every now and then, but in reality, I'm listening to the girls, interested to find out more about Kate.

"Hey, Emmett!" A few girls greet me as they pass by the table, just as we all get up to go to our next class.

"Ladies," I nod, and they start to giggle.

As soon as they're out of sight, Becky rolls her eyes.

"What?" I ask.

"Nothing." She turns her attention to Kate. "What do you have next?"

"Umm..." Kate smooths some of her runaway strands. "Trig, I think?"

"That's what I have now." I look down at her. I haven't noticed so far, but she's a small thing, probably a whole foot shorter than my six-foot-two.

"Excellent!" Becky claps her hands cheerfully. "Then you can make sure to show Kate to class. We don't want her to get lost. It's her first day, after all."

Kate looks between the two of us, shaking her head. "That's unnecessary. I'm sure you have better..."

"I'm going there anyway."

"See? No need to go alone." Becky smiles brightly. "I'll see you guys later, then."

Everybody waves their goodbyes as they go to their next class.

Shifting my weight from one leg to another, I hoist the strap of my backpack higher. "Is it me, or are you usually this stubborn?" I ask, the question nagging at me from earlier.

"I'm pretty sure I'm capable of finding my own way to the classroom. It has nothing to do with you."

To prove her point, she starts walking. In the wrong direction, no less. My lips twitch, but I school my features as I hurry after her.

"Are you telling me if it were Becky who shared the next class with you, you'd have tried to get rid of her too?"

She turns over her shoulder and glares at me. "Of course not!"

"Then it *is* me," I point out, unsure if I'm happy or disappointed with the confirmation of my suspicion.

"Ugh." Kate stops in her tracks for a moment. "Are you usually this infuriating, or is it me?"

This time I can't help the grin that spreads over my lips. "What can I say? You bring out the best in people."

Kate narrows her eyes at me. "Does everybody usually fall at your feet?"

"Umm... Usually, yeah."

Just not her, apparently, literal falling not included.

"I'm not one of your groupies."

My brows shoot up. "Never said you were. Besides, how do you even know I have groupies?"

"Don't all football players have groupies?" She waves her hand. "Doesn't matter. Either way, you can ease up on the charm; it's not going to work on me."

I look around. "What charm?"

"That charm." She points at my face. "Right there."

"My face? What's wrong with it?"

"Not just your face, but the whole package. Those eyes and that smug grin, ugh."

I chuckle. The grip that was clenching around my gut easing a bit as the meaning of her words set in. "What you wanna say is, you like me, but you don't want to like me?"

Kate huffs, crossing her arms over her chest defensively. "I don't like you."

"Say that again." My grin grows wider. "Try being convincing this time around, Kitty."

She presses her lips in a tight line. "I'm serious."

"Mm-hmm..."

The warning bell rings.

"We should go. I don't want to be late on the first day."

She turns around and continues walking.

I shake my head at her retreating back, laughing quietly. That girl is something else.

"Kitty?" I call after her.

"I'm serious, Emmett, I can't..." She turns around and finds me standing in the spot where she left me.

"What are you doing? We're going to be la—"

"Late if you keep going in the wrong direction," I finish for her. "I know."

Kate blinks, looks in the direction she was going, and then back at me. "You've gotta be shitting me."

"Afraid not." I laugh. "C'mon. As you keep pointing out, you don't want to be late."

She turns on her feet and sashays toward me. Her footsteps are long, hips swaying from side to side as she crosses the distance between us. For a while, I think she'll power through me, but she stops when we're toe to toe, jabbing her finger in my chest. "You did this on purpose."

"Who? Me?" I give her my most innocent smile. "I thought you said you know where you're going."

"I. Hate. You," she says, and to accentuate the statement, she pokes me in the chest with each word.

Laughing, I wrap my fingers around her wrist, stopping her from making a hole in my chest.

"Keep trying, Kitty. Keep trying." With her hand safely in mine, I pull her in the right direction. "Let's go. Time's a wastin'."

Chapter 4

KATHERINE

"Morning," I say as I enter the kitchen and go straight for the coffee maker.

"Good morning." Aunt Mabel turns around and leans against the sink. "Did you sleep well?"

"'S okay," I mumble, grabbing the biggest cup out of the cabinet and pouring the black gold. I drop two sugars into it, then a dash of creamer, stirring the contents before taking a sip.

Heaven.

"Your light was on until late."

I look up at her, surprised by her comment. There is nothing in the way she says it that demands attention. She isn't reprimanding me or nagging, but it still makes me feel unsettled. I'm not used to people actually... caring. Even using the word feels weird in my mind.

Don't get me wrong; I know Mom loves me. That was never the issue. But she's always been too stuck in her own world to ask questions. Random, boring mom questions that I so often hear my classmates complain about. With her, there's always something, her new boyfriend, her asshole boss, or a role she was preparing for and was certain she'd get when she never did.

Mabel is her complete opposite. There are some physical similarities, like our dark blue, almost purple eyes. Bluebonnet eyes, Mom always said. One trait that all Adams girls share. Aunt Mabel also has the same brown hair like Mom and me, only hers is cut in a short, practical bob and is streaked with a few grays, something Mom wouldn't ever let happen. Hell, she's been coloring it platinum for the last decade, insisting blondes are more popular in Hollywood. But Mabel isn't Mom. She's older, dependable, practical. Everything I wish Mom was, but know she never will be.

"Yeah." I run my free hand through my messy hair. "I was working on some homework."

And then I couldn't fall asleep because my thoughts were filled with a boy. And not just any boy.

Emmett.

The way he smiled at me, his eyes crinkling in the corners. The warmth of his hand as it enveloped mine when he pulled me to the classroom. Just thinking about it makes my heart race faster.

"That's good." Mabel nods, taking a sip of her coffee. "How's school going?"

"It's okay." I shrug, not really knowing what to say. School's school. "Different."

Mabel smiles softly, almost regretfully. "Not really used to small-town life, huh?"

"No." I shake my head. "I guess not."

Mom left Bluebonnet Creek the day she turned eighteen, and she never looked back; at least that's the story she always tells.

We've never come here, not even for a short visit. There was always something. Either Mom was too busy with her work, too stuck on her flavor of the month, we were at school, or we didn't have enough cash to fly here, and the bus ride just takes too damn long. There was always something.

I didn't question it—after all, you can't miss something you never knew existed. Until things with Penny, my younger sister, went south this past spring, and this small town seemed like the perfect place to escape to.

I knew that we needed to get away from the toxic environment that surrounded us. A new start, and help, definitely help, but Mom didn't want to hear about it. We fought for weeks, and it wasn't pretty. For years, she's been pushing Penny's issues back, ignoring the fact that she's different and needs professional help.

I'm not sure what she hoped her ignoring would do, but that was Mom. Always pushing problems to the back and hoping they'd solve themselves or disappear. Finally, I'd had it with her, and I promised her that if she wasn't going to let me do this, I was going to do it all on my own, consequences be damned.

Mom, I can deal with, but I wasn't sure Penny could battle her demons. Not without some help.

I'm not sure if she took me seriously or if she was just sick of us fighting, but she gave in, and that was all that mattered.

"It's only been a day; give it some time."

I hum, taking a sip of coffee. "People seem nice. Nosy, but nice."

Aunt Mabel laughs. "They'll grow on you. It's our southern charm."

Southern charm. Dark eyes and a wicked grin flash in my mind. *That's one way of putting it, that's for sure.*

Mabel's phone beeps. She goes to the table and grabs her phone, mumbling something softly. "Do you mind going to check on Penelope? I just got a message that I should come in early if possible."

"Sure, no problem." I give her a curious look as she keeps frowning at her phone. "Is everything okay?"

"Yeah, sure," she says distractedly. Sighing, she locks her phone and looks up at me. "Will you be fine if we drop Penelope first?"

"Of course. I don't mind walking if you have to hurry."

She walks to the sink to rinse her cup before putting it in the dishwasher. "This stupid sink is dripping again," she mutters, probably more to herself than to me.

"I did notice it the other day."

"Charms of living in an old house. There's always something that needs fixing," Mabel sighs. "I'll call a friend and see if he can stop and check it. Just another thing on my to-do list."

"Is there anything I can do to help?" I feel so bad because we're imposing on her, but she didn't even take a moment to consider it when I called her to explain what happened and ask if she would take us in.

"No, that's okay, but thank you, Katherine." Mabel smiles softly.

"Okay." Holding onto my cup, I go toward the door. "I'll check on Penny and get ready quickly."

———

"Are you sure you don't want me to drop you at school?" Mabel looks at the clock on the dash, and although she's doing her best to hide it, I know she's already late.

"Nope, that's fine. You go ahead. I have more than enough time. Might as well stop to grab a cup of coffee on my way."

Mabel turns to face me. "But you just had some."

"Your point being?" I quirk my brow at her.

Mabel laughs. "Fine, go grab your coffee. I'll see you girls later."

Penny and I get out of the car. We wave goodbye as we watch her drive away.

"You good?" I ask, looking at my sister.

Although just a few years separate us, I've always taken it upon myself to be her protector.

Penny nibbles at her lip, her eyes fixed on the school in front of us.

"I guess." Penny tries to smile, but I can see right through her. She's been through a lot—way more than a thirteen-year-old girl should go through—in these last few months. Maybe even longer.

The anxiety I feel every time I think about what could have happened comes rushing back, but I shove it away.

Not now.

I push a strand of her hair behind her ear. "It's okay to be nervous."

"I know. People seem nice, though."

"Do they?"

She nods, her platinum strands tickling my hand. "It feels good to be somewhere where people understand. Where you can belong, just the way you are." She turns to me. "Not that I don't believe—"

"I know exactly what you mean, Penny." I pull her in for a hug, inhaling her sweet strawberry shampoo. "You're amazing, just the way you are. And you will charm the hell out of all your classmates."

"You think?"

"I'm sure." With one final squeeze, I let her go. "See you later?"

"Sounds like a plan. Bye, Kate."

I stay behind, making sure that Penny makes it safely inside. She'd roll her eyes at my overprotectiveness, tell me I'm treating her like a baby—and maybe I am—but she's my little sister, so if I want to make sure she's okay, I'd like to see the person who'll get in my way.

Sighing, I turn to the road ahead.

I mean, how hard could it be?

I ignore the little voice that reminds me of what happened yesterday, as I hoist the strap of my bag higher on my shoulder and start walking.

I haven't been to town much yet, but from the little that I saw, it seemed like one of the towns you can see in Hallmark movies. Picturesque. I think that's the right word.

As I walk, I look around for something that resembles a coffee shop. The main street—it's legit called that, *The Main Street*—is filled with different kinds of little shops that have probably been standing there for ages, owned by the local families. People walk around, stopping to greet their friends and neighbors as they pass. One older man even slowed down so he could talk to somebody who was cleaning in front of his shop.

It feels as if I'm walking in some kind of dreamland or something.

Shaking my head, I look before crossing the street.

Is there no Starbucks here?

I stare at the shop windows and signs until I spot one with a coffee cup.

Bingo.

I hurry up my steps, reaching for the door handle just as the door swings open, and I come face to face, or more like face to chest, with a man.

"I'm so sorry," I say, my cheeks flushing.

"No, it's my fault."

We each move to step out of the way but just end up colliding all over again. Our awkward dance lasts for a little while. I chuckle, moving away from the door. "Well, this is not awkward at all."

The man gets out but keeps holding the door open. He's older, probably in his forties, dressed in a flannel shirt, jeans, and cowboy boots, which I've noticed are something a lot of people wear around these parts. He's tall, but the hat sitting atop his head gives him a few extra inches.

"It's okay, darlin'. Happens all the time." He looks at me carefully. "Do I know you?"

I push a strand of hair behind my ear. "I don't think so. I'm Mabel Adams's niece. You probably know her."

His brows shoot up. The hat is throwing a shadow over his face, which makes it hard to read him. "Mabel Adams, of course, I know her. We went to school together."

"She always had a sweet spot for you, that one," comes from the inside.

"I don't know what you're talking about, Letty," the guy says with a smile, looking over his shoulder just as a small woman comes into view.

"Don't listen to him. It's that Jones charm. Gets to the best of us." She looks at me. "Mabel's niece, you say?"

"Yes, ma'am."

The woman takes me in from head to toe, stopping at my face. "Yes, I can see it. It's those eyes. Bradley, don't deter my customers."

"Yes, ma'am," he echoes.

The woman, Letty, grabs my hand and pulls me inside the little diner. It's nice, cozy, and there are quite a few customers for this time of the morning. "What can I getcha?"

She pushes me into one of the empty chairs at the counter before getting behind it.

"Just coffee would be nice. If you can make it to go, that'd be great." I check my phone. "Gotta make it to school."

Letty's brows shoot up. "You going to Bluebonnet High?"

"Yes, we just got here not that long ago."

I watch as Letty works behind the counter, grabbing a to-go cup and pouring some coffee inside. "Your momma too?"

"No, she's back in California." Letty looks at me expectantly. "Work."

"Oh, right."

I'm not sure if I'm imagining it, but her smile falls a little.

Letty puts the cup on the counter in front of me, then grabs one of the muffins from the display window. "On the house."

"What? Oh, no, I ca—"

"Nonsense." She covers my hand before I can give her the cash. "This one's on the house. Now hurry so you won't be late getting to school."

By the time I arrive to school, the hallways are already buzzing with activity. Keeping my head down, I walk through the people until I get to my locker, where I make a quick exchange of books.

Zipping my backpack, I let it slide back down and close the door.

"You're the infamous Katherine Adams."

"Holy shit." My hand flies to cover my racing heart as I turn around and face the girl that's legit ambushed me behind my locker.

How's that for southern charm? I want to ask, but I bite my tongue as I look at the girl.

She's beautiful. I have to give her that. Dressed in a flirty knee-length dress, her makeup and hair done to perfection, she's what you'd imagine a perfect southern belle to look like.

"And you are?" I ask, my brows rising. Surprisingly, so far, most people have stayed back and watched, commenting on all the things they found out, or they *thought* they found out about me, behind my back.

Two girls behind her exchange a look. They almost look like perfect carbon copies of the one standing front and center.

"Rose Hathaway."

Her tone might be soft, but there is an underlying bite to it that indicates it's something I should have known.

So much for the warm welcome.

"Well, nice to meet you, Rose." I look up and add, "And friends. Now, if you'll excuse me, I have a class to get to." I smile as I walk around her.

"Wait."

I stop, debating if I should actually listen. But then I remember this is a small town where everybody knows everybody, as I just witnessed, and I'm the odd one out. Maybe her mom or somebody is friends with Mabel, and the last thing I want is to offend somebody or cause trouble for my aunt.

"Yeah?"

"I'm a part of the Bluebonnet welcome committee, and I just wanted to wish you a warm welcome to our school." Rose smiles sweetly. "I wish I were there yesterday to help greet you, but something came up."

So, she's the one who ditched me.

"No problem, really. I found my way around."

I'm about to get on my way when her words stop me yet again. "Yeah, I saw you were sitting at the football table."

The way she says it has goosebumps rising on my skin. "Oh, did you?"

I knew people were watching; hell, they're still watching as this unfolds. I can feel their curious eyes on me, but the way she says it sounds like she's implying something that I can't decipher.

"You're the only thing everybody's been talking about. It's a hard thing to miss."

There it is again, that tone. I'm not sure what she's trying to get at. Oh, I know all about high school hierarchy and cliques, but I never thought too much about it. I don't care about popularity, who's hanging out with whom, or who's sitting at what table. Hell, I wouldn't even have gone to that table if it weren't for Becky, who was in the line behind me and saw me looking for an available place to sit.

"Well..."

Before I can think of what to say, Becky slides next to me as if I called her out of thin air. "Pull in your claws, Rose. There is no actual territory for you to mark."

A frown appears between Rose's perfect brows. She crosses her arms over her chest, a sour smile twisting her lips as she takes Becky in.

"Becky Williams, I'm not sure I understand what you're talking about."

Becky rolls her eyes at Rose. "Oh, you understand all too well. Let's not fool ourselves."

Rose huffs and flips her hair over her shoulder, lifting her chin up just a tad to look at us down her nose. "No, I don't think I do." Tuning Becky out, she turns toward me. "Well, I'd love to show you the school and town, give you a proper welcome. You should join us for lunch today and we can discuss it."

"I—"

Becky loops her arm through mine, pulling me closer. "I don't think it'll be necessary. She already has a place to sit, Rose." And then, if that wasn't clear or territorial enough, she adds, "With us. At the football table."

The tension fills the space between us so much it's almost tangible. Rose's lips twitch. She looks at me as if waiting for me to say something different and accept her offer. She seems like one of those people you shouldn't turn down. It's a shame I'm not one to give in easily.

"I guess I have a place to sit." I shrug helplessly.

Rose's eyes narrow at me. "Fine. C'mon, girls."

As one, they turn and sashay away, leaving Becky and me standing by my locker.

"Did they practice that trick in the circus?"

Becky turns to me, eyes wide. We exchange a look and burst into laughter so hard people start turning in our direction to see what's going on.

"I can see we're going to be very good friends." Becky bumps her shoulder into mine playfully. "And to answer your question, I wouldn't be surprised. Just ignore her. She hates that she's not the center of attention *and* that she was never offered a place at the football table." Becky shakes her head. "Welcome committee, my ass. People move here once in a decade or so."

Together we start walking down the hallway.

"She doesn't seem to like me," I point out.

Becky waves her hand nonchalantly. "Rose doesn't even like her own reflection. Plus, you've got Emmett's attention."

I raise my brows. I try to act casual, but there is a slight twist in my stomach. "Are they a thing?"

"Rose and Emmett?" Another shake of her head. "Only in her dreams, bless her little heart."

Becky seems certain, but something about the way Rose was looking at me makes me question if there is more to it than meets the eye. Either way, I can see that Rose has trouble written all over her, and there is no way I'll get in the middle of it. The last thing I need is to start off by making enemies in a place that should be our sanctuary.

Chapter 5

EMMETT

"All I'm saying is, maybe we should do something together as a team." Nico nods his head and takes a huge bite of his sandwich.

"We have a good ratio of seasoned versus new players, but it would help us mesh better out on the field," Tim, our quarterback, adds. "What do you think, Santiago?"

I swallow my bite and look at the expectant faces around the table. It's a bit unnerving, the way they all look up to me like I hold all the answers. I didn't sign up for this. I'm just a guy who wants to play the game he loves. But that's not how it works.

"I mean, it wouldn't be a bad thing," I agree, already trying to figure out when I'd be able to put that in my schedule.

Although my parents don't expect me to help on the ranch, and more often than not, they tell me to concentrate on school and football, I love doing it. I love working out in the fields, side by side with my dad. There is something peaceful about working on the land and tending to the animals. It's grueling work, but at the end of the day, satisfying.

"Maybe we should try and figure out what kind of activity..."

"I have something in mind."

All eyes turn to John, and the asshole is eating up the attention. "Some kind of outdoor adventure rink opened on a farm between Bluebonnet and Bravo. They have paintball, among other things."

"Hell, yeah!"

"Sweet."

More agreement comes from people sitting at our table as they start talking about logistics, like on what day we should go.

"Why so quiet?" Miguel asks, nudging Becky with his elbow. She's been looking over her shoulder since we sat down.

"Huh?" Becky turns her attention to the table.

Miguel tips his chin toward the entrance, chuckling. "Why are you glaring like that at the door? You'll crick your neck if you keep at it."

The guys are still immersed in their discussion about paintball, and they barely pay us any attention.

"Just looking for somebody."

There is a frown between Becky's brows as she stabs her fork into her mac and cheese. If there is any indicator she's acting off; it's the way she tries to kill one of her favorite meals.

"Does that somebody's name start with a K?" Miguel asks, chewing loudly.

Becky's nose furrows in disgust. "What if it does? Worried I'm going to replace y'all with somebody with better manners?"

Miguel rolls his eyes. "Yeah, right. Fat chance of that happening."

"You just keep thinking that." She peeks over her shoulder once again. Not that I can blame her. My own gaze has strayed toward the door more times than I'd like to admit in the last couple of days, but Kate is nowhere to be seen. "She should have been here."

"Who?" John looks around the cafeteria.

"Kate," Miguel explains, not even bothering to avert his gaze. "But seriously, why are you so stuck on her?"

"I'm not stuck on anybody, Miguel. I just like her." Becky's answer is followed by another hard stab at her pasta.

"I think Becs has a girl crush on her or something," Miguel sing-songs.

"Like, *like* her, like her?" John wiggles his brows. "I didn't take you for that kind of girl, Becs."

Becky balls up her napkin and throws it at Miguel's head.

"You two are disgusting. She's my friend." She pushes off the table and stands up. "I think I need some air."

"Becs, don't..." I try to stop her, but she's already walking away.

I turn my attention to Miguel and John, who are still snickering. I extend my leg and kick one of them from underneath the table.

"*Ouch*," John protests. "What was that for?"

"What was that for? Seriously?" I glare at them, shaking my head.

I expect shit like that from John, but not Miguel.

"What? I was just—"

"Save it." I get up. "I'm going to check on her."

I grab my backpack and throw it over my shoulder, picking up my half-eaten tray off the table.

"It was just a joke," Miguel calls out after me.

I look over my shoulder. "Maybe you should be careful with things you joke about."

I walk across the room, ignoring all the people who call my name and dispose of my tray before heading out into the hallway.

There are still ten-ish minutes left of the lunch hour, and most of the people are either in the cafeteria or in class, so the hallway is almost empty.

Except for Becky, that is.

She lifts her head when she hears the door open and close, but sighs when she realizes it's just me.

"He makes me so mad sometimes," she says quietly, her fingers curling into fists.

"He can be a real asshole sometimes," I agree, leaning against the wall next to her but making sure to keep my distance in case her fists start flying. "Most guys are."

"Not you." She thinks about it for a moment. "Well, at least not toward me."

I poke her softly in her side. "I tease you, too."

The corner of her mouth twitches, but she bites the inside of her cheek to prevent from laughing. Instead, she swats my hand away.

"There is a difference between teasing and being an asshole."

"There is also a difference in how you react to different people." I push off the wall and turn to look at her. "Who are you really angry at, Becs?"

Her brows furrow. "What do you mean?"

"Who are you angry at?" I repeat slowly, wanting her to understand. To look at this situation from my perspective. While, yes, Miguel and Becky have always been at each other's throats, it was all just teasing. But lately, it feels different.

"Miguel, of course..."

"But not John?"

"John is just being John."

I raise my brows. "Yet, you're angry with Miguel?"

She huffs and crosses her arms over her chest. "Your point being?"

"That maybe you should ask yourself why it makes you so angry when Miguel says something, but John's just being John."

"I expect better from him. I—" Becky presses her mouth in a tight line, the words dying on her lips.

"Just think about it." I push a strand of her wild hair behind her ear. "I don't want to see you get hurt, Becky."

I don't want to see either of my two best friends hurting, and that's exactly what they're doing. Only it's worse because they're fighting against each other when it was always us against the world. I don't know what to do about it, how to make it right.

Becky forces a smile out. It's small, barely visible, but it's there.

"My feelings are bruised, that's all. I'll be fine." She looks at the door leading to the school backyard. "I think I'll go out. Get some air."

"Want me to come with?"

"No, I just need a moment alone."

"Okay." I pull back, letting my hand drop to my side. "But if you need anything, I'm here."

"I know." Becky gives my hand a squeeze. "Thanks, Emmett."

With that, she walks away.

Lifting my hat off my head, I run my fingers through my hair. They better figure their shit out, and fast, because otherwise, they'll drive us all insane in the process. I wait until she's outside before letting out a sigh.

I push off the wall and start walking down the hallway.

Might as well go to my next classroom.

The hallways are still quiet, but that will change soon enough, and I don't feel like talking with anybody.

I peek through the little window in the door of my classroom. I don't want to barge in only to find there is a class underway. But the classroom is empty.

Well, almost empty.

Turning the doorknob, I enter the room. Kate is sitting in her seat, her back to me.

So this is where she's been hiding.

Her head bobs to the music that's playing in her ears as she scribbles something down in the notebook in front of her.

Closing the door behind me, I move forward. After all, my seat is right next to hers since those were the only two left that first day when we came in together.

"Hey there," I say, putting my hand on Kate's shoulder. She jumps at the touch and turns around to glare at me, her hands covering her chest.

"Jesus Christ!" Kate whisper-yells and pulls out her earbuds. "Why does everybody keep doing that?"

"Doing what?" I look at her, confused, but she just shakes her head.

"Never mind. You were saying?"

"Nothing." I take my seat next to her, letting my backpack slip to the ground. "I'm just surprised to find you here, that's all."

Her cheeks blush, and she looks away, slipping a strand of her hair behind her ear. I've come to realize it's a nervous habit of hers. Something she does when she knows she's guilty of something but doesn't want to admit it. But it has a completely different effect, or maybe it's the right effect all along.

Her face opens up, rosy color creeping up her neck and over her cheeks. The curved bow of her lips and thick dark eyelashes cast a shadow over her cheekbones. I want to reach out and trace that line with the tips of my fingers, see if it feels as soft as it looks.

"And where would I be?"

"Not sure, but you've been MIA the last few days." I shrug. "Maybe you got scared of small-town life and ran away?"

Kate tilts her head to the side, those dark blue eyes looking at me. "Are you telling me you guys are so scary you ran people out of the town before?"

I nod my head, trying to keep a serious face on. "The scariest."

"Oh yeah? Who else did you manage to run off?"

"People here and there." I lean in to whisper conspiratorially, "Didn't you know? The small towns are usually the ones hiding the biggest secrets."

"Oh, please." Kate rolls her eyes but laughs nonetheless. The sound, low and melodic, leaves me breathless.

I shake my head. *Get a grip, Emmett.*

"But seriously, this is where you've been hiding?"

I didn't really know what to think when she didn't show up. I was disappointed, sure, but I managed to hide it better than Becky. At least, I hope I did. I probably would never hear the end of it if the guys caught me moping, so I guess I'm safe. For now.

I have to give it to Kate though, it takes some serious skill to hide in our school, so there is that.

"I haven't been hiding," she protests.

I lift my brows at her and wait. It doesn't take long.

"I haven't," she insists. "I just needed a little breather, that's all."

"And that breather was just supposed to be during lunch these past few days?"

"I can't exactly ditch school in general, now can I?"

I pretend to think about it for a moment. "I mean, you could have, but I see your point. Becky was disappointed, though."

I feel like a dick as soon as the words are out of my mouth because Kate's face falls.

"It wasn't my intention to hurt her feelings, but this is all just... too much, I guess? I can feel people stare, hear their whispers behind my back. I'm not used to it, and I don't particularly like it. Hallways are manageable because we're all rushing to one place or the other, but during lunch..."

I nod my head in understanding. I can't imagine how she must feel with all the attention on her.

"Well, I just wanted to make sure you're not running away from me and my famous charm." I grin.

"Yeah, right." Kate rolls her eyes at me. "If that's the scariest thing about Bluebonnet Creek, I think I'll survive."

"I don't know about that. You looked pretty scared the other day."

"In your dreams, buddy."

We just stare at one another for a while. There is a small tug at the corner of her mouth. It's not a smile, not exactly, but it's a beginning.

I open my mouth, wanting to tell her just what my dreams have been about since she came to town, but the door opens, letting in the cacophony from the hallway as people start rolling in.

We pull back instantly, each of us turning forward in our seats.

"Hey, Emmett!" Tim yells as he takes his seat two rows behind me. "We agreed on this weekend. John will call to see if they can fit us in, but I figured I'd tell you."

Paintball, right. Can't forget about that.

"Sounds like a plan. Keep me posted."

Chapter 6

KATHERINE

"Katherine Adams!"

I turn around and find Becky storming toward me, determination written all over her face. When Emmett told me yesterday that she'd been waiting for me to come, I felt like the worst person ever. It's not Becky's fault that I don't like to be the center of attention. She's been so nice to me since the first day, and the last thing I wanted was to hurt her feelings.

Sighing, I stop to wait for her. It's not like I'd be able to escape now that she's seen me anyway.

Becky stops a few inches away from me, propping her hands on her hips. I wait for her to rip me a new one, but she just tilts her head to the side and purses her lips. "That doesn't sound half as threatening without adding your middle name to it, dammit."

She seems so serious, and I can't help but start to chuckle. "I'm sorry to disappoint you, but I don't have one."

"You don't have a middle name?"

"Nope, just Katherine."

Becky narrows her eyes at me. "Everybody has a middle name."

"Not me, I'm afraid." I shrug. "But I can invent one if it'll make you feel better."

Becky sighs. "Doesn't matter. The effect is lost anyway." She hooks her arm through mine, and together, we start climbing the stairs to the school. "However, you, missy, have some explaining to do."

"I'm sorry about missing lunch," I say instantly.

No sense in beating around the bush, now is there?

Becky stops and looks at me. "How do you know about that?"

Somebody that was walking behind us crashes into us, stopping me from responding. I stumble a little, and Becky has to put her hand on my shoulder to help steady me.

"Hey, watch where you're going!" the person protests, the irritation clear in their voice.

A somewhat familiar voice.

Becky turns around. "Well, you're the one who crashed into us, Rose."

Yup, I knew I recognized that voice from somewhere. Slowly, I turn around.

Rose pushes a lock of her hair back into place, glaring at us. "Maybe if you didn't block the entrance, I wouldn't have."

Just then, the door opens—the second wing of the big double door—and a girl walks out, giving our little group a curious glance as she passes by.

"Again, if you watched where you were going, you'd see there is this whole other door available for you to pass through," Becky says sweetly, pointing at the place where the girl just exited.

I nibble at the inside of my cheek to prevent myself from bursting into laughter. The sarcastic Becky always manages to crack me up. Rose apparently doesn't feel the same because I can see the fumes coming out of her ears.

Rose takes a step forward, getting in our space. "Listen you..." she starts, pointing her finger at Becky as her voice drops low.

"Hey, I didn't realize we were meeting up in front of the school today."

A shiver runs down my spine at the sound of his voice. Rose immediately takes a step back as Emmett joins us, his eyes taking in our group.

"Ladies," he says, nodding at Rose and her friends.

"Hey, Emmett." Rose smiles extra wide as she looks at him. It's unnerving the way she can just flip the switch and turn into a completely different person when she's talking to him. "How is practice going?"

"Good." He nods, a smile on his face. "We're getting there."

"I'm sure you guys are going to be amazing." She puts her hand on his bicep, giving him a squeeze. Seriously, can she be any more clingy? She's so obvious.

"They're already amazing." Becky loops her arm through Emmett's, brushing Rose's off. Rose's smile falls, and I have to admit, I enjoy every second of it.

I'm not sure what the deal is between Rose and Becky, but there is some serious history between these two. Ignoring Rose's scowl, Becky tugs Emmett toward the door. "Let's go inside. I have to grab my books before class."

Emmett looks between Rose and Becky one last time. If he can sense the tension in the air, he doesn't say anything. "Sure thing, Becs."

He pulls the door open for us, and Becky waves me over. "C'mon, Kate. We don't want to be late."

"Kate," Emmett says as I pass by him. His voice is low and husky, barely a whisper.

"Emmett."

Amusement dances in his eyes. "I see that Becky finally got her hands on you."

I open my mouth to reply but don't get a chance.

"And I'm not letting go until she promises that she'll join us for lunch today." Becky jabs me in the arm before turning her attention to her best friend. "And you shouldn't have told her that I was upset yesterday."

"I said no such..." Becky gives him a pointed look. "I haven't!"

"Then why did she apologize?"

Emmett turns to me for help, but I just shrug. His eyes narrow at me. "Because she felt so bad for missing lunch?"

A group of young girls, probably only freshmen, passes us by, and they greet Emmett on their way. Seriously, how is this real? Does he also have grannies and babies wrapped around his finger?

"Well, I don't want anybody's apology if they don't mean it." She looks between the two of us, settling finally on me. "As for your reluctance, I really do get it, but the only way people will stop talking is when they get used to you, and they can't do that if you're hiding away, God only knows where."

"I guess you have a point there."

"Of course I do." Becky grins.

"So humble," I tease.

"Do you see now what I have to deal with every day?"

I turn to the side to look at Emmett. "Poor baby, I'm not sure how you manage."

Our eyes lock, and I can see the amusement dancing in his irises. They are brown, but from up close, I can see a few deep green speckles scattered over them.

"Neither can I."

The warning bell rings, breaking us from our eye lock.

I look away and take a step back. "I guess we better hurry to our classes."

"Kate?" Becky calls out, making me stop in my tracks.

"Yeah?" I tuck a strand of hair behind my ear, turning toward her.

She's watching me with a big smile on my face. "You forgot something."

"Fine," I sigh. "I'm going to join you for lunch today."

Becky looks at me expectantly, tapping her foot, her smile not wavering.

Emmett leans down and whispers in my ear. "You have to promise."

His warm breath touches my skin, sending a current of tingles running through my body.

"I promise," I add, my voice coming out breathy.

"Great!" Becky claps her hands. "Now that's settled, I'll see you guys later."

Emmett and I stay by my locker and watch Becky leave.

"She's something else."

"She most definitely is," Emmett agrees.

***

"Look who's here again." I look up to find the guy from last week standing by my table. Bert? Ben? No, Bradley.

Bradley Jones.

The same cowboy hat he was wearing then is sitting on top of his head; this time matched with a different plaid shirt, washed-out jeans, and cowboy boots.

"It's the only place that sells coffee in town." I lift my almost-empty coffee cup in the air and take a little sip from it.

"Ain't that the truth," he chuckles. "I guess you're used to something more fancy, though, coming from California?"

My brows shoot up. I don't remember mentioning where I was living before, but then again, this is Bluebonnet Creek we're talking about. For all I know, he probably heard it from somebody while he was stocking up on milk at the store.

"As long as it's good coffee." I shrug, letting the rest of the sentence hang in the air.

"Letty's good people." He looks at the table, where my books are scattered around, taking up most of the surface. "School done?"

"Yup, I figured I'd grab some coffee and finish my homework here before I have to go pick up my sister."

I grab my phone to check the time.

"Oh, shit." I jump to my feet and start closing the books and shoving them into my backpack.

"Is something wrong?"

"The time just got away from me, that's all."

Putting one last book into the bag, I zip it and drink the rest of the coffee. No sense in wasting good fuel.

"Are you in a hurry?" He throws his finger over his shoulder. "My truck is right there—"

"It's fine, really. It's not that far, so I should be good."

"If you're sure."

"Yup. But thanks." I slip the strap over my shoulder. "I guess I'll see you around."

He looks at me for a moment, a serious expression on his face. "Yeah, sure."

With one last smile, I push my chair back into place and hurry outside. I don't like Penny to wait for me any more than she has to.

Once outside, I look both ways before crossing the street and hurrying toward Penny's school.

It takes me roughly fifteen minutes, and Penny is already

sitting on the bench outside, her golden retriever, Henry, lying by her side.

"I'm here," I pant as I stop in front of her. "I lost track of time."

"It's okay." She gets up, pushing a strand of her blonde hair behind her ear.

Most people don't think we're related, not with her being blonde and fair-skinned, and me dark-haired and tanned, but if you look closely enough, you can see the small resemblance that we both get from our mom's side.

"How was the piano lesson?"

"It was good!" Penny beams. "I had so much fun. Miss Ginny said if I practice this piece and play it to her from start to finish without a hitch, we'll switch to something harder next time."

"That sounds like fun." I loop my hand through hers. "You can practice when we get home to show me what you've been working on."

"Sure thing! Henry," Penny calls, her grip tightening on the harness. "Let's go home."

Chapter 7

EMMETT

"Everybody ready to go?" I ask, looking around to count if all of our teammates got here.

"Not yet." John doesn't even bother to lift his head, all his attention on his phone and the message he's typing.

I frown, my eyes scanning the space. "But everybody's here."

Just as I say the words out loud, more cars start to pull in.

What the—

"Hey, guys!" Rose calls out as she slides out of the car, followed by more girls from school. All of them on the cheer team.

"What are they doing here?" I hiss quietly, looking at Miguel.

He lifts his hands in the air defensively. "Don't ask me. This wasn't my idea."

"That wasn't the plan." Tim's appreciative gaze takes the girls in. "Do they actually plan to participate wearing that?"

Some of the girls are wearing dresses, others shorts and skirts. Seriously, what were they thinking? And how did they know we'd be here?

"They wanted to come," John says—as if that explains everything—and goes to greet them, but I place my hand on his shoulder and pull him back.

"And you let them?" Is this guy for real? "What happened to team bonding?"

John's eyes narrow into tiny slits, the irritation rolling off of him in waves. He shrugs my hand off and glares at me. "They're cheerleaders. If that doesn't make them part of the team, I don't know what does."

Plastering a smile on his face, that fucker, he goes to greet the girls.

"Easy now." Miguel places his arm around my shoulders. To most of the people, the move would look casual, but we both know he's actually the only thing that's holding me back from pummeling some sense into John with my fists.

"I seriously can't stand the guy."

"It is what it is." Tim shrugs. "Not like we can ask them to leave."

Not like he actually looks sorry about how things turned out. Do they all think with their dicks? I rub my temples, feeling a headache approaching. Of course, they do.

You wouldn't be this irritated if the one person you wanted to see were here.

I look up and scan the crowd, but as expected, only cheerleaders are here. So, no Kate and no Becky.

Rose catches my eye and lifts her hand in a little wave. One of her friends leans in and whispers something in her ear, both of them laughing.

"I guess not."

"Look on the bright side." Miguel slaps me on the shoulder. "Now we'll suit up, and you can kick his sorry ass in paintball."

That does sound appealing.

"Yeah, I guess you're right."

Together we join the group of our friends, who are already discussing who's going to be on what team.

"I guess that leaves Frannie and me on your team." Rose turns around with a big smile on her face.

"You're playing?" I ask, surprised.

Some of the girls decide to stay on the sidelines to cheer us on, but a small number of them have opted to participate. I didn't expect Rose, of all people, to belong to the second group.

"What's with that face?" Her hand brushes my upper arm. Rose leans in, her voice dropping so only I can hear her. "We're still friends, right?"

I look down at her expectant face.

"Sure, Rose. Friends."

A smile spreads over her lips. "Amazing! Let's go kick some butt."

KATHERINE

"There's a little flower shop just on the corner," Becky says, pointing in the direction of the shop. "Mrs. Timothy has owned it for as long as I can remember. And across from her works Mr. Wilson. Technically his son owns the place now, but old Mr. Wilson still comes by every day." She leans in and whispers conspiratorially as the old lady in front of the shop lifts her head, shields her eyes from the sun, and after a moment waves at us. "I think it has more to do with Mrs. Timothy than his shop." Becky waves back. "Hi, Mrs. Timothy!"

"Do you know everything about everybody?" I laugh.

"Just about. And that sums up the tour of Bluebonnet Creek." Becky turns around and takes my hands in hers. "Can we go eat ice cream now?"

"Sure thing."

"Yes!" Becky fist-pumps and starts dragging me back up the street.

"You're the one who insisted on doing the tour first," I remind her.

"Well, you can't live here and not know anything!"

I guess she's right. This place is our home now, might as well start getting used to it.

"For what it's worth, thank you for showing me around. Bluebonnet is a lovely town."

"Well, I've gotta show you all the good stuff before they chase you away with their questions. But, you're welcome." She tips her head to the side. "C'mon, let's get that ice cream before I melt from this heat."

The walk to the shop is short, thankfully, because it feels like it's hell outside. When we get to the little ice cream shop, Becky pushes the door open, and we enter. A blast of cool air hits me in the face instantly, making goosebumps appear on my skin.

There is a group of kids in front of us, so we wait in line while a girl who looks like she's a few years older than us serves them before getting our own ice cream.

Once we each get two scoops, we go back outside and find an available table on a little terrace overlooking the main square.

"Seriously, you're so lucky to have a sister. My brothers drive me crazy all the time! Can you believe my younger brother actually locked himself in the bathroom just so I couldn't finish getting ready? I swear, one of these days, I'm going to strangle him."

"That seems like a typical boy thing to do." I laugh at the image of Becky pounding against the door and yelling at her little brother. She wasn't joking when she said she's surrounded by boys. I scoop some ice cream and put it in my mouth. "Oh, my Gawd." I close my eyes to savor the rich chocolate taste.

"Good, right?"

"Amazing."

"It's the best ice cream in the whole county," Becky says proudly.

"I'll take your word for it. Is every flavor this good?" Not waiting for her answer, I scoop a little bit of cherry ice cream.

"Yup, I've tried them all, and I can never settle on which one's my favorite."

"Can't blame you. This is so good! You should have started the tour here."

"As if! I knew if we started from the ice cream shop, I wouldn't get you anywhere else today."

"It's good ice cream."

"That it is." Becky nods. "I'm actually glad that we got to spend some time together outside of school. Without boys too. I love those guys but they drive me insane." She looks up at me. "I just realized I say that about all the boys in my life."

"Well, if the shoe fits..."

"Oh, it does. But it's all I've ever known." She shrugs. "I live on a smaller ranch between Emmett and Miguel so it's always been the three of us together. You know, before we went to school. Then there are my brothers, of course. It's nice to have female company for a change. You know, somebody who doesn't barf and thinks it's an accomplishment."

"Got it, no barfing."

We both chuckle. But it's amazing how different our lives have been. While Becky has been surrounded by guys, in my life, it's always been us girls. Mom, Penny, and I. And a string of faceless guys Mom's dated, but that doesn't really count.

I never spent much time with any of them because I knew they'd be gone before long. Well, except Penny's dad. He stayed for a while, but when the reality hit of what it's like to have a child, he ran for the hills too.

"So it's always been you and the guys? Even when you started going to school?"

"Yeah, by that point, it felt natural for me to hang out with the boys. I've been doing it my whole life. I had some girl-friends too, but I always felt more at home hanging out with the guys."

"That does make sense."

"So, what's going on with you and Emmett?"

"What do you mean?" I ask slowly, unsure of what she's getting at.

"Don't play innocent. I know my boys, and that guy has it bad for you. And I mean real bad."

"He doesn't!" I protest, but my cheeks betray me. I feel heat creeping up my neck, so instead of facing her, I look down at my bowl.

"Umm... yes, he does. Have you seen the way he looks at you?"

A shiver runs through my body, but I ignore it. "Don't know what you're talking about, Becky. Emmett is just being nice to the new girl, that's all."

"Since we've established that I'm the one who's known Emmett the longest, let's assume I know better, and that boy is smitten with you! And let me tell you, you won't find a better guy than Emmett. He's the most amazing, kind, talented guy in this whole town."

"Even better than Miguel?" I lift my brow at her in chal-lenge, happy that I can finally turn the tables on her.

A frown appears between her brows, her lips pressing together.

"I don't see what one has to do with the other."

"Seriously, that's the card you're going to play? I mean, I

know I'm pretty new here, but even I can see there is something going on between you two."

Becky pushes a strand of her hair behind her ear. "We're friends, that's all. And we're not talking about Miguel and me here."

"Well, we weren't talking about Emmett and me either. Because there is no Emmett and me."

Becky rolls her eyes. "All I'm saying is that he's a good guy. And he seems to like you. You should give him a shot."

"He's the golden boy of Bluebonnet Creek, Becky," I point out. "Even if I was interested, and I'm not, I'm just a girl passing by."

"So, what? You're not good enough for him?"

Not even close.

"He's going places. He has people looking up to him, and I can't stand in the way of that. Not with everything else I have going on right now."

"I get it." I lift my head to look at her. There is understanding in her eyes, but her mouth is pressed in a tight line. "I don't like it since I think you'd be good together, but I get it."

Just then, a commotion over her shoulder catches my attention. I look up, grateful for the distraction. Cars have taken over the parking lot that weren't there just a minute ago, and people are getting out, guys and girls who I vaguely remember from school.

Emmett gets out of his truck. He's the first one I notice. I'd be able to pick him out of a crowd any day of the week, and it's not just his height. It's just him. The way people gravitate toward him like he's the sun. And I'm no exception.

His feet have barely touched the ground when two girls, Rose and one of her friends, join Emmett and Miguel, bright smiles on their faces.

I watch as they talk and laugh at God only knows what.

Rose lifts on her toes. My throat dries as she reduces the distance between them. I expect her to kiss him, but instead, she swipes her thumb over his cheek, cleaning the red smudge off his skin.

"See what I've been telling you?" I ask calmly. My voice sounds foreign even to my own ears, but if Becky notices it, she doesn't say anything.

Confused, Becky turns around, her eyes landing on the group. A deep scowl appears between her brows. "What is going on here? They were supposed to go to that team bonding paintball something or other."

I guess that explains the color.

"I guess they're done."

Becky crosses her arms over her chest. "What's with them? Since when are the cheerleaders part of the football team?"

I shrug, turning my back to the parking lot and grabbing my things. "Maybe they needed moral support to bond."

"Of course, they did. Seriously, I'll never understand these guys."

You and me both, I want to say, but I hold the words in. "Ready to go?"

Becky crosses her arms over her chest and huffs. Unable to resist, I take a peek and see Rose's friend plastered to Miguel's side.

I guess that explains it.

Turning her back to the group, Becky grabs her bag. "Sure, let's go."

Chapter 8

EMMETT

"So, how did the team bonding go yesterday?" Becky asks, looking out the window.

Miguel and I exchange a look at her question; I'm pretty sure we look like deer caught in the headlights. Becky's been in a mood since she got into the truck, but for the life of me, I couldn't figure out what could have happened to make her upset.

"It went okay, I guess." I look up in the rearview mirror, but she's still stubbornly ignoring us. "Why?"

"Oh, it seemed to me that it went more than okay."

There is something in her tone that makes me pause for a second. Thankfully, the traffic light turns red, so I can give her my attention without risking killing us in the process.

Shit, Miguel mouths, but I just glare at him.

"What do you mean?"

Finally, she turns to look at us, her lips pressed in a tight line. "Since when are cheerleaders part of the football team?"

"How did you know?"

"Does it even matter?" She waves her hand dismissively. "You know shit like that always comes out. Even if I didn't see you with my own eyes when I was having ice cream with Kate..."

"You were there with Kate?" I ask, just as somebody honks behind me. I look up and see that the light has turned green.

Fuck.

"Of course, you'd hear that part." Miguel rolls his eyes.

"It doesn't even matter," Becky huffs. "It was all over Instagram since the girls posted the whole event in their stories."

"We didn't know they'd be there," Miguel says defensively. "It was John's brilliant idea to invite them."

"And you found it such a hardship that you went out to town afterward?"

I look up and find them glaring at one another.

"Jealous you weren't there, Becky?"

"Yeah, because I don't have better things to do with my life." With an exaggerated eye roll, she crosses her arms over her chest and looks out the window.

Miguel curses silently.

"Don't be like that, Becky." He nudges her knee. "Nobody knew they'd be there. Do you seriously think we wanted to hear them squeal and moan every few seconds because it hurt too much to be hit?"

"Of course, they would. God forbid they break a nail."

"Well, technically, John was the one who protested the most."

Miguel turns to me with an evil grin. "Did you actually go for his crotch?"

A smile tugs at the corner of my mouth. "Not sure what you're talking about. It was an accident."

Becky gasps, her eyes wide. "Emmett James Santiago, you did not!"

"Of course not. It was an accident."

"Of course, it was."

Miguel gives her another nudge. "So, you're not angry?"

"Of course not, it's not li—" Something draws her attention. "Hey, is that, Kate?"

I look up and see her walking down the street, just as Becky rolls down the window.

"Hey, Kate!" Becky yells, leaning out.

"You're going to fall out, Becky."

"Am not!"

Kate turns around at the sound of her voice; a backpack is slung over her shoulder, a coffee cup in her hands. I check in my rearview mirror to see if anybody's behind me before pulling up by the side of the road.

"Hey, guys," Kate greets us as she stops by the car. "What are you doing here?"

"The guys didn't have practice this morning, so we're going to school later. Wanna ride?"

Becky doesn't actually wait for an answer before opening the door and motioning Kate in.

"Well, if you don't mind." Kate gives me a quick glance.

"Of course not."

After Kate slides inside, I pull out onto the road. "So, how did you girls spend yesterday?"

Kate's brows shoot up in surprise as she and Becky exchange a glance.

"It was good. I think Becky introduced me to half the town, and she fed me the best ice cream I've ever eaten in my life. Now, I might never want to leave."

"It's damn good ice cream, that's for sure."

I look up, my eyes finding Kate's in the reflection in the rearview mirror. Becky nudges Kate with her elbow, drawing her attention.

"The guys were just telling me all about how they destroyed John out on the paintball field. Apparently, there was a ball that 'suddenly,'" Becky makes a point of drawing air quotes, "went off-course and landed in his crotch."

"Suddenly, huh?"

"It was an accident," I protest, taking the turn to the school parking lot.

"Accident, my ass." Miguel turns around to look at the backseat. "Emmett almost strangled him when the girls showed up."

"It was supposed to be a team bonding exercise, not a damn party!"

"It seems like you guys had fun."

"There were some good moments, but we'll see if it was effective at all."

I spot a place and hurry to park the car before somebody else grabs it.

"Your destination, my ladies," I say as we get out of the car.

Kate hops out and hands me my backpack that was on the backseat. "Thanks for the ride."

I take it, my fingers brushing against hers. "Anytime."

KATHERINE

I'm just unlocking the door when I hear the soft rumble of an engine nearing. Although I'm not expecting anybody, I turn around just as a Range Rover pulls into the driveway.

My brows furrow as I watch a man kill the engine and get out.

"What are you doing here?" I ask as recognition sets in.

Bradley Jones tips his hat to me, a smile curling his lips. Dressed in classic cowboy attire—a plaid shirt, jeans, and boots —he looks like any other guy in this town.

Is he stalking me? He doesn't seem like the type, there are

no creepy vibes surrounding him or anything like that, but out of all the people I've met in Bluebonnet, he's the one that keeps popping up at random times.

"Your aunt didn't tell you?" he asks as he goes to the back of his truck and pulls out something from behind.

"Tell me what?" I ask suspiciously.

Why would Mabel tell me anything?

"She asked me to look at the sink. I told her I'd come by one day when I had time."

"You're the friend?" I remember her mentioning she'd have somebody look at it. I just never really thought it'd be Bradley Jones.

"I'm the friend," he confirms with a chuckle and comes closer. "You mind if I take a look?"

"I guess?"

With one final look at him, I push open the door and enter. "Hey, Penny!" I call out, toeing off my shoes. There is a faint sound of footsteps coming from the kitchen, and then she pops her head through the doorway, Henry by her side.

"Hey, you done for today?"

"Yes, just got here." I can feel Bradley's looming presence behind me. "And we have company. Aunt's friend is here to check the sink."

She looks around, unsure. "Oh, okay."

"This is my sister, Penelope. Penny, this is Mr. Bradley Jones." I step aside to let Bradley in and close the door.

"So nice to meet you, Mr. Jones," Penny says shyly, her hand burrowing in Henry's fur.

"Likewise, Penelope."

The tension in the room seems to grow as Bradley looks at her with curiosity. I leave my backpack by the door and clear my throat. "Do you want something to drink?"

"No, thank you, I'm fine. But I'd like to get a look at the sink if that's okay with you girls."

"Sink, right." I nod. "It's over here."

I go toward the kitchen and wave him over.

"I'll clear away my things so you can work."

Penny is the first to enter the kitchen. She goes to the table where she's been reading something and picks up her things before she and Henry leave the kitchen.

Bradley watches her go. Only when she's out of the room does he sigh and go to the sink, placing his toolbox on the counter.

"She seems nice."

"She is nice," I correct him instantly.

"She doesn't look much like Mary."

"No, she took mostly after her father." I was too young to remember much about him either. I just remember a guy with floppy, almost white hair and a smile. Out of all Mom's boyfriends, he was one of the nicer ones. "And before you ask, yes, we have different fathers. Not that either of us knows much about them."

His piercing eyes stare at me, and I'm not sure how to interpret the look in them. I'm familiar with people's curiosity and insensitive questions, but there is something different about the way Bradley Jones observes us.

Unable to hold his stare for much longer, I turn my back to him and go to the fridge. Pulling the door open, I take a pitcher of iced tea, then grab two glasses from the cupboard and fill them. Leaving one on the counter, I take mine to the little island so I can watch Bradley work.

"You knew Mom?" I ask, ready to change the subject.

"We all went to school together. Mabel, Mary, and I."

Well, that's a surprise.

I never gave much thought to the idea that these people

ANNA B. DOE

know my mom, or well, they *used* to know my mom back when
she lived here. But it's hard to wrap my mind around that other
person I never knew.

"How was she? Back then?"

Mom doesn't really like to talk about the past, especially not
her time in Bluebonnet. I never understood why. What is so bad
about this place that she had to run away and never wanted to
look back?

"Like any other teenager, I guess."

Bradley doesn't even bother lifting his head. He inspects the
sink before crouching down to open the cupboard beneath it.

"Are we really talking about Mary Adams here?"

That gets his attention. A small smile tugs at the corner of
his lips. "I guess you're right. Mary was wild. Her aspirations
and dreams were always too big for a small town like Bluebonnet. I guess that's why she decided to leave. You guys still live in
California?"

"We do, well, we did, but she's still there, yes. Still dreaming
of making it big."

I try to keep my bitterness at bay, but it's useless. Deciding
I'm done with talking about Mom. I change the topic.

"So, you and Mabel? Are you guys close?"

"We are, we have been since we were in school since we're
the same age. Why?"

"Hmm..." I trace the tip of my finger over the rim of the
glass. "I just find it interesting that she didn't mention you, that's
all."

"Why would she?" He peeks out, those dark eyes of his
fixing on me. "Did you tell her you know me?"

"Touché. In my defense, there was never actually a reason
for me to mention you."

"Was there a particular reason why she should have
mentioned me to you?"

68

"You went to school together," I point out.

"We did, bu—"

"Hey, guys!" Mabel says as she rushes into the room. "I'm so sorry I'm late. It took forever to wrap up at work. But I can see that Kate let you in."

"Bradley arrived just when I was coming home," I explain, as the man in question stands up.

"Hey, Mabel, no worries." Bradley closes the cupboard and puts away his tools. "I'm actually just done."

"Did you manage to find the issue?"

"Yes, you should be all good now."

"Thank you." Mabel smiles at him, and I swear I see her eyes flutter a bit. *What's with that?* "What do I owe you?"

Bradley shakes his head. "It's on the house."

"You always say that," Mabel protests.

"Because I mean it. Seriously, it's all good."

She moves to him and places her hand over his. "Well, you should at least stay for dinner."

"Rain check?" He gives her a small smile, and her cheeks turn pink. "I promised Keith I'd go back to the ranch to check on something."

"Okay, but I'll hold you to that."

"I didn't think otherwise." He grabs the toolbox and takes a step back, his eyes meeting mine for a moment. "I guess I'll see you ladies later."

"Yeah, sure. Later."

"I'll walk you out," Mabel says, leaving her bags in the chair.

I take a sip of my tea as I watch them leave, talking about something in hushed voices. I can hear Mabel laugh at something Bradley says.

Sighing, I get up and go grab my things so I can change and start on my homework. Just as I'm about to climb the stairs, Mabel comes back inside.

"What was that about?" I ask, taking her in. Her cheeks are flushed, and a smile still plays on her lips. She's usually a happy person, but there is something more to it now that I don't see every day.

Mabel pushes a strand of hair behind her ear. "What do you mean?"

"You and Bradley?" I prompt. "Are you like a thing?"

"What?" Her eyes bug out. "Of course not."

"Really? It's okay if you are, you know. You don't have to hide your boyfriend..."

"Really, Kate. Bradley and I, we're just friends, always have been."

It didn't seem like that only minutes ago, but who am I to protest? "Okay, if you say so."

Chapter 9

KATHERINE

"Kate!" My head shoots up at the sound of my name. I look around until my eyes land on Becky waving at me from the bleachers. "Over here!"

I wave back, looking around for an excuse to continue on my way, but there really isn't one. Sighing, I walk slowly toward her.

"You're here early," I comment as I come within hearing distance.

She tips her head to the side. "I occasionally come to watch the guys practice."

Climbing up a few steps, I sit on the bench next to her, and together we watch the guys out on the field. They're divided into smaller groups, one half wearing gold while the other has purple jerseys, and they're obviously working on something. A play? Drills? I'm not really sure.

I have never been a sporty girl or interested in jocks, in general. Okay, I've never been interested in *boys*. Don't get me wrong. I like them just fine. When they're not stinky or overall gross. I guess a part of my reluctance toward them comes after watching my mother fall for losers all my life.

I might have never met my father, but I've met all the guys since, including Penny's dad, and they've been just a bunch of idiots who'd storm into our lives, cause some ruckus and then walk right back out, leaving me to pick up the pieces.

"That one is Emmett," Becky says, breaking me out of my thoughts. She points to the group in gold jerseys that's taking one half of the field. They're all wearing helmets, so I'm not sure I'd have recognized him even if I tried. Then she points out another guy. "And Miguel."

"You guys finally talking again?" I ask, my eyes glued to the field. The last few days have been... tense. Becky and Miguel haven't avoided each other, but there's a silent hostility in the air any time they're together.

"We're..." Her voice has a funny tone to it that makes me turn my head to look at her. She tilts her head back, thinking. "Us, I guess." She flashes me a quick smile. "Don't worry. We always find our way back to normal."

I nod as if I understand. I don't, but I'm not about to ask more questions. Instead, for a while, we just sit quietly under the Texas sun and watch the green field.

Coach, at least I think it's Coach, blows the whistle, and the boys fall in line. One guy in a gold jersey stands on one side of the line, while two in purple stand on the other. They're all in that weird half-bent, half-crouching position you always see football players in as they face each other across the line. Coach blows the whistle one more time, and the guys facing each other clash together. I wince at the sound of pads crashing into each other, accompanied by grunts and growls.

"He's really good, isn't he?" I ask as Emmett brings the first guy down and then catches the second before he manages to slip past him, wrapping his arms around him and clenching tightly until they both fall to the grass.

"One of the best." Becky smiles, and this time it's genuine. "If somebody's got a shot at going all the way, it's probably him."

I turn toward her. "You mean like, pro?" My voice drops to a whisper, and I can feel my eyes widen. I mean, I knew he was good. There's just something in the way Emmett carries himself. In the way people react to him. But pro kind of good? I didn't see that one.

"Yeah, he already had college scouts watching him play last year. He's *that* good."

I look back onto the field, where they're working on the same thing over and over again. Guys switch so that everybody takes a turn to practice, but there is just something when Emmett's on the field. Something...

My tongue darts out, sliding over my suddenly dry lips.

"Pro, huh..." I whisper, more to myself than for Becky's sake. She's not even listening because she's on her feet cheering loudly as Emmett once again takes two of his teammates down.

Is it really surprising, though? No, not really. I just watched him play, even at practice, he has that air about him that demands people's attention. Something about him screams *born leader*. Then there's that charm of his. So natural. Effortless.

I could totally see it, see *him*, going all the way. He'd be amazing. A golden boy from a small town in Texas making it big and showing people that it's actually possible. That hard work pays off, and dreams do come true.

I should be happy for him. Why does just the thought of it make my gut clench?

"What is all of this?" I ask a little while later when we get ourselves to school, my eyes darting around the unusually busy hallway.

"Watch out," Becky laughs, pulling me to the side just as the banner falls down.

"Sorry!" a guy yells from up the ladder.

"Be careful, or you'll kill somebody!" Becky shakes her head as she glares at the group hanging up the banner. "Seriously, these people."

"Are they preparing for a parade or something?"

"No, we're preparing for the pep rally." She must see my blank face because she explains. "First game of the season? Football, Kate, we're talking about football here." Becky shakes her head, laughing. "What did you think they were doing out there? Training just so we can drool over their sculpted butts in those tight pants and their shirtless bodies in the heat?"

My cheeks heat as I remember the end of practice and how they started to take off their clothes before even hitting the locker room.

"No idea." I shrug. A strand of hair falls into my face, and I don't bother pushing it away. "I don't really follow the football schedule. Football, well *sports,* just aren't my thing."

Becky's eyes bug out.

"You what?" She looks around as if she's afraid somebody can hear us. Grabbing my arm, she pulls me to the side. "You can't say stuff like that around here."

"Umm... okay?"

She snaps her fingers in front of my face. "I'm serious; this place lives and breathes football."

"Okay, okay, I got it." I roll my eyes, laughing. "I'll keep the fact that I don't give a shit about football to myself."

"Hey, there."

My head snaps to Becky, my smile falling as I hear his voice behind my back. We both probably look like deer caught in the headlights. Becky shoots me an I-told-you-so look, which earns her a glare.

Slowly, I turn around to come face to face with Emmett and two of his football friends.

"Hi?" I say weakly, plastering on my most innocent smile.

"Were you guys watching practice?" Emmett smiles at us.

"Who cares about that?" The annoying one—Jack? Justin? No, John. I think that's the one—crosses his arms over his chest and stares at me. "Did you just say you don't like football?"

"Umm…" I tuck a strand of my hair behind my ear. "Sports just aren't my thing?"

"Girl, you just haven't watched the right sports yet." He throws his arm over my shoulder and pulls me into the crook of his arm. "But no worries, there's still hope for you."

He starts pushing me down the hallway, all the while talking about football. I look over my shoulder at Becky and the rest of her friends following after us. I catch her gaze and mouth, "Help," but she just grins and shakes her head no.

So much for us being friends.

EMMETT

"She doesn't like football," John yells in my ear, all the time shaking his head like somebody just told him Santa isn't real. "Like where did she live? Somebody needs to teach that girl what the real sport is."

"Not everybody likes football," I mutter, not even looking at him. My eyes are scanning the crowd that has gathered in the gym for the pep rally.

There is that familiar excitement going through the air like it always does before the first game of the season. The principal is giving a speech about hard work, love for our school, community, and the game, but you can still hear the hushed voices of our classmates in the background. John isn't wrong though, the people of Bluebonnet love the game. On Friday nights, during the fall, businesses close, and people come to the games to cheer on the team.

"And nobody really cares what you think, so shut it," Miguel adds, and I give him a thankful smile. I'm so not in the mood to discuss Kate with anybody, least of all John.

"And now, let's welcome to the stage our Bluebonnet Eagles!"

The crowd roars as the marching band starts with our school fight song, and we come out on the stage one by one as our names are called.

"Emmett Santiago!"

If it's possible, the chanting becomes even louder as I step out, the bright lights of reflectors shining over me.

There is a loud whistle coming from the back. A grin spreads over my face as I look over the crowd until my eyes land on Becky and Katherine.

Becky has always been Miguel's and my biggest cheer-leader. I don't think there was one game she missed in all the years since we started playing. Practice or game, she's been a constant in the stands, urging us on when we thought we couldn't move a muscle, and one of the rare people there when we'd lose, reassuring us that it's not the end.

And now there's Katherine Adams.

Sweet, slightly infuriating, non-football-loving Kate Adams.

She turns toward Becs, looking stunned by the sound, but Becky just laughs and hoists her onto her feet before waving enthusiastically from the bleachers. Kate shakes her head at Becky's silliness, but when she turns around, she sees me watching. Our gazes meet, and for a moment, everything fades back. All the noises and all the people become irrelevant. My heart tightens a little. I reach up, rubbing the spot.

Kate smiles and lifts her hand for a wave of her own. It's small, over before it began, but I'm certain it was there. Directed at me.

A grin spreads over my mouth.

Things lately have been going well. Kate's more amicable than she was just after she got here. She started integrating more into our little group, mostly thanks to Becky, who took it upon herself to make her feel welcomed.

Miguel elbows me in the gut, drawing my attention back. We listen to Coach give a speech, followed by our quarterback, Tim.

I try to listen to them talk, but all the while, I keep sneaking glances at the bleachers and the girl sitting there.

Will she come to the game?

Sports just aren't my thing—her earlier words ring in my mind. Probably not. It's not surprising, but I can't say I'm not disappointed.

"Go Eagles!" Tim finally finishes, and the whole school joins in on the chant.

"Are you ready for tonight?" Becky asks later that day as we walk to the parking lot. On game days, if we're playing on home turf, we usually have a pep rally instead of our final class, and then we're off the hook until we have to get back to prepare for the game.

"As ready as I'll ever be," I say, unlocking my door and throwing my duffle in the back.

Becky lifts her brows. "Where did the confident Emmett disappear to?"

We both enter my truck. Becky has her own car, but she rarely drives it, instead choosing to go with either Miguel or me.

"He's still here." I lift my ball cap and run my hand through my hair. "I'm just tired, I guess. It's been a long day."

"Mm-hmm... does this have anything to do with a certain brunette?"

I look up, my eyes falling on my best friend getting into his car. He sees us and tips his chin before disappearing inside. I turn to Becky. "Does your sour attitude have anything to do with a certain football player?"

Becky glares at me. "We're not talking about me now."

"But we can talk about me?" I challenge right back.

"Of course we can! If I can't put my nose all up in your business, who can?"

"You're something else, Becs." I shake my head, laughing. I start the car, check the rearview mirrors and pull out.

"That's why you love me," she says playfully, jabbing me in the bicep.

"True."

For a while, we drive in silence. Becky plays with the radio, changing the station until she finds her favorite one, and then she leans into her seat, humming happily to the song.

"Do you think she'll come?" I finally ask, unable to hold it in.

"Kate?"

"Yeah."

Didn't we just talk about her? Seriously, and they say guys are clueless.

"I'm not sure." Becky shrugs. "She did say that football isn't her thing."

She doesn't have to like football to come to the game, I want to point out, but bite my tongue before the words can get out.

"She's different from us."

And that's part of the problem. I don't know what to make

of her. I don't know how to explain why I'm so preoccupied with this girl I don't even know. Not really.

"She is, but that doesn't have to be a bad thing. Change can be good sometimes." Becky turns toward me, looking at me contemplatively. "Do you want her to? To come, I mean?"

I shrug, keeping my eyes firmly on the road. I know that if I turn toward her, she'll see more than I want her to on my face.

"Maybe." I try to play it cool, but as always, Becky sees right through me.

From the corner of my eye, I can see a smile tug at her lips. "You like her."

"Don't know what you're talking about," I mutter, my fingers clenched tightly around the steering wheel.

"You actually like a girl!"

I roll my eyes. "I've always liked girls."

Thankfully, I'm just pulling up to Becky's house, so this torture should soon be over. I love her, she's one of my best friends, but God, sometimes she drives me insane.

"Not *liked* liked them."

I shake my head. "You make no sense, Becs."

I pull the car to a stop. Becky unbuckles her seatbelt and grabs her bag.

"I do, and you know it." She pats my knee. "No worries, leave it all to Becky."

Right, leave it all to Becky.

Not sure if that really is the best idea, but before I can protest, she's already jumping out and rushing inside her house.

Chapter 10

KATHERINE

"Becky," I breathe as I open the front door. I look at her and then over her shoulder. There is a Jeep parked by the curb in front of Aunt Mabel's house that wasn't there earlier. "Did you forget something?"

Turning my attention back to her, I notice for the first time what she's wearing—a blue-purple jersey with Bluebonnet Eagles written in gold over it, a pair of cutoff jean shorts, and cowboy boots. Her hair is curled, and her makeup complements her outfit completely, all the way to 67 and 42 written in gold and purple one next to the other over her right cheek. How I didn't notice it at first, I have no idea.

"Nope." Becky shakes her head, her smile widening. "I'm here to pick you up."

"Pick me up?" I scrunch my nose up in confusion. "What for?"

"For the game, silly!"

I scratch the back of my head. "Umm, I didn't realize I was going."

"Everybody's going." She waves me off. Apparently, "everybody" includes me too. Becky takes me in from head to toes.

"Although you might consider changing into something with more school spirit."

More school spirit? Is she high? I blink, but nope, she's still here, looking at me expectantly.

"I didn't realize that was a thing."

Becky tsks. "Seriously, you've got so much to learn. C'mon, time's a wastin'." Becky pushes past me and enters the house.

"Becky, I'm not..."

But before I can think to protest, I'm interrupted yet again, this time by my aunt.

"Who is it, Katherine?" Aunt Mabel comes out of the kitchen, wiping her hands on a towel.

Sighing, I look at Becky, who's standing by the door, smiling extra wide. "Aunt, this is Becky, one of my classmates. Becky, my aunt Mabel, although I'm pretty sure you both know more about each other than I do."

"Kate!" Mabel chastises, looking stunned by my blunt comment. "I'm sure she..."

"Oh, don't worry, I totally agree with her. But it's so nice to see you again, Ms. Adams. How have you been?"

"Good." Mabel nods her head. "It's been lively since the girls came to stay with me."

"I'm sure it's exciting to have them here."

"Of course, I always asked Mary to bring them, but..."

My whole body tenses at the mention of my mother. I can see Mabel give me a side glance as if she noticed it too. Thankfully she lets the subject go. "Anyway... What are you girls up to?"

I open my mouth, but Becky is faster. "Today's the first game of the season, so I figured Kate should come with me to see what this town is all about. Plus, there will be a little get-together after the game. Nothing too wild."

"The first game, right. It completely slipped my mind."

Slipped her mind, right. I want to roll my eyes. Since I've come here, I don't think I've ever seen Mabel watch TV, much less watch *sports* on TV.

"I don't mind staying here and helping you with dinner; I know you have a lot of work..."

"No, no." Mabel shakes her head. "Becky is right. You girls should go. Have fun."

"But, Pe—" I try to protest, but Mabel isn't having it.

"Go and have fun, Katherine. We'll be okay. Hell, I'm not even going to cook. We'll order pizza. More time for me to finish my work."

I look between the two of them, finding two pairs of hopeful eyes staring at me.

"Are you sure?" I ask, still hoping that maybe, *maybe,* she'll change her mind. But Mabel just smiles and gives me a little pat on my shoulder.

"Positive. Have fun, but be home by midnight."

EMMETT

The crowd screams as we run on the field. There isn't anything quite like the first game of the season. The grass seems greener, the year full of possibilities. Friday night lights shine brightly, illuminating the stadium, and every step I take is in tune with the blood pumping through my veins.

"This could be our year," Miguel murmurs next to me. His eyes are taking in the scene, too, trying to memorize it for eternity.

This will be something we'll remember once we're older. The smell of freshly cut grass, the roar of people, the adrenaline rush going through our bodies as we're stepping onto the field, playing the game everybody loves as much as we do.

"It could be," I agree.

Our team's solid, but Bluebonnet High hasn't won a State Championship in years. But maybe, just maybe...

"Don't get all mushy now," Nico says as he punches me in the shoulder. "Let's get out and make these assholes remember who we are."

"For once, you're right, Nico."

"I'm always right, you jackasses just don't want to admit it."

Miguel shakes his head. "He's an idiot."

"True, but there is something there. One game at a time."

Miguel looks to the stands. "You might want to make this one count, though." He tips his chin forward. "It seems we have company."

I look up and see Becky sitting in the last row, her usual seat, but what's different this time is that she's not alone.

"She actually did it," I mutter, shaking my head. *She actually fucking did it.*

Kate is sitting next to Becky and laughing at something she said. Her head is thrown back, ponytail swaying. She's the odd one out, the only one sitting in a black shirt in the sea of purple and gold, but it doesn't matter.

She's here.

Not because she likes the game.

Not because she likes you, either, a little voice reminds me.

Yet, she's here.

Just then, the announcer says it's time for the national anthem. Kate turns toward the field, her eyes instantly finding me. She lifts her hand in a small wave, and I wave back.

"Dude, you've got it bad," Miguel chuckles, shoving me.

I shove right back. "Like you're one to talk."

"Don't know what you're talking about." Miguel looks away, which makes me chuckle harder. We all stand on the sidelines.

"Yeah, right, keep telling yourself that," I mumble quietly.

Whatever he thinks, I'm not dumb. I can see there is something going on between Miguel and Becky. I'm not sure what or how it'll unfold, but I'm interested to see how things play out.

John glares at us. "Are you done talking shit? We've got a game to win."

Today he's more unbearable than usual. This year will be one royal pain in the ass if he continues sulking because he's warming the bench.

"We know, we're going to play in it," Miguel shoots back instantly.

John huffs, standing a bit taller. Like that'll change anything. "Just don't screw up the game."

Miguel glares at him. "We never screw up the game; that's why we're starting."

John mutters something, but Coach glares at us, making us all shut up.

The national anthem starts playing, and I try to get back to my game day mindset, pushing all the other things back and concentrating on what's about to happen on the field.

Once the song ends, the team captains go out on the field for a coin toss. Our opponent, St. Lewis High, wins the toss, and they opt to receive.

I put my helmet on.

It's game time.

Miguel and I run onto the field, with the rest of the defense team behind us. St. Lewis's offensive guys do the same on the other side of the field, some of them smirking knowingly as we meet on the line of scrimmage.

Smug assholes.

Miguel plays the position of the defensive end, meaning he's first in the line, right in front of me.

The referee blows a whistle, and offense and defense clash. Guys are grunting, cusses flying everywhere, as everybody tries to keep the dominance to their team.

I keep my eyes on their quarterback as he pulls into the pocket, the ball falling into his hands, trusting Miguel to hold the line. The quarterback holds the ball for a second before he lets it fly safely into the hands of his receiver, who quickly slips past Nico, and almost past me, but I catch him at the last second, pulling him to the ground.

The crowd cheers as one of my teammates offers me his hand and pulls me up.

A grin spreads over my lips.

It's good to be back.

Chapter 11

KATHERINE

"C'mon, we're late!" Becky yells as she walks around the hood of her Jeep to the passenger side before I can even get out.

"How can you be late for a party?"

I have to admit, Becky's excitement is infectious, and even I'm not immune to it. She's been like that all evening, jumping and cheering like her life depends on it. I'm surprised she can talk considering the amount of screaming she did—to cheer the guys on, to trash talk the rival team, or complain about the call a referee made. The girl knows her football, and she isn't afraid to show it.

Becky loops her arm through mine and starts pulling me toward the fire beckoning us from the clearing. She's like a kid on a sugar rush, overly excited and hyped up.

Shaking my head, I thank God for my trusty pair of red chucks. Keeping up with Becky would be impossible in anything else.

"Everybody else is already here."

"Maybe they're just here early," I point out.

She gives me an unamused look. "Yeah, or maybe we're actually late."

"It's all in the eyes of onlookers, Becs. Besides, do I need to remind you that you wanted to stop by your house before coming here?"

"Yeah, yeah." She rolls her eyes. "Don't remind me. Let's go find the guys. I'm sure even they are here somewhere by now."

We walk between different cars and trucks parked all around and come out on the clearing. A big fire is built in the middle of it, illuminating the darkness of the evening. Somebody brought huge speakers, and country music is blasting at max. A few people are dancing, others sitting in the beds of trucks parked around the bonfire, chatting and drinking.

Before I can take it all in, Becky squeals loudly and lets go of my hand. I turn around to search for what might have caused her reaction, just as she jumps at both Emmett and Miguel, wrapping her arms around their shoulders and pulling them in for a group hug. Since they're both taller than her, her legs hang in the air.

She looks like a cute little monkey.

"You did it! One down, nine more to go!"

Miguel laughs. "It's just the first game, anything can happen."

"It's the first game that you *won* this season," Becky points out. Letting go, she jumps back to the ground and jabs her finger into his chest as if to accentuate her point. "That's the difference. I'm telling you, I can feel it. This is our season."

"Well, if you say so." Emmett ruffles her hair.

My heart squeezes a little, just standing here and watching them interact. I'm not sure what to make of the three of them. The love and friendship they share are so obvious; it hurts a little to watch.

As if he can feel my eyes on him, Emmett lifts his head, his gaze landing on mine. My tongue darts out, sliding over my lower lip. Nervousness creeps in as his sole attention is on me. I shift my weight from one foot to the other, pushing a strand of my hair behind my ear and feeling self-conscious at being caught watching them.

"Hey," I say, lifting my hand in an awkward wave.

"Hi." Emmett's grin widens as he looks at me. His voice seems deeper, making the goosebumps rise on my skin. We stare at each other for a while. I wait for him to say something, anything, but he stays silent, just looking.

Becky and Miguel are still talking, probably discussing the game, and completely ignoring us. We're not alone, not in the least, but in a way, it feels like we are.

Emmett moves closer.

He must have taken a shower after the game because he smells fresh and citrusy. His purple football jersey clings to his shoulders like it was made for him. I wonder, how many of those he has? Probably a dozen, at least.

"Congrats on your win," I say awkwardly, the first one to break the silence.

"Thanks." Emmett lifts his eyebrow at me. "What? No tackling to the ground?" He points behind his back at Becky, who's standing next to Miguel, his arm casually thrown over her shoulder. "I figured that was your doing."

"My doing? How would it be my doing? She's your best friend."

"Your doing because you specialize in bringing people to the ground."

"For God's sake, how many times will I have to say..."

"Just kidding, Kitty." Emmett puts his hands on my shoulders, effectively shutting me up. He's so close I have to tilt my head back to look at him. "No need to bring out the claws."

Emmett's looking at me so intently; it's getting hard to think. I suck in a shaky breath, reminding myself I need to breathe if I don't want to embarrass myself further by passing out. But it's so hard to act normal when he's standing so close to me.

I'm wearing a tank top so I can feel Emmett's warm skin touching mine. I can smell his cologne or shampoo or whatever the hell he put on after the shower with every breath I take, intoxicating me.

A shiver runs down my spine, making the faint hairs at the back of my neck rise and my skin pebble.

"Cold?" Emmett asks.

It's unnerving, the way he notices things. The way he notices *me*. I don't think anybody's ever noticed me as much as he does.

His big palm rubs over my upper arm, warming me up.

I shake my head no. Definitely not cold. More like burning from the inside out.

Get a grip, Kate.

I look around, needing to find something else to concentrate on. Something that's not Emmett Santiago. Or his big, warm hands. And definitely not his thumb that's sliding over my skin in slow circles.

Biting the inside of my cheek, my attention returns over his shoulder, back to Becky and Miguel.

"They seem to have made up."

Emmett peeks over his shoulder and then shrugs. "That's Becky and Miguel for you."

"Have they always been like that?"

I find their dynamic curious. In groups of three, there almost always seems to be one odd person out. For some reason, it's usually even worse when it's a mixed group. Two guys and a girl? It has love triangle written all over it. Not that *they* give off that vibe. It's pretty obvious to anybody looking that there is nothing more than sibling love happening between Emmett and Becky. Miguel and Becky, on the other hand...

"More or less. They drive each other crazy, but they can't stay mad at each other for long either."

"Hmm..."

They're definitely not driving each other crazy now. Becky's cheeks are flushed, and she's giggling at whatever Miguel is telling her.

"Do you miss your friends from back home?" Emmett asks, drawing my attention.

"We moved a lot, so..." I shrug, not in the mood to talk about that. Thinking about home just brings out bad memories that I'd rather leave behind.

"I'm sure you had friends."

"I did. When you move a lot, you learn how to adapt, but also, since you never stay in one place for too long, you realize that forming meaningful relationships is pointless."

Forming connections has never come easy to me. It was too hard when you never knew when that person would leave your life for good. Or if you'd be the one leaving.

Emmett slips his finger under my chin and lifts my head up. "Good friends are always worth your while."

Becky's laughter rings in the night, and I can hear Miguel saying something, although all the noises prevent me from hearing what.

"Says the guy who grew up in the same small town, surrounded by the same people since before he was born."

Yeah, I could see how he'd think that. Being here, even for a short while, surrounded by his friends, had *me* believing that I could belong. That maybe this was finally a place I could call home.

"True, but I know that even if our paths went in different directions, they'd have my back. Hell, *once* that happens, because it will happen eventually. We all have our dreams and wishes for life, we'll most likely end up at different colleges, and then, God only knows where, but we'll stay in touch. That's what friends do."

The silence settles over us. Maybe in his world, that's true, but they had years to build their relationship. The bond between the three of them is so strong; it's almost palpable. But the reality is, those kinds of bonds are rare, and only some people are lucky enough to find them.

"What are you two whispering about?" Becky asks, nudging me with her hip when she joins us.

I've been so focused on Emmett that I didn't hear her coming.

I pull back, thankful for the interruption. "Nothing, just chatting." I look around, needing to find something to change the subject. "So this is what all the fuss is about?"

"Yes, thanks to Emmett's parents, we get to have parties out here without people getting in our business."

I turn back to the group and find Emmett watching me. It feels like he's always watching. "This is yours?" I ask, surprised.

It took us forever to drive here. The road was dark and dirty, but Becky didn't seem worried, so I didn't ask any questions.

"Not mine." Emmett rubs the back of his neck. "But my family's, yes."

Becky rolls her eyes. "They own one of the biggest cattle ranches in the state."

"You're making him blush, Becs," Miguel chimes in, joining our conversation. He thrusts a cup each at Emmett and Becky.

"Oh, please, it's not like it's some big secret. You should come once when it's still light outside, it's really pretty. There's even a pond further back where we go swimming when it's hot." She takes a quick sip. She must notice me looking because she offers it to me. "Want some? It's just water. No drinking since I'm driving you home, so don't worry."

I shake my head. "I'm good, but thanks."

"I'd have gotten you something, but I wasn't sure what you drink." Miguel grins apologetically. He takes a sip from his cup, which I'm pretty sure has beer inside. "But seriously, you're good with Becs. She drives like an old lady anyway."

"Hey now!" Becky protests, shoving him away hard enough that a little bit of the beer splashes over the rim of the cup. "I don't drive like an old lady."

"Oh please, you forgot who taught you how to drive."

"Well, if my driving sucks, then we know who's responsible for it, now don't we?" Becky huffs, putting her hands on her hips.

Here they go again.

I look at Emmett, and I'm pretty sure his expression mirrors mine.

"C'mon now," Miguel groans, his smile falling. "That's totally unnecessary."

"What is unnecessary is that you think you can talk to me like that, Miguel Luis Fernandez." Shaking her head at him, she turns on the balls of her feet and walks away.

"Becky!" Miguel yells after her, but she doesn't bother slowing down. He looks at Emmett, who just shrugs. Swearing, he runs his hand over his face. I expect him to go in the opposite direction, but instead, this time, he goes after her.

"Well, that escalated quickly," I mutter, looking in the direction the two of them disappeared to. "Will they be okay?"

"Yeah, we've been roaming around these fields since we were little. They're good. Well, they won't get lost. I don't know about *good*. They seriously need to get their shit together." Emmett lifts his ball cap and runs his hand through his hair before putting it back in place and looking down at me. "So... Want to get away while they sort their shit out?"

With one last look toward the darkness, I turn my attention to Emmett, who's waiting for an answer. He's the only other person I know here except Becky, who conveniently disappeared and probably won't be back for a while.

Yeah, that's definitely the reason.

My decision doesn't have anything to do with the cute boy standing in front of me, nor his hopeful smile.

"Yeah, sure."

EMMETT

"Is this where you take all the girls?"

I jump up on the bed of my truck and turn around. Kate's looking at me from the ground, her brows raised in question. While most of the people want the prime spots just around the bonfire, I love staying back. Away from the smoke of the bonfire and probing eyes looking at your every move, so instead, I always park farther in the shadows.

It took us a bit to get here, with all the people wanting to congratulate me on the win and most of them interested in meeting Kate. To a lot of them, she's still an enigma. Somebody they see walking around the school hallways but don't get a chance to talk to and definitely don't mind gossiping about.

"Har-har. Nope, and before you ask, this is totally Becky's doing. She always complained that the bed was too hard, and since we didn't listen, she took matters into her own hands and brought a blanket and some pillows that she forces me to keep in the back just for moments like this." I lean down and offer Kate my hand. "C'mon, hop on."

Placing one leg on the bed, she takes my hand. With one hard pull, I help hoist her up. She crashes into my chest, swaying on her feet. I put my free hand on her shoulder to help steady her.

"I've got you," I whisper.

My heart is beating furiously in my ribcage at her nearness. This close, I can smell the faint scent of apples in her hair, see the way her skin pebbles under my touch.

Slowly she looks up. Her dark blue eyes, so dark they almost seem purple, are wide as they stare into mine. Her tongue darts out, sliding over her lower lip.

"Thanks," she whispers, and I swear her voice is a little shaky.

Kate takes a step back, and although it pains me, I let her go. I notice that about her, and not just when it comes to me, but Becky too. For every two steps forward, there is one step back. It's like she's afraid to get close to anybody.

Grabbing one of the pillows, I throw it into the corner and sit down, leaning my back against the back of the cab.

Kate looks around, carefully taking everything in, and by the look on her face, weighing where to sit.

"I don't bite," I tease.

Her eyes meet mine, narrowing slightly. "I never said you did."

My brows shoot up, a smirk playing on my lips. "Then why are you still standing?" I challenge.

Kate glares at me, her lips pressed in a tight line. I hit a nerve, but I'm not planning to apologize for it. Kate moves closer, sitting by my side. She, too, grabs one of the throw pillows and pops it behind her head, her mouth falling open as she looks up.

"The sky is so pretty here."

Turning to my side, I observe Kate. Her head is tilted back, her dark ponytail swinging over the edge of the truck, her creamy neck exposed, making me wish I could trace my finger over the soft skin. My mouth. My tongue.

"It really is," I agree, not even bothering to look up.

I've looked at this sky so many times I can see it even if I close my eyes. But not Kate. I don't want to look at the sky when I have Katherine lying here next to me; the look of genuine bewilderment on her face is better and more beautiful than any night sky.

"There are so many stars here. You can't see that in the city."

"Nope," I agree readily.

There is definitely nobody quite like Katherine. Is that the real reason for my fascination with her? Because she's different from all the girls from around here?

No, it can't be. Whatever this thing happening between us is, it's real. It's not infatuation. Or the need for change. It's just her.

There's something about her that draws me to her.

Obviously, there is the physical beauty, but it's also more than just that.

I'm not sure what, but I want to figure it out.

Figure *her* out.

Kate must feel my eyes on her because she turns to me. Her eyes shine brightly even in the dim light. My fingers itch to cross the distance and touch her, but I worry that if I do that, she'll pull back, so I keep my hands to myself.

"You're not even looking!" she accuses, making me chuckle.

"I've seen it every day for the past seventeen years."

But not her. And I don't want to miss anything that's Katherine.

"How can you say it's pretty when you're not even looking at it?"

"Because I wasn't talking about the sky."

She sucks in a breath as my words settle in. The way she reacts to me mesmerizes me. The flush in her cheeks, her eyes widening as her mouth forms a perfect little O in surprise.

Shifting forward, I close the distance between us.

"W-what are you doing?" she stutters, her voice cracking.

The corner of my lip twitches as I fight the smile that wants to spread. "Nothing."

I extend my hand, my fingers tracing the outline of her cheekbone. Her skin is silky smooth under my fingertips, and while most girls have overexaggerated their appearance, Kate is just... Kate. There is no glitter on her eyelids or mouth, and the blush covering her cheeks is one-hundred percent natural. One-hundred percent my doing.

Her throat bobs as she swallows. Kate looks up at me through her long eyelashes. "It doesn't look like nothing."

"What does it look like then?" I ask, my finger tracing down the column of her neck and then back up just like I wanted to do, and I can feel her shiver under my touch.

She can pretend all she wants that I don't affect her, but her body betrays her every single time.

"Emmett," she breathes, her eyes falling closed. She places her hands on my chest, to pull me closer or push me back? I'm not sure, but neither is she, because her hands just linger there, not doing either of those things.

"Katherine," I whisper back, leaning closer. For a while, we stay like that, just staring at one another, only inches separating us. I can feel her hot breath on my skin as her breathing hitches. "I want to kiss you now."

I brush the tips of my fingers over her skin, cupping her cheek with my palm. My lips brush against hers with every word I say. My whole body screams for me to do it, to place my mouth on hers and claim her as mine, but I hold myself back.

"I-I..."

"You what?"

"I can't," she finishes finally, tilting her head to the side.

The rejection, although not unexpected, still stings.

I huff, pulling back. "Can't or won't?"

She wraps her arms around herself. "I'm not the kind of girl you're looking for."

"And what kind of girl is that?"

She glares at me. "The kind of girl who'll be okay with kissing you now and then watch you flirt with other girls later."

I grit my teeth to hold back my irritation. "I wouldn't do that."

"No? Can you seriously tell me you've never done it?"

I rip my cap off my head and run my palm over my face in frustration. "Why does it even matter? I wouldn't do it, not to you."

"Well, I still can't." She scoots away. "I'm not even sure how long I'll stay here." She shakes her head. "Besides, I have more important things to worry about. I can't fool around."

I put my hand over hers to prevent her from leaving. "More important things like what?"

"Family and school and..." Kate shrugs. "Just things."

"And you think I'll get in your way? I like you, Kate."

"That's just it! How can you like me? You don't even know me!"

"I like what I've seen so far, and I want to know more." I want to get to know *all* of her, but I don't say it because she's skittish enough as it is. "You know, when you're not driving me batshit crazy, that is."

"I—" Kate pulls her hand from underneath mine, scoots to the edge of the bed, and hops off. "I'm sorry. I think I'll go look for Becky, it's getting late, and I should go home."

She can't just leave like that.

I jolt forward, wrapping my hand around her wrist and pulling her back toward me.

"I'm not giving up, Katherine," I say softly, so soft it's barely audible, but I need her to know this. I need her to know that this is far from over, whatever she might think.

"You can't change my mind."

"I'm damn well going to try," I promise, and it's a promise I'm planning to keep.

"Emmett…" Kate sighs, and I can hear the uncertainty in her voice.

It's not that she doesn't want me. She does, and that's what's scaring her. She doesn't know what to do about it. About me. About us. We don't belong in any of her carefully crafted boxes, and it's unnerving her.

I pull her closer. With me sitting in the bed of the truck and her standing on the ground, we're almost eye to eye.

"I'm not giving up, Kitty." I push her hair behind her ear. "And once you realize that and decide to give in to this—" I point at the space between us, the invisible pull I've felt ever since I saw her—"you'll have to be the one to make the first move."

"What?" I'm sure that if I weren't holding on to her hand, she'd stagger back.

Didn't see that one coming, now did you, sweetheart?

"Yup." My grin grows wider as I nod decisively. This is what she needs? Fine, I can wait, give her time to adjust, get her to fall. "I'll wait for you, Kitty, but you're going to be the one to make the first move."

"What are you talking about?"

"I'll wait for you to kiss me first."

"I-I'm…"

I place my finger against her lips, effectively shushing her.

"But once you do, all bets are off."

With one final slide over her lip—for now—I pull back.

"It won't happen," she says with such conviction I almost believe her. Almost, but not quite.

Because what Kate doesn't know is that when I play, I play to win. Nothing else is an option.

Letting go of her, I cross my arms over my chest. "I guess we'll have to wait and see, won't we?" I look up when I see the movement behind her. "Oh, look, Becky and Miguel are here."

KATHERINE

"What was that?" Becky's wide eyes meet mine as we pile into her Jeep, and she starts the car.

"What was what?" I ask innocently, looking out the window.

The party is still in full swing, but when I was in Emmett's truck, it felt like it was just the two of us. It's dangerous. The way he can make me forget about everything around me and just concentrate on him.

His hands.

His voice.

His mouth.

"Don't play like you don't know. I'm talking about you and Emmett!"

"We were just waiting for *you* to show back up after disappearing with Miguel only God knows where." I turn to look pointedly at her. "Which took an awful lot of time, if I might add."

"We were fighting." Her voice is steady, but I can see a blush creeping up her neck.

"And it was important for him to smear your lipstick and ruffle your hair during that fight?" I lift my brow. "Plus, it's dark, but I believe I can see a hickey at the base of your neck, just barely covered by your shirt. You might want to take care of that before you get back home."

"Katherine!"

"Yes, Becky?"

She peeks at the rearview mirror. "God, I hate when you're right."

We both laugh at that.

"So, I presume the make-up went well?"

"I..." There is a brief pause as she makes a turn to the main road. "I don't know. We're friends. And then we piss each other off with something. Then we get angry. Then we try to talk, which leads to more yelling until we just burst from all this pent-up tension, and we kiss. But when the kiss ends, the reality and doubt set in."

I'm not sure who she's trying to convince because I'm fairly certain it isn't her who has doubts.

"But we weren't talking about me! We were talking about you, and what exactly we walked into earlier?"

"It was nothing."

"It ain't looking like nothing."

"Emmett has this weird obsession with me, and he thinks that he can get me to feel the same."

"What you mean is he likes you." She gives me an I-told-you-so look before returning her attention to the road just to take the turn onto Mabel's street. Well, my street, technically.

"What I mean is, he *thinks* he likes me. I've only been here for a few weeks. He doesn't even know me."

"Love doesn't know a timeframe."

"My skepticism does." I sigh in relief when I see my house, the only light on the one illuminating the front porch.

Becky parks in front of my house and turns to look at me. "Just promise me something."

"What?" I ask carefully.

"Whatever happens, don't break his heart."

Her words ring in the space around us, making my throat close up.

"He's a good guy, Kate, and I'd ha—"

I cover my hand with hers. "I know, Becky. I'll try my best. The last thing I want to do is hurt anybody."

A small smile appears on her lips, and she nods.

"See you at school on Monday?"

"Sure thing."

We say our goodbyes, and I get out of the car. Becky lifts her hand and waves before driving off. I climb the few steps onto the porch and pull the key out of my bag to open the door.

The house is quiet, so I slowly toe off my shoes, not wanting to wake up anybody.

"Fun night?"

I jump a little, completely startled. My hand covers my chest to calm my fast-beating heart as I turn around.

"Aunt Mabel! You scared me."

She's dressed in her pajamas and robe, her glasses perched on her nose.

"I was watching TV." The living room faces toward the backyard, which explains me not noticing the light. "Plus, somebody decided to stay out late."

Looking down at my phone, I notice it's past midnight. "Sorry if I kept you waiting."

The words feel foreign on my tongue. I don't remember a time Mom waited up for me to see if I got home okay.

Mabel looks at me for a moment but finally waves me off. "Did you have a good time?"

"Yeah, I did. Becky just dropped me off." I scratch the nape of my neck. "Anyway, I think I better go off to bed. Night, Aunt Mabel."

"Night, Kate."

Chapter 12

EMMETT

"Hey, is that the new girl?" John asks, narrowing his eyes somewhere over my shoulder.

I turn around, my eyes landing on Kate instantly. It's like my body knows she's there even before I see her.

"Katherine," I correct immediately. "Seems like it. But who's that with her?"

Kate's walking in front of a bench where a blonde girl with a dog is sitting, a few bags next to her. She's wearing another pair of jean shorts that leave all that skin exposed. Seriously, doesn't this girl have anything else in her closet?

Nico doesn't even bother to look her way. "Who the fuck cares? You guys coming or what?"

There are grunts of agreement, but I don't move my eyes from Katherine. Her mouth is moving a mile a minute, but she's too far away for me to decipher what she's saying.

"Emmett?"

"Huh?" I look back to see the guys already walking down the street.

"You coming or what?"

I shake my head no. "I'm good, I promised my dad I'd bring him some stuff for the ranch."

"Whatever man. Later."

We say our goodbyes, and I look at the road, making sure there isn't anybody around before I run to the other side.

Kate has stopped in front of the bench and is texting something on her phone. Her back is to me, so she doesn't see me coming, which gives me a moment to listen in before she realizes I'm there.

My body buzzes with anticipation as I get closer.

It's been less than twenty-four hours since I last saw her. Last touched her. I didn't want to let her go yesterday, but I knew it was the right choice. I don't know her story, but I can see her reluctance to get close to people. Even just as friends. I know she has to be the one to make the first move. But fuck it, I'm not used to waiting.

"It's going to be okay, Kate," an unfamiliar soft voice says, and it takes me a moment to realize it belongs to the blonde girl. She reaches for Kate's hands, trying to reassure her. Kate gives in, although it's obvious that she's restless. She looks down at her phone clenched in her free hand, cursing silently.

"She should have been here by now."

"She'll come, we can wait for a bit longer."

"It's already been half an hour."

"If she doesn't show up in the next fifteen minutes, we can go home on foot. It's not that far."

Figuring I've listened enough and not wanting to be caught eavesdropping, I clear my throat before asking, "Trouble, ladies?"

Kate's back stiffens at the sound of my voice. She slowly turns around to face me, blocking the girl on the bench from my view in the process.

"Emmett, fancy seeing you here." Kate crosses her arms over her chest.

"It's a small town," I comment, trying my best to ignore the fact that the motion lifts her tits just a tad higher, and the snug top she's wearing definitely doesn't help.

"Too damn small," she mutters quietly.

I blink, focusing my attention back on Kate's face. "You were saying?"

"Nothing. What are you doing here?"

I try to look over her shoulder, but she moves closer, drawing my attention back to her. Today her hair is piled atop her head in a messy bun, and she has a gray tee with *Cute but psycho* written on it. "Should I be afraid?" I ask, motioning to her shirt.

Kate rolls her eyes. "Yes, you should always be afraid. Now was there a specific reason you stopped by?"

Instead of answering her question, I ask one of my own. "You're not going to introduce me to your friend?"

"Wasn't my plan."

"Where are your manners, Kitty? I don't bite."

"Emmett..." There is a clear warning in her tone, but do I listen? Of course not.

For a bit, we struggle, but finally, I manage to get through her and face her friend. The blonde sits on the bench looking at us curiously, her hand clenching the dog's leash.

"Hey there, I'm Emmett. Kate and I go to school together," I say, offering her my hand.

She looks up and gives me an uncertain smile, but doesn't accept my hand. She looks young, probably two or three years younger than me, if not more. She's wearing a summer dress that shows off her pale skin. Her long blonde hair is braided and falling over her shoulder, and those eyes...

"Nice to meet you, Emmett. I'm Penelope, Kate's sister, but friends call me Penny."

Kate mutters something behind my back, then loudly clears her throat.

"Oh, sorry." Penelope extends her free hand and, after a bit of stumbling, grabs mine for a handshake.

"No problem. I didn't know Kate has a sister. And one so sweet." I take a quick glance at Kate. "Are you sure you two are related?"

"Har-har-har." Kate rolls her eyes.

"It's just an innocent question, Kitty." My hand drops to my side. My eyes fall down to the dog, a golden retriever, who's observing me carefully, but makes no attempt to socialize. "That's a cool dog you have. What's his—"

I start to reach for him to pet him.

"Don't touch him!"

I freeze mid-motion. Kate's hand is on my forearm, holding me back.

"What's the big deal?" I turn over my shoulder to look at Kate. I don't get her reaction at all. The dog doesn't seem dangerous, so what's the problem? "We have a dog back at the ranch. It's not like he'll bite my hand off."

"It's not that. Just don't…"

"He's working," Penelope's soft voice interrupts us.

"Penny, you don't have to…"

"It's okay, Kate." I turn around to look at Penelope. She's watching me, but her eyes don't quite reach my face. It's more like she's looking at my chest. "He's a seeing-eye dog, and he's working. Nobody should touch him right now except me. Plus, we're still kind of getting used to one another."

"A seeing-eye dog?" I ask, rubbing at the back of my neck. My mind is working a hundred miles a minute as I work out what she's saying. "But, that's…"

"Because I'm blind," Penelope finishes, that soft smile of hers not wavering once.

Blind?

"Oh, wow..." I know I probably sound like a complete idiot, but I'm at a loss for words.

Kate's sister is blind? She doesn't look blind.

As soon as the thought registers in my mind, I want to smack myself over the head. At least I didn't say it out loud. Because seriously, what does a blind person look like?

But I didn't see that one coming. Not in the slightest, although now that I look at her, actually *look*, it makes so much sense. The handshake, the whole watching while not quite meeting your eye thing.

Thankfully, Penelope doesn't seem to take it personally, or if she does, she doesn't show it.

"Didn't see that one coming?" Penelope offers kindly. I guess this isn't her first rodeo.

"No, I really didn't. Sorry for being weird."

Kate lets go of my hand and goes to her sister, looping her hand through her free one. Instantly, I regret losing her touch. She obviously doesn't because she's back to ignoring me.

"Maybe we should go. Mabel just texted that it might take a while, and she isn't sure when she'll be able to pick us up."

Seriously, Kitty?

"Where are you girls going?" I ask, not ready to be dismissed. "I can give you a ride."

"Oh, no, that's not..." Kate starts, but Penelope interrupts her. "That would be great!"

"Penny!" Kate hisses in warning, but Penelope either doesn't care, or she's used to it.

"What? He's offering to take us home."

"He might be a serial killer!"

"Is he?"

"Well, no, but that's..."

I look between the two sisters as they discuss me like I'm not standing right here. It's like watching one really intense tennis match. The part that really surprises me is that Penelope isn't just giving in to her sister, quite the contrary.

"Perfect." Shaking Kate off, Penelope stands up and moves closer, the dog moving in perfect sync with her, pulling her to a stop when they're right in front of me. "You and Kate are friends?"

I look over Penelope's shoulder, where her sister is scowling at us. Kate lifts her brow in challenge, which makes the tips of my lips rise.

"Yeah." I look down at Penny, giving her my full attention. This close, I can see even more similarities between the two sisters. They share the same round blue-purple eyes. The same pouty lips and stubborn tilt to their chins. They also have similar builds, which means they're awfully short, barely reaching my collar bone. "I think of her as my friend."

A friend with really sexy legs and a really, *really* stubborn streak that I'd love to kiss really badly.

"See?" She looks over her shoulder at Kate, smiling brightly.

Watching Penelope is fascinating. I now know she can't actually see Kate, yet she looks almost right at her. "Friends help friends, Kate."

"Fine," Kate huffs. She looks at me, and I can see it pains her to be nice. "We'll take you up on that offer *if* it's not too much trouble."

We stare at each other for a moment, and then there it is, that stubborn tilt to her chin. As if she's daring me to... I'm not even sure what.

Tell her I was just joking, and I'm not going to do it?

Actually take them home?

"No trouble at all," I grin, unable to look away. "Never when it comes to you."

Color creeps into her cheeks, turning them rosy. Her throat

bobs as she swallows; looking away, she nibbles at her lower lip. "Well... thanks."

Walking around Penelope, I come toe to toe with her sister. I tuck my finger under her chin and lift it, so she looks at me. "I mean it, Katherine."

She lets her lip pop, color rushing into the flesh. "That's what I'm afraid of."

Chapter 13

KATHERINE

"Sorry for the wait," Emmett says as he slides into his seat. Once we piled into his truck, he told us he had to make a stop at a store to grab some stuff for his dad.

We waited patiently—well, Penny waited as I gave her a piece of my mind—for Emmett and one of the workers to load the back of the truck with bags of God knows what. And all the while, as I was reprimanding Penny for asking Emmett to drive us, I couldn't help but watch him as he worked. The way his biceps flexed every time he grabbed one of the bags and threw it over his shoulder. Seriously, how does a guy in high school look like that?

Thankfully, Penny couldn't see me staring at him, but Emmett could. At one point, he caught me ogling him, and one of those grins of his appeared on his lips.

So. Not. Fair.

"No worries, you're doing us a favor," Penny says with a smile.

It's surreal the way he has her wrapped around his finger, and she couldn't even get the full effect of his charm.

Emmett starts the truck and checks the rearview mirror before pulling out on the road.

"So, Emmett, how do you know Kate?" Penny asks as soon as we're on our way.

"Oh, she ran over me," Emmett says so matter of factly that I almost believe him too.

"She what?" Penny shrieks, her wide eyes turning toward me.

"Yup." Emmett nods his head, dead serious. "It's true. She ran me over the first day of school."

I roll my eyes. "It was an accident. He turned around just when I was leaving the administrative office. And it was me who ended up on my ass, so I don't know who ran over whom," I point out for the umpteenth time. "Take a right turn here."

He gives me a quick glance, a grin flashing on his lips, before moving his attention back to the road. "It's not my fault that I'm all ripped, and your plan backfired."

I guess there is something to say about manual labor. Not that I'd ever admit that out loud.

"Ripped? What are you, a bodybuilder?"

"Nope, darlin'," Emmett drawls, his accent thickening. "Just a good ol' footballer."

Another grin. A shiver runs down my spine, goosebumps rising on my skin. That grin should be forbidden by law. As if he can read my mind, Emmett chuckles quietly.

"You play football?" Penny asks. Of course, that would get her attention.

"Sure do, Little Adams."

"Apparently, football equals religion around these parts," I mutter, unable to resist poking him, if only a little. But neither of them cares as they continue their conversation, ignoring me.

"What position do you play?"

"Linebacker."

Her brows furrow. "Are you any good?"

This time Emmett full-on laughs. "You can say that, yeah, I guess."

He makes the turn onto our street. Just a little bit more, and we'll be home, and Emmett will be gone. No more sexy grins and little taunts.

My eyes fall down to his mouth.

I'll wait for you to kiss me first.

The words I couldn't get out of my mind all night long ring in my mind once again. I hoped I'd get more time to compose myself, but of course, he had to be the one to find us stranded with bags of groceries to carry back home and our aunt MIA.

Get a grip, Kate!

"You guess?" Penny frowns. "That doesn't really sound convincing."

"Penny," I hiss quietly, elbowing her in the gut. The only thing it does is upset Henry, who gives me an unamused look.

"No, it's fine," Emmett reassures me.

"This is us." I point at the house.

The driveway is empty, so Emmett pulls in and kills the engine. Taking his cap off his head, he rubs the back of his neck before putting it back down.

"Have you ever been?"

"What?" I ask, my hand already on the door handle.

"To a football game?" He looks at Penny, and I realize the question was aimed at her. "Have you ever been?"

"Oh." Penny shrugs. "No real point in going since I can't actually see?"

"Maybe, but maybe not. Football is so much more than just watching an actual game."

Penny tilts her head to the side. "Like what?"

"Smell of grass." Penny furrows her nose in disgust, making Emmett laugh. I have to admit he has a nice laugh—loud and cheerful, it pulls you in, making you want to join in on the fun. "Okay, but there's also the crowd. The way they cheer you on to victory. Yelling, trash talk, stomping feet."

"Okay, I guess that does make sense."

"You should come."

"What?"

"No, really, the football season has just started, and we'll be playing every Friday. You should come." Emmett looks up, his eyes meeting mine. "Both of you."

The intensity of his gaze has chills running down my spine.

Stop it, Kate.

"I don't know."

"Think about it," he urges.

Nibbling on my lip, I nod once, not ready to give him an answer. Instead, I turn to my sister. "Ready to go?"

"Sure."

I hop out of the car and watch as Penny slowly does the same with the help of Henry. My heart is in my throat as she almost misses the step but manages to find her footing at the very last moment.

"Do you need help with the groceries?" Penny asks, rubbing softly between Henry's ears.

"I'm good," I assure her just as Emmett chimes in too.

"I'll help her carry the things inside, don't you worry about a thing, Little Adams."

"You know I'm not actually that little, right?"

"Of course, but you're Kate's little sister, hence you're Little Adams."

Penelope tilts her head to the side, thinking about it for a moment.

"Okay." Penny nods, her grip on Henry's harness tightening. "I'll prepare us some sweet tea. You like sweet tea, right?"

Emmett chuckles. "I'm southern, love. We live for sweet tea."

"Great. C'mon, Henry. Let's go to the house."

Emmett stops by my side, and together, we watch the two of them make their way to the house.

"How do you do that?" he asks quietly after a while.

"Do what?" I ask, my attention still on Penelope and Henry. They've stopped in front of the stairs, and Penny has to pat a bit until she finds the railing. Holding onto it, she takes a few steps to the porch.

"Just stand here and watch."

Once Penny unlocks the door and is safely inside, I breathe out and turn to Emmett, who's watching me. "I keep reminding myself that this isn't about me, but about her and that she can do it."

He nods his head. "Does she see anything at all?"

"Not sure." I shrug helplessly. "Penny was born with some nerve damage due to the fact that..." I look away, my throat closing up. I never talk about Mom's addictions. She might not drink her body weight in alcohol every day, but she has a soft spot for it, drinking way more than she should. Then there was a time when she experimented with drugs. Anything just to fit in with the movie crowd and get in. Did she do it when she was pregnant with Penny? I was too young to know, but knowing her patterns now, it seems very likely. "Well, anyway... Sometimes she says she can decipher shadows, but if so, it's very little."

"Is there anything that can be done to help her?"

Isn't that the million-dollar question? One I asked myself a hundred times in the past.

"I'm not sure, really, but even if there is, it probably costs a bunch of money, something we don't have. And I'd rather help her with something that she might find useful, like making sure she goes to a school that specializes in working with blind and visually impaired kids and getting her a guide dog to make things easier on her than giving her false promises."

Emmett turns toward me and just looks at me for a moment. I'm not sure how to decipher the look on his face. "You're a good sister, Kate."

A lump forms in my throat, but I push it down. "She's my little sister. There isn't anything I wouldn't do for her, no matter how crazy she drives me sometimes."

Emmett chuckles. "I like when she drives you crazy. Especially, if it ends up with you in my truck."

His eyes darken, if only slightly, and I know he's thinking about last night.

"Emmett," I sigh.

"Katherine."

"Why... I can't do this." I'm not even sure what *this* I'm referring to. Maybe I'm totally out of line here, but I need him to understand this. "Now you know about Penny, I can't..." I shake my head. "I *won't* risk somebody hurting her."

He frowns, seeming taken aback by my words. "And you think I'd hurt her?"

"What? God, no."

If I've learned something about Emmett in this short time we've known each other, it's that he's kind, and he wouldn't hurt a fly.

"Then?"

"You're... well, you." I push a strand of my hair behind my ear, suddenly feeling awkward.

"And what does that have to do with anything?"

"I might be new to town, but I see how people look at you. You're the golden boy around here. People look up to you, and I..."

Emmett takes my hand in his. "You matter to me."

I suck in a breath. "You can't say things like that."

"Why?"

Because you barely know me.

Because this is too fast, too soon.

Because I might believe you.

"Because it's not right."

"How can it not be?"

I shake my head. "It just can't be."

"So, all the things I'm feeling, they're what? Wrong?"

"They'll go away. You're just infatuated with the new girl in town. But that feeling? It'll go away sooner or later."

With his free hand, he grabs my chin and tilts my head back. Our gazes meet, and I can see the frustration on his face. "Don't tell me how I feel, Katherine."

My throat bobs as I swallow. He lets go, his fingers tracing the column of my neck. "There has never been anyone that made me feel as crazy as you do. Since the moment I first saw you."

"Emmett..."

"The worst part?" he interrupts me. "I don't want it to go away."

"I can't," I say softly. *Please, don't make me.*

"You're lucky I'm a patient man." Emmett cups my face, his thumb sliding over my lower lip. "And you, Katherine? You're worth waiting for."

With that, he pulls back, his hands falling by his side.

We're silent as he helps me get my things out of his truck and take them inside. Penny offers him sweet tea, but he apologizes and tells her that his dad called him and he has to leave. It's a lie, but I don't stop him when he turns on the balls of his feet and walks back to his truck, leaving me standing on the porch, looking as he drives away.

"I didn't do something wrong, did I?" Penny asks quietly from behind me.

I turn around to face her. "No, of course not."

It's been all me.

But, it's better that way.

Chapter 14

KATHERINE

"What has you all scowling like that?" Becky asks, nudging me with her elbow.

"What?" I ask, startled. I force myself to turn around and look at her instead of staring at her best friend.

Since her previous class is right next to my locker, she has a tendency to pick up her things quickly before meeting me so we can walk to AP English together. Something I don't appreciate right this moment.

Becky's head is tilted to the side as she observes me carefully. She tips her chin toward me. "What's with that face?"

Pushing my hair behind my ear, I shrug. "Not sure what you're talking about," I mutter, doing my best to act nonchalant.

I turn my back to her and blindly start grabbing books from my locker. I'm not even sure if I'm grabbing the right ones, I just need something to hold on to, and then I'm getting the hell out of here.

And you, Katherine? You're worth waiting for.

So much for that being true.

The book I just grabbed slips through my fingers and falls on my foot. Pain spreads through my leg.

Ouch, that hurts.

"Oh, please, you all but drilled a hole through Emma's head."

Emma, Emmett, it's all the same. I crouch down and pick up the book forcefully.

"Who's Emma?" I ask instead, deciding to play dumb. My voice is tight even to my own ears, my throat closing in.

"That girl standing with Emmett and the guys? Perfect blonde waves and big blue eyes, wearing too short of a skirt Emma? Ring any bells?"

"Not really." I grab the rest of my books—hopefully, the right ones for the remainder of my classes—shove them into my backpack and shut my locker before turning to Becky. "You coming?"

"Not really?" She frowns. "Is that all you have to say?"

Knowing she won't move if I don't do it first, I start walking. "What do you want me to say?" I ask defensively.

"I don't know, something?" She catches up to me, the two of us hurrying through the throng of people that are also rushing to get to their next class before the bell rings.

Not Emmett, though. He's too busy flirting with the Barbie.

I'll wait for you to kiss me first.

Yeah, right, I see how he's waiting. Seriously, what was I thinking? I wasn't. That's the problem.

That's what you wanted anyway, I remind myself.

"They have US history together," Becky says, bringing me out of my thoughts. "Emmett and Emma. They're probably been talking about the class or something."

"Or something," I mutter, entering the classroom.

People are already mingling around the room, getting ready for our next lesson to begin. I sit down in my seat, letting my backpack slide to the floor next to my desk. "You don't have to explain Emmett to me. What he does is none of my business."

From the corner of my eye, I can see Becky's brows shoot up. "Is that why you're acting so weird?"

"I'm not acting weird," I protest quickly. Maybe a little too quickly.

"Mm-hmm... right. I figured after Friday..."

"Nothing happened Friday." I force a smile out. "Seriously. Emmett can do whatever he wants, with whoever he wants."

"If you say so..."

She doesn't seem convinced, but thankfully, she lets it go.

"Can we talk about something else, please?"

"Like what?"

"What's new with you and Miguel?"

"Shh!" Becky hisses at me, then looks around frantically to make sure nobody is listening.

"What?"

"Not so loud."

I look around, but everybody is, for once, minding their own business. "Nobody's looking."

"Still, I think we've already established nothing's going on. We're just friends."

"Mm-hmm, if that's what you call it around here, then, sure."

"I'm serious, we're just..."

But she doesn't get to finish because the bell rings, and our teacher starts the class.

I give her a look. "Saved by the bell."

―――――

EMMETT

"Are you planning to tap that?" Nico asks me as we hurry to get to the gym on time, so Coach doesn't kill us.

I look at him over my shoulder, but the dude seems completely serious. "Don't be an idiot."

"What? She seemed more than willing, and you didn't exactly correct her."

I was about to, but then I saw Kate and Becky together. Kate caught a glimpse of me, but before a smile could form on her mouth, she saw Emma standing there next to me. Her smile was gone before it even appeared, replaced by a scowl.

I knew it was wrong, a completely asshole thing to do, but I couldn't help myself. I was still so pissed at her for not even giving me a chance. For assuming that I'd want to hurt her sister, all of it. So, I might have let Emma hang on my arm a bit too much, and my smile might have been a bit bigger than usual.

Kate was the one who said no, after all.

"We were only talking," I say defensively, as we get to the locker room, just as one of our teammates is coming out in a hurry.

"Dude, hurry the fuck up because Coach's pissed."

Shit, just what I needed.

I let my backpack drop on the bench in front of my locker and quickly work on changing my clothes.

"What he's trying to say is that he was trying to make Kate jealous." Miguel grins knowingly.

"The new girl?" Nico frowns.

"Her name's Kate," I mutter, pushing down my jeans and grabbing my shorts.

How hard is that to remember?

"See? He gets all irritable like that when she's in question."

I pull my shirt on and glare at my soon-to-be ex-best friend. "Seriously?" Does he really have a wish to lose one of his teeth today? "And all that coming from a guy who can't find common ground with his best girl friend?"

"Shut up." He shoves me away as we all start toward the

door and gym. "It's not my problem that girls act so freaking weird."

"She's *Becky*," I point out.

"I know, that's why it's even more weird than usual. You'd think she'd be used to it by now."

"Girls are just weird, bro." Nico shrugs.

"Maybe if you tried not to piss her off so much..."

"I'm not doing it on purpose."

I give Miguel a pointed look.

"What? I'm not. At least, not *most* of the time."

"And then you wonder why she's pissed at you *most* of the time." I roll my eyes.

"Hey, it's not like you're any better. I remember seeing Kate storm away as fast as she could just now."

"For the hundredth time, I wasn't the one who asked Emma to come and talk to us."

It's not like I intentionally wanted to make her jealous. It just kind of, sort of, happened.

"Sure thing."

Miguel pushes open the door to the gym, and we go inside. The door makes a squeaking noise as it always does, making the coach turn around toward us.

"Oh, look who finally decided to join us. Guess we know who'll be cleaning today after we're done."

I want to groan, but with Coach's narrowed eyes still on us, I hold it in.

"Now, get your asses to work."

Chapter 15

KATHERINE

"Why is it still so hot?" I groan loudly as I wave a hand in front of my face in hopes it'll help me cool off. No such luck. "Shouldn't the temperature start falling by now?"

Becky chuckles. "This is Texas, honey."

"So, not fair. It feels like all I do is sweat, and it's frigging September. Did Texas not hear about fall?"

Becky, on the other hand, looks amazing as always. Her hair isn't frizzy from the heat, and there's not even a drop of sweat on her face.

"Not likely. It's like there are two seasons around here, summer and winter, and that's about it. Are you sure you don't want to go back inside? There is AC in the cafeteria."

And be forced to spend my lunch break with Emmett and the guys? Highly unlikely.

"The quad's fine. I think a little bit of air will help me clear my mind."

Becky gives me a skeptical look. "Suit yourself."

Together we find a little piece of ground that's in the shade of a tree, so we settle underneath it, pulling our lunch out.

"You'd think that you'd be used to heat coming from California of all places."

"I am, but I guess after a while, you just get sick of it? I'm so ready for cooler weather." I pull my chicken wrap from the bag. "What about you? Been anywhere outside of Bluebonnet, Texas?"

"Actually, yes."

I listen as Becky tells me about her mom's sister who lives in Ohio, and how they occasionally go there to visit.

Her phone beeps just as she's finishing telling me about the time her family went fishing and her older brother ended up in the lake. Although phones are technically prohibited inside the school premises, I don't think anybody actually follows that rule.

Becky checks the screen, and whatever's on it has her rolling her eyes.

"What is it?"

"Miguel." She rolls her eyes. "He's asking where we are."

"If you want you can go inside," I offer, knowing she's here because I asked her.

"What? Of course not. I'm not leaving you."

"But they're your friends. It wasn't my intention to put you on the spot."

"You're my friend too. And you aren't putting me on the spot. Besides, chances are even if I go back, we'll pick a fight or something again. I love those guys, but sometimes they drive me bonkers."

I chuckle. "I think the feeling is mutual."

"Oh, I know that. We've known each other since we were just kids. My family owns a ranch next to Emmett's. We've been next-door neighbors our whole lives. With two brothers, I've always been surrounded by boys, so it felt natural to make friends with Emmett and the guys."

"It's strange that you didn't turn out to be a tomboy."

Becky smooths out the edge of her skirt. "Oh, I was a tomboy for a bit there, but even though the boys are my best friends, I always loved girly stuff too. Dresses, high heels, makeup, dolls." She looks to the side, a smile curling her lips. "I remember one time I was really sick with the flu. Once I finally felt better, Miguel and Emmett came for a visit, and I made them play Barbies with me."

"Did they do it?" I ask, laughing at the image of the three of them playing with dolls.

"They sure did. They were grumbling the whole time, but they did it."

"Who did what?"

We both turn as one at the sound of the new voice. Emmett and Miguel are standing there, looking at us expectantly. I'd been concentrating so much on the story that I didn't hear them arrive.

"I was just telling Kate about that time when you came to visit me, and we ended up playing with Barbies together."

Emmett groans.

"Seriously, Becs? That's so freaking low. And here we were worried about you since you didn't come to the cafeteria."

Becky looks at me and makes a face before turning her attention back to Miguel. "What did you think happened?"

"How the hell should I know? You didn't show up." There is a frown between Miguel's brows. He kicks a rock, sulking. "You always show up."

"That's my fault," I interject, not wanting Becky to take the blame. "I thought it'd be fun to eat outside for a change."

Emmett's brows raise. "In this heat?"

"It's not that bad," I say defensively, but don't look at him. There is no way I'll admit that not that long ago I complained about the exact same thing, but would rather spend time outside than have to look at him flirting with Barbie Emma or one of her friends.

"Yeah, right."

Emmett doesn't seem to believe me one bit, not that I can blame him. Even I don't believe myself.

"It's not. Besides, I'm from California. It's basically the same."

Becky gives me a look but doesn't comment out loud.

"Sure thing." Emmett throws his backpack on the ground and sits next to me.

I pull back a little, creating some space between us. "What are you doing?"

"We're here." Emmett shrugs, pulling his lunch out of his backpack. "Might as well eat."

He takes one of my chips.

"Hey," I protest. "That's mine."

Emmett's hand stops just short of his mouth. His full, lush mouth. The mouth that I still dream about brushing against mine.

He lifts his brows. "Want me to give it back?"

I shake my head to clear my mind and glare at him. "Keep it."

"How come you two decided to come outside?" Becky asks, taking a sip from her water bottle.

"When you didn't show up, other people decided to take your spots," Miguel says as he sits cross-legged next to her.

"What other people?" Becky asks, her eyes narrowing.

"Just oth—" Becky pinches him. "*Ouch.* Fine, some of the cheerleaders."

"Why am I not surprised the vultures came?" She rolls her eyes.

"They're not all bad." Miguel takes a huge bite of the first slice of his pizza; out of *three.*

Becky turns to him. "If they're not so bad, why did you come here?"

"And here they go again," I mutter to myself. Becky and Miguel are too busy fighting, so they don't hear me, but Emmett does, and he chuckles softly.

"Nothing to say?" Emmett whispers so only I can hear him.

Unable to resist it, I look up at him. His face is serious as he observes me. My tongue darts out, wetting my lower lip. "What is there to be said?"

The silence stretches between us as we just stare at one another—

a silence filled with tension that seems to last way longer than the few seconds it actually does.

"Nothing, I guess." Emmett shrugs and looks away, concentrating on his food.

I do the same, but I can't erase the look of disappointment that crossed his face before he looked away.

"Hey, I'm home," I yell as I enter the house. I let my backpack drop to the floor and toe off my shoes.

The music stops, and a soft voice calls out my name. "Kate?"

"It's me." I grab the strap of the backpack and follow the sound of my sister's voice to the living room. "What have you been up to, Penny?"

Her fingers swiftly move over the ivory keys, melody filling the space. "Playing."

Dropping my backpack by the couch, I go and sit next to her on the bench. Henry opens one eye from his place next to the piano and looks at me. I swear I can feel his judgment sometimes. I scratch him behind his ears for a bit until he's content and goes back to sleep. "How was school?"

"Good."

"Nobody giving you a hard time?"

"I'm thirteen, not a baby, Kate," Penny groans. Shifting in her seat, so she's turned toward me, Penny takes my hand in hers, giving it a squeeze. "You don't have to worry so much."

She tilts her head, making her braid sway and fall over her shoulder.

I push a strand of pale blonde hair behind her ear with my free hand. "You're my little sister, of course, I worry."

"You don't have to worry. People are nice here. It's not like in the city."

I know she's right, but the fact is, there are bad people everywhere. And just because so far we've only encountered good folk doesn't mean there isn't an asshole hiding here somewhere.

"There are mean people everywhere, Penny," I voice out loud. I need her to remember that and not let her guard down.

"Why are you always so pessimistic?"

"Realistic," I counter, at which she just rolls her eyes.

"Tomato, tomahto."

"Yeah, yeah, smartass."

"How was *your* school?"

"It was..." Emmett's disappointed face flashes before my eyes, making my heart sink a little. I hated seeing him like that. I hated even more that I was the reason behind that look. "Good," I finish weakly, but Penny doesn't notice. Instead, she nudges me with her elbow playfully.

"Seen a certain football player?"

I groan. "Don't say it like that."

"Like what?" That innocent look she's sporting isn't fooling me. Not in the slightest.

"Like that. Like there is something going on."

"It's not?" she asks, a frown between her brows deepening.

"Of course not."

"Emmett said you guys are friends."

"We are," I confirm. "Sort of."

Penny quirks a brow. "That doesn't sound convincing."

That's because I'm not. But I'm not about to admit that. Instead, I play a few keys, hoping it'll draw her attention from a certain boy. "C'mon, play something for me. I so rarely get a chance to hear you play."

Penny gives me a look that tells me she sees right through me. "You have to start letting people in." She presses one of the keys, the sound ringing in the room. "There are some good things about Texas, you know."

"I do, but don't get too comfortable."

I've had my life uprooted one too many times to let myself believe this is forever. A rug can get swept from under your feet before you can even blink, so it's better not to get too comfortable.

"And you don't be so moody."

Not waiting for my retort, Penny turns to the piano. Her fingers hover in the air, just above the keys, and then she slowly puts them down, creating a soft melody.

Penelope has always had a thing for music, ever since she was a baby. All she wanted to do was bang against things as hard as her chubby little hands would let her. But while all she created before was noises that most of the time drove Mom and me mad, now she's gotten better. So much better. It was all thanks to one of her previous teachers who took her under her wing and gave her free classes one year.

Looking back, I think her love of sound came with her inability to see. To compensate—in a way—for her lack of sight, she had to rely on her other senses to fill in the void that was inside her.

The melody slowly grows in intensity as her fingers move

faster and faster over the keys, creating a haunting sound that touches your soul.

Penny moves in time with the notes, her whole body flowing with the melody. As the piece reaches a climax, her head falls back, more of her hair slipping the confines of her braid. Her breathing is rushed, color filling her pale cheeks as she slowly brings the piece to an end.

"That was beautiful." I wrap my arms around her and pull her in for a hug.

"Thanks," she says, a smile curling her lips. "I've been practicing every chance I can; maybe if I get really good, that could be my ticket to college, since I know..."

I take her hands in mine, giving her a reassuring squeeze. "You'll go to college, Penny. I know you will."

"It's not the same, and you know it."

My heart squeezes painfully at the sorrow in her voice. "I do, but I also know any college would be lucky to have such a smart, talented girl like you."

"Fingers crossed, right?"

"Fingers crossed." I give her another squeeze and then get up. "How about you play for a bit more while I go up and change? Then we can do something fun together."

"Yeah, sounds like a—"

The rest of the sentence dies on her lips as the doorbell rings, making Henry jump to his feet and start barking excitedly.

Penny and I exchange a look.

"Are you expecting somebody?" Penny asks, brows furrowing.

I shake my head and get off the bench.

"Not that I know of." I head to the door, Henry at my feet. "Be right back."

Pulling open the door, I come face to face with the last person I expected.

"Becky." I look over her shoulder, but there is just her Jeep parked in the driveway. "What are you doing here?"

Henry barks excitedly, happy to have company. Seriously, if somebody were to break into the house, Henry would welcome them with open arms or paws, in his case. Completely useless as a guard dog, that one.

"Nope, I'm here to get you." Henry nudges her with his head, drawing her attention. "Oh, who do we have here?"

Becky crouches down and scratches Henry behind the ears, all the while cooing excitedly, and Henry, the traitor, enjoys every second.

"Ummm..." I lean against the door. "Get me for what?"

Becky looks up and gives me an extra big smile. "You know how you complained you were hot earlier?"

"Vaguely," I admit, unsure where she's going with this.

"Yeah, well, you're not the only one. That's why we decided to go swimming!"

"Swimming?" I frown. "And who exactly is 'we'?"

"Yeah, silly, swimming. You know that thing where you get in the water to cool off when it's extremely hot outside?"

Henry gives another nudge to Becky since she stopped petting him.

"I didn't realize there's a pool here in Bluebonnet."

A secretive smile curls her lips. "There isn't."

"Then how are we going to swim?"

"The old-fashioned way, how else?"

Before I can ask her what she means by that, I hear rustling coming from the living room. Henry's head snaps up at the sound. He tilts it to the side, as if listening carefully, and then dashes to the living room without a backward glance.

I guess he's good for something after all.

"I didn't realize you have a dog." Becky lifts her brows in question, just as Penny walks to the doorway, Henry by her side.

"Kate? Who is it?"

"He's not mine," is my only explanation as I turn toward Penny. "A friend of mine."

"Oh." Penny pushes a strand of her hair behind her ear, a nervous smile flashing briefly over her lips. "I didn't realize you'd have company."

"Becky just stopped by to invite me for a swim, although I'm still not sure where," I explain, glaring at the person in question. "Becky, this is my sister, Penelope. Penny, this is Becky, one of my classmates."

"Hi." Penny waves her hand.

"Hey, it's so nice to finally meet you!" Becky gives me a quick glance. "Kate told me a little bit about you. What grade are you in? You look around my brother's age. Maybe you know him..."

"Oh, I don't attend school here," Penny says quickly.

"No?"

"No, I—"

"Penny, you don't have to—" I start, but she just shakes her head at me.

"It's okay, Kate. She's your friend, right?"

From the corner of my eye, I can see Becky give us a curious look.

"She is, but so was Julie."

Penny takes a few steps toward me. She reaches for my hand but misses it, so I wrap mine around hers instead. "Not everybody is Julie."

"They aren't," I sigh. "Still, I worry, Pen."

Penny shakes her head. "No, it's okay, really. It's not like it's a big deal. I go to St. Lucy's."

Becky blinks. "But that's..."

"School for the blind and visually impaired, yes," Penny finishes.

I wrap my arms around Penelope, pulling her into my side. It's almost an instinctual reaction. I don't believe Becky is mean or that she'd do anything to hurt Penelope—or anybody else for that matter, okay except maybe Miguel—but I'm insanely protective of my sister.

"Penny's blind," I supply. "St. Lucy's was a part of the reason we moved here."

"Oh." Becky looks at Penny like she sees her for the first time. "So you don't see anything?"

Penny chuckles a little. "Nope, not a thing."

"And you were born like this?" Becky blushes. "Sorry if that's inappropriate. I don't think I've ever met a..."

"Blind person." The words fall off Penelope's lips easily. There is no judgment in her voice. It's actually funny. People always ask similar questions when they first find out about Penny's eyesight. Sometimes we'd bet which one they'd ask first. It was a game of ours. Then again, we've lived like this our whole lives. "It's okay to say it. I'm blind. It's just the way I am. The way I've been my whole life."

"Wow, okay." Becky looks around, seeming lost for a moment. Her eyes fall down to Henry and then come back to me. "So when you said the dog's not yours..."

"Henry, yes." At the sound of his name, Henry's ears perk up. "He's Penny's guide dog. As you could see he's pretty social, but he shouldn't be distracted while he's working."

"No distractions while he's working." Becky nods. "Gotcha."

I take a deep breath.

This went... well.

Maybe Penny is right after all. I do always expect the worst from people, but after everything that has happened, it's not surprising I'm wary.

"About swimming, I don't think that's the best idea, Becs. Besides, I just told Penny we'd go and do something together."

Becky looks between the two of us. "She should come too."

"What?" I pull back, stunned. *Is she for real?*

"No, I'm serious." She turns to Penny. "You should come. It will be so much fun."

Penny's eyes widen. "But I don't know how to swim."

"It's not a problem." Becky waves her off. "Half the people come to be seen anyway. Or drink beer. That too."

Does she think that's encouraging?

"I'm not sure that's the best idea." Penny turns to me. "But you should go, Kate. We can always do something together later."

"No." I shake my head. "I promised. If you're not going, I'm not going."

"Kate..." Penny groans.

"Don't *Kate* me, Pen. We're in this together, remember?"

It was a promise I made her, and I planned my damnedest to keep it. I failed her once, and I'm not about to do it again.

"God, can you both get a grip?" Becky crosses her arms over her chest and glares at us. "You're both coming."

"But..."

"But nothing, you're coming." Becky snaps her fingers. "C'mon, put on some swimsuits, day's a-wastin'."

"Is this..." I ask, looking at the dirt road in front of us some twenty minutes later. Once Becky started snapping fingers; there wasn't anything that could be done to change her mind. You don't mess with Becky once she sets her mind on something, there is no way you'll come out a winner, so you might as well give in and not waste your breath.

Becky gives me a quick glance before returning her attention to the bumpy road. "Emmett's place, yeah."

My heart skips a beat just at the mention of his name.

Seriously, this is crazy.

Penny's head peeks between the seats. "We're going to Emmett's?"

Of course, that'd get her attention.

Becky lifts her head and looks at Penny's reflection in the rearview mirror, clearly surprised. "You know Emmett?"

"Yeah, we met recently. He gave us a ride home the other day when our aunt had to stay late at work and couldn't pick us up."

"Oh, really?" Becky gives me a curious glance, but I look away, not really in the mood to explain that one. And knowing Becky, she'll want details.

Chuckling knowingly, she shakes her head at me but thankfully doesn't probe further, for now. "Yeah, this is Emmett's. His family owns a ranch."

Penny's face lights up. "Like a horse ranch?"

"Cattle, but they have a few horses too."

Penny nods like that makes sense. "That sounds like fun."

"It's a lot of work, that's what it is, but it's our way of life." Becky shrugs. "You like horses, Penny?"

"I like animals in general."

"I'm sure if you asked him, he would show you."

Penny thinks about it for a moment. "You think he wouldn't mind doing that?"

"Penny," I warn. I hate being the one to tell her no, but want it or not, we're both aware of her limitations. Riding horses definitely being one of them. Just the idea of her sitting on a horse makes a shiver run down my spine.

"It's not like I want to ride, Kate. Just meet the horses, that's it."

"I know, I just..."

"Worry," she finishes on a sigh. "I know, but you can't baby me for the rest of my life. I know what I can and can't do better than anyone."

Her little stab stings more than I'd like to admit, but she's right. More often than not, I feel like I act more like a mother than her sister, but it's been like that since we were little. You can never rely on our mother, so somebody had to take the role of an adult, and that somebody turned out to be me. I know I'm too protective, but I can't help myself.

"Okay, sorry. I'll try to chill."

"Thank you."

Penelope extends her hand between the seats. I take her hand in mine and give her a little squeeze. While some sisters could communicate with their eyes, we do so by touch. "I just want you to be happy."

"I'm happy."

I turn around so I can see her better, trying to figure out if there is truth in her words, but she genuinely seems okay. She's been smiling more often, laughing even, and she seems like she's excited about things again. All the things that were lacking there for a while.

"We're here," Becky says, cutting the engine. "Ready to go?"

I look out the windshield and see a group of kids hanging out around the pond that's more like a small lake. Some I recognize from school, although not all. Not that that's anything strange. Some are in the water, while others play with the football out on the grass. The group is mixed, with both boys and girls hanging out together. Beautiful girls dressed in bikinis that reveal more than they hide sunbathing on the dock.

I swallow the lump in my throat. "I didn't realize there'd be such a crowd."

They must have heard the car coming because people are already watching us curiously, Emmett being one of them. I sink my teeth into my lower lip.

This was such a bad idea.

"Oh, that?" Becky shrugs, opening her door. "That's nothing; usually there are more people."

Not helping, Becs. Not helping.

"Great."

Forcing a smile, I get out with Penny following my lead. I watch as she, with the help of Henry, gets out of the car.

"Here you go." Becky hands me my backpack, in which I quickly put our towels and a quick change of clothes before Becky ushered us out of the house.

"Thanks." Throwing it over my shoulder, I look at Penny. "You good?"

"Yeah." Penny tightens her hold on the harness. "Lead the way."

Before we even get halfway to the pond, Emmett and Miguel are there to greet us.

"Look who finally decided to show up," Miguel muses, throwing the football in the air and catching it.

Becky crosses her arms over her chest. "Some of us had to pick up company."

I'm not sure how she does it because I'm at a loss for words.

Holy mother of Jesus, is that what's been hiding under his shirt? No wonder he's so cocky.

I mean, I saw him at practice that one time, but looking at shirtless Emmett from a distance versus all up close and personal isn't nearly the same.

Emmett runs his fingers through his slightly damp hair. He

must have already been in the pond at some point earlier today, and a part of me is sad I didn't get to see it.

How is this guy only seventeen years old? It seems so unfair. Shouldn't teen years be an ugly duckling phase? Apparently not for Emmett Santiago because he's as far from an ugly duckling as possible.

Even at seventeen, he towers over most of his classmates. His shoulders are wide, muscles firmly defined, and although there's no six-pack on his stomach, I swear I can see the slight outline signaling he's not that far from getting one. His skin is golden, probably from hours spent outside, playing football and helping his family with the ranch, and there is a little patch of dark hair covering his lower stomach and leading into his swim trunks.

"Kate?"

Penny's voice makes my head snap up, my cheeks heating in embarrassment. "Huh?"

I find four pairs of eyes, five if we count Henry, looking at me curiously. How long was I out? My God, did I stare at Emmett's stomach as if it was calling my name?

Becky tilts her head to the side. "Are you okay?"

"Yup, fine. Totally fine," I mumble, hoping I sound half-coherent.

"You sure?" Emmett grins. "You seem a bit flushed."

I glare at him. "I'm fine."

He lifts his hands in surrender. "I'm just asking." His attention shifts to Penny. "I see you brought company. Hey, Little Adams, so nice to see you again."

Penny shifts in Emmett's direction, smiling at him. "Hi, Emmett."

"I hope we're not intruding," I say, putting my arm around my sister's shoulders.

"No way, the more, the merrier. If I'd known you'd be here, I'd have brought Rex too, or is that a no-no?"

"Henry's working."

"Poor pup, all work, no play." Emmett shakes his head. "I hope you at least give him all the treats."

Penny giggles. "We play when we're home."

"And he gets too many treats, courtesy of this little rebel."

"I don't know what you're talking about," Penny giggles, petting Henry between the ears.

"I have no idea what you guys are talking about, I just know it's freaking hot, and I'm ready to dive in."

Before I realize what Miguel's about to do, his hands are around Becky's waist. He throws her over his shoulder and runs for the pond.

"Miguel!" Becky shrieks. She starts punching his back, but the only thing it does is make her backpack slide down on the ground. "This is a new dress, and I swear to you if you throw me in the water with it on, I'm going to k—"

The words die on her lips as he jumps in the water, Becky in tow.

"Did he—" Penny's fingers dig into my forearm.

"Mm-hmm..."

Just then, they both surface. Becky pushes her hair out of her face and turns around to Miguel, who's shaking his head like a dog.

"Kill you," she hisses, pointing her finger at him. Then she jumps on him, dunking him underwater once again.

"She seems quite serious about it," I note, my eyes glued to the two of them. Part of me wonders if I should intervene. Nope, I'm definitely not getting in the middle of *that*.

"Oh, she *is* serious," Emmett chimes in. His brows rise as he looks at me. "You wanna go swim?"

Swiftly, I turn toward him. *Is he insane?*

"No, thank you very much."

"You sure?" He almost looks disappointed.

"Positive."

"Oh, well..." Emmett grabs my hand and throws his arm around Penny. "Let's get you at least settled then."

"You're not going to go and help your best friend?"

"With that?" He tilts his head in the general direction of the pond where Becky and Miguel are trying to outmaneuver one another. "Yeah, I think not. He made his bed and all that jazz."

"Some best friend you are."

"Becky wouldn't think so."

"Well, Becky is acting just a bit crazy."

"Hey!" the person in question yells. Jumping on Miguel, she dunks him underwater and throws her head back to get her wet hair out of her face so she can glare at me. "I heard that."

"You were supposed to!" I shout right back.

"I'll remember that, just so you know."

"I'm all about getting your revenge, but I draw the line at murder. Maybe you should let him get some air? Torture works better if the person is alive."

She tilts her head, thinking. "That," she says and points her finger at me. "That's the kind of friend I need."

I chuckle at her, shaking my head. Peering over my shoulder, I look at Emmett. "Seriously, what kind of people do you hang out with?"

His eyes are still glued to his best friends like he doesn't recognize them. "Sometimes, I wonder too."

Chapter 16

EMMETT

"You sure you don't want to dive in to cool off?" I look over my shoulder to where Miguel, Becky, and a few others are playing volleyball in the shallow part of the pond. "They're not killing each other any longer."

"I'm not sure about that," Kate says warily, squinting in the direction of the two. She's sitting on the dock, her legs dangling over the edge, her toes dipped into the water. Kate nibbles at her lower lip, her attention returning to me. "Truth?"

"Always," I say instantly, moving closer toward her. So close that I'm standing between her legs, my hands leaning against the dock on either side of her.

"I've never swum in anything other than a pool."

"What?" I ask, surprised.

"I know," Kate groans loudly, burrowing her head in her hands.

"Don't hide from me, Kitty." I pull her hands away gently and find her pink cheeks.

"Our mom never took us swimming, and the one time I did go, it was for a birthday party for one of the girls in my class. To say it was a disaster would be an understatement."

"So you don't know how to swim?"

"I can manage." There is a slight pause as she looks away. "Probably."

I shake my head, not knowing what to say. "What about you, Little Adams?" I ask, turning my attention to the other sister. She's been quiet so far, sitting by Kate's side and petting Henry, who's lying next to her.

She shakes her head. "I never learned."

"I honestly don't know what to say." I'm completely baffled. They never learned how to swim? For real? I still remembered those summer days when my dad took me riding with him, and we'd eventually end up at the pond.

"Don't worry, we won't go drowning on your land or anything like that," Kate says teasingly. Or at least I hope she's teasing.

"Nobody's drowning on my watch." Especially not her. Just the thought of anything happening to her sends chills running down my spine. "I could teach you."

"Teach me what?" Her brows furrow. "How to swim?"

"Yeah."

Or anything else you'd like me to teach you. Even better if it involves my hands on you. Or my mouth.

"Like right now?" Kate looks around, her eyes wide.

I shrug, trying to play it cool. "Or we could do it another day."

When it's just her and me.

Kate nods in agreement. "Another day sounds like a plan."

I hold her gaze, wanting her to know I'm serious. "I'll hold you to it."

Kate's throat bobs as she swallows. "Okay."

"Okay," I say, smiling.

I was surprised when I saw them come, not sure why exactly. I should have known Becky would take it upon herself to invite Kate. Hell, I wanted her here. I just didn't know how to ask, not after the debacle that happened earlier.

I hate this tension that has grown between us in the last few days, and what for? I know Kate is closed off and doesn't trust easily. And what was the first thing I did when it was directed at me? I ran, pissed off at her.

"What are you two grinning at?" Becky asks as she swims next to me.

"Just talkin'." I raise my brow at Kate but she just shakes her head.

"Mm-hmm..."

Reluctantly, I turn away, giving my attention to Becky. "What about you? Done playing?"

"Yup, I want to get dry before the sun goes down."

Becky places her palms on the dock and hoists herself up.

"Hey, Emmett?" Penny asks softly, so softly, I almost don't hear her.

"What's up, Pen?"

She's looking out toward the pond and fussing with the tip of her braid nervously.

"Becky told me you have horses on the ranch."

Kate groans. "Penny..."

I glance quickly at Kate, and then turn back to her sister. "Sure, we do. Why?"

"Could I meet them?"

"Emmett has friends here, Penny, he can't just—"

"It's not a problem." I wave Kate off. "Wanna go now?"

Penny beams at me, her smile so bright it's almost blinding. "Really?"

What is it about these Adams girls, really? Just one smile, and a guy doesn't stand a chance.

"Sure thing." Pulling away from Kate, I move so I can also get out of the water. I can feel Kate's eyes on me as I push out of the pond and get on the dock. "Mind if I borrow your towel?" I ask her, already grabbing it.

"N-nope."

"Thanks." I wipe my face with it and throw it over my shoulder. "You coming, Penny?"

She gets to her feet, and Henry follows her in tow. "Yes!"

"You wanna come too, Kate?"

"She'll stay with me. I need somebody to prevent me from killing Miguel," Becky says before Kate can even open her mouth.

"I thought you guys are good."

"That can change pretty quickly," she mutters, glaring at the pond, where Miguel is flirting with one of the girls.

"You guys are so fucked up." I shake my head. "C'mon, Penny, let's get out of here."

Kate grabs my hand before I can take a step. I look down at her, hoping that maybe she changed her mind. "Take care of her, okay?" she asks softly, so only I can hear it.

I nod. "Of course."

"His hair is so rough," Penny says, running her hand down the animal's neck. He shies under her gentle touch.

"Shh..." I soothe quietly, gripping the reins tighter. The horse's brown eyes stare at mine, and he doesn't look the least bit amused. Not that I can blame him. "Good boy."

"What's his name?"

"Thunder." His ears perk at the sound of his name. "He's an Appaloosa. We've been buddies since he was a foal. We grew up together in a way, right boy?"

Thunder lifts his head and huffs, which has me rolling my eyes. Sometimes he acts like he's the freaking king of the stables.

"Did you ride him when he was a baby too?"

"Sure did. When you grow up on a ranch like this, you learn how to ride before you can even walk. Do you want to give him a carrot?"

Penny tilts her head toward me, her whole face lighting up. "Can I?"

"Sure thing, here." I grab the carrot from my back pocket and hand it to Penny. Thunder's greedy eyes follow the exchange. Penny's slender fingers carefully wrap around the vegetable as she takes it from me.

"Will he bite me?" she asks, looking unsure, those big blue eyes of hers that remind me so much of her sister turning to me for reassurance.

"Nah, just be..."

But before I manage to warn her, Thunder's already stealing the carrot from her, munching on it happily.

"He's one greedy bastard," I say, glaring at him. "But don't worry, he won't hurt you."

Once he's done chewing, Penny extends her hands toward Thunder, carefully examining his face. I'm not sure if he can sense something's different about her, but he isn't as fussy and stubborn with her as he usually is.

"You're a pretty boy, aren't you?" she coos.

Thunder extends his neck as her fingers run through his mane. He leans forward, his brown eyes staring directly into her face. My body tenses. Rationally, I know he won't hurt her. Thunder might be stubborn to the point of being an asshole, but he never ever did anything to hurt me or anybody else. Still, a part of me can't help but worry. Penelope Adams is the sweetest person I've ever met. There is this gentleness to her that draws you in, and you can't help but fall for her, if only a little bit. And I'm not talking about a romantic kind of falling either. No, she isn't the Adams sister who evokes those kinds of feelings in me; these are more of a protective, brotherly variety.

Her magic must not only work on people, though, because the next thing I know, Thunder leans closer and nuzzles her cheek.

"Hey!" Penny giggles. "That tickles!"

Her happiness is infectious, and I can feel myself smile too. "I think he likes you."

"I like him too." Penny nuzzles closer to Thunder, their heads touching. "I wish I could ride him."

"Ehh..." I scratch the nape of my neck, unsure of what to do. When Kate let Penny and me go, she gave specific instructions that included no riding. I can't blame her for worrying; hell, I'm worried too. But I also don't think I can say no to Penny if she asks.

Seriously, between her and Kate, I'm screwed.

"Don't worry," she chuckles, as if she can read my mind. "I won't get you in trouble with Kate."

"For what's it worth, I think it wouldn't be that big of an issue. You could ride with somebody."

"Maybe, one day." Penny turns to me, her unseeing eyes staring at my face. "Could I..."

She nibbles at her lower lip nervously, looking away.

"Could you...?" I prompt, unsure of what she's trying to ask.

"It's probably silly, but could I touch your face?" She blurts out the question, her cheeks turning red.

"My face?"

"I told you it's silly, let's just forg—"

Penelope tries to walk around me, but I place my hands on her shoulder to stop her. "It's not silly."

Dropping my hands down, I place them over hers and lift them up to my face.

"This is how you get to know people, right?" I ask softly.

Penelope inhales sharply as her skin touches mine.

"Y-yes. I don't actually do it often; it's just so weird to ask of people."

Her fingers are gentle as she slides them over my skin slowly. She starts from the top, her fingers gliding over my forehead and brows, down the bridge of my nose, and over my cheekbones.

"You're scratchy," Penny giggles.

"Just a few hairs here and there; don't tell anybody."

"It'll be our secret," she promises as the tips of her fingers slide over the bow of my mouth and then lips.

"I get it now."

"What?"

There is a small smile on her mouth.

"Why Kate gets all flustered when we talk about you."

"Oh, yeah? Do you talk about me often?" I wiggle my brows playfully.

"Not too much. She usually tries to avoid it." With one final brush of her fingers against my cheeks, Penny pulls back. "Thank you for letting me do this."

I wrap her in my arms. "Anytime, Little Adams. Anytime."

After that, we stay in the stables for a little while longer. Penny keeps petting Thunder, and I give her a couple more carrots to feed him. I swear I can see smug satisfaction in his irises with every bite he eats. I'd relish the attention too if the other Adams sister would give it to me, so it's not like I can blame him.

When we finally emerge, dusk is coloring the horizon in different shades of pinks, purples, and reds. With Penny holding onto my forearm with one hand while holding Henry's harness with the other, we walk back to the pond where we left the rest of the people.

Even from a distance, you can hear the yelling and splashes of water coming from the pond.

"Do you think Becky is still trying to kill Miguel?"

I narrow my eyes, trying to decipher the shapes in the distance to see what's going on. "Wouldn't put it past her, that's for sure."

"She seems nice."

"Who? Becs?"

Penny nods in confirmation. "Well, at least when she's not trying to kill somebody. Then she's scary."

"Yeah, there's that tidbit. But seriously, she's the best. We've been friends for as long as I can remember. Her family lives on the ranch next to ours."

"Do they own cattle like you do?"

"Nah, they actually sold a big chunk of the land to my dad shortly after her dad passed. Now they mostly just keep things for the family. A little garden, some chickens, that sort of thing."

"Oh, I didn't know her dad passed." Penny's smile drops. "That's so sad, though."

"Shit, I'm sorry, I'm so used to people knowing things around this town that I spaced out."

"It's okay. Was he sick?"

I shake my head. "Accident, drunk driver pushed him off the road."

"That's terrible."

"It is," I agree, the memories of those days just after the accident coming back in full force. Becky was always so cheerful; she had one of those smiles that could make you happy even when you were feeling like shit, but not after her dad died. It was the first and only time I saw her break. She was inconsolable, and no matter what Miguel and I tried to do, we couldn't help her because we couldn't understand. Not really.

"We were barely ten when it all happened. The whole town was shaken."

"At least she had friends by her side."

"Always."

Townspeople called us the three musketeers, Miguel, Becky, and me. We've been best friends since we were just kids, and there is nothing that could change that. No matter what, we always have each other's backs.

"I'm glad Kate has friends too. She's been keeping to herself a lot lately."

That gets my attention.

"She told us you guys moved a lot," I comment, fishing for any information I can get since Kate herself is a closed book. You know, like one of those from Harry Potter that has to be tied up, so it doesn't bite your hand off? Well, she's just like that, only she chooses to be all closed off. It's like she's afraid if she lets people in, she'll scare them away.

"We did, but usually, Kate had an easier time adapting. Before..."

"Before?" I urge, wanting to know more.

Penny shakes her head. "It doesn't matter."

I want to ask more questions, but just then we get close enough for people to start noticing us. Kate, who's sitting on the dock with Becky by her side, looks up, her eyes meeting mine. Her cheeks are pink from the day spent under the sun, fine hairs that slipped her ponytail curling around her face.

Her whole face lights up when she sees her sister. I get that she's protective of her; hell, I'm protective of her, and I barely know the girl. But if I'm to believe Penny, she wasn't always like that. What had to have happened to make her so guarded?

Kate gets to her feet, dusting off her shorts before walking toward us.

"Did you have fun?" she asks as soon as she's within hearing distance.

"Yes!" Penny lets go of my hand and goes to Kate with Henry's help. I watch in amazement as she takes Kate's hand, and they go toward their towel, Penny talking animatedly all the while about her visit to the stables. "Emmett introduced me to his horse. He's called Thunder, and he has a weakness for carrots."

"And women, apparently," I say quietly, following after them.

It's amazing seeing them together, so similar yet so different. While one is light, the other is dark, but if you look close enough, you can see similarities in the lines of their faces. And the eyes, definitely the eyes. That's not including the way they act when they're together. The love they share for one another is undeniable.

Kate must have heard me because she looks over her shoulder. "What?"

"Nothing."

Her brows raise in a silent challenge, but thankfully she doesn't ask further, instead concentrating on her sister.

I look around, noticing that the crowd has dissipated a bit since we left, but there are still a dozen or so people mingling around. Becky is on the dock while Miguel is playing ball with a few of our classmates, Rose and a few of her friends cheering them on.

Rose turns around and sees me, a smile curling her lips. "Emmett!" she yells, getting to her feet. She wobbles a bit, but then seems to regain her balance before striding toward me.

Shit.

I'm not sure who invited her, but once she was here, it's not like I could have asked her to leave. So, instead, I tried my best to avoid her all afternoon, not wanting to cause any trouble, but it seems my luck is running out.

"We missed you!" She gives me a big smile as she takes a hold of my arm. I try not to look down since she's still only wearing her bikini that reveals way too much, and I don't want to give her the wrong idea.

"Did you?" I look up; two of her friends who are still sitting on their towels try to pretend not to watch while at the same time giving us inconspicuous side glances and whispering between themselves. "You girls seem like you've been having fun."

Rose giggles loudly. "The beer John snatched from his father's stash sure did come in handy." Suddenly she turns serious, her mouth twisting into a pout. "Where did you disappear to?" She points her finger at my face, poking me in the cheek in the process. "The host shouldn't leave his guests unattended, it's not nice."

"Rose, how much of that beer did you have to drink?" I ask carefully. While she occasionally has a flair for the dramatics, she's never acted like *this*.

"Not nearly enough."

AKA way too much. I don't think I have ever seen her drinking before today.

Fuck. Just what I needed.

"You're drunk," I say, trying to gently remove her hand from mine so I can send her to her friends, who are hopefully sober enough to take her home. "You should go home."

"Don't wanna! I want to stay here with you. You should drink more. We had fun last time when we were at the pond." She moves closer, her teeth grazing over her lip as she presses her body against mine. She bats her eyelashes, her voice dropping in what should sound seductive, but just has the hairs rising at the nape of my neck. "Maybe we could have it again."

Definitely, not.

Before I can try to push her away once again, a throat clears behind me. My whole body freezes for a moment. Then, slowly, I turn around and come face to face with scowling Kate.

Fuck. Fuck. Fuck.

Just when things were starting to get better...

"Kate..." I start, but she interrupts me before I can even think of what to say. How to explain.

"I was just coming to say goodbye since we're leaving. Thanks for taking Penny to the stables. She loved it." Her tone is even, almost emotionless, and the whole time she's speaking, she looks somewhere over my shoulder, pointedly ignoring me. "I guess I'll see you at school."

"Kate," I try again, but nails dig into my flesh, holding me back.

Kate's eyes fall down to where Rose is holding me. Then, with a shake of her head, she turns on the balls of her feet, and I stay there watching her walk away.

Chapter 17

KATHERINE

My forehead is pressed against the window, the cool glass feeling nice on my skin. I watch as nature slowly turns into concrete as we move farther away from Emmett's ranch and closer to town.

"I seriously can't stand that girl."

"Huh?" My head snaps up, and I turn to look at Becky. She was unusually quiet as we gathered our things and left Emmett's place.

"Rose." Her fingers grip the steering wheel tighter. "I can't stand her."

A weak, *oh*, is my only answer. I'm not sure what to say to that. Did I like seeing her hang all over Emmett? Well, no, but who was I to say anything to that really? Apart from that one interaction I had with her the first week of school—which honestly didn't give me the best impression of her, but still—I don't even know the girl, so who am I to judge?

"I can't believe I was actually friends with her once." Becky shakes her head.

My brows shoot up. "Rose?"

"Yeah, we were friends when we were younger."

Well, I didn't see that one coming. It actually makes me realize how little I know about Becky in general. Some general stuff that most people with good cognitive abilities would be able to patch together, but who's Becky beneath all the surface stuff? If I were a better friend, I'd know by now. At least some.

"What happened?"

I glance quickly at the rearview mirror, only to find Penny and Henry dozing off in the backseat.

"I'm not sure really. One day we were friends, but the next..." Becky shrugs, her words lingering in the air. She stops at the red light and turns to look at me. "We were confiding secrets and running after boys, playing Barbies, but suddenly she changed. It didn't help that around the same time my dad died, so I just didn't have it in me to put much effort into getting out of bed, much less trying to figure out why she wasn't interested in hanging out with me any longer."

Now I feel like even more of a dick. Her dad died? And who leaves their supposedly best friend at a time like that?

"I'm so sorry, Becky."

She shrugs once again, a sad smile playing on her lips. "It was a long time ago," she says and starts to drive once the light turns green. "But sometimes it still feels like it was only yesterday."

"Was he sick?"

"Nope, car accident. He kissed me on the forehead that morning when he was leaving, and then he was gone."

There is sadness in her voice that makes my heart squeeze.

"I'm so sorry."

My answer sounds lame even to my own ears. What do you say to a person who lost their loved one? Nothing seems like enough.

At least she had a dad—a dad who loved her. I can't say I know the sentiment since I've never met mine.

"Thank you, but enough about the sad stuff." Her face twists in a scowl. "Or about the harpy. She's just jealous because she wants what she can't have."

I remember Rose clinging to Emmett like there is something going on between them. The way she leaned in, her hand possessively wrapped around his. It wasn't even the first time. Did something happen between them to make her feel like she can do it? Or is Becky right, and Rose just wishes it to be true?

"Like how desperate do you have to be to come to a guy's house, get drunk, and then hang all over him when he already told you he isn't interested?" Becky shakes her head. "Get a grip, girl."

So much for stop—

"He what?" I ask as Becky pulls into our driveway, her words finally registering in my head.

Becky, completely oblivious to my turmoil, takes her sweet time parking the car, her tongue peeking from the corner of her mouth as she does so. Only when she's happy with the result does she turn off the engine and look at me.

"He told her he wasn't interested. That first day of school? It actually happened a little before you guys crashed into each other."

My heart does a little flip inside my chest.

"She seems to have a thing for him, though."

Becky turns to me and gives me a pointed look. "She's had a thing for Emmett since we were kids, but he never returned her feelings."

"Well, sometimes we want things we can't have."

Becky looks at me for a moment, quiet.

"He likes you. You know that, right?"

I can feel my cheeks heat, so I look away.

"I think he's just fascinated with me. I'm new and different."

"Maybe, but I think it's more than that. I've never seen him try so hard to get a girl's attention. Don't get me wrong, there have been other girls, but nobody who he was quite so interested in."

At least she's honest, but I still can't quite believe that anybody would find me so fascinating.

"What about you? You guys have been friends forever."

"*Friends*. That's definitely not the same. I'm like an annoying little sister to these guys. Always was, and always will be."

"Not to all of them," I point out. No matter what she says, there is no way she and Miguel are just friends. Not after everything I've seen in these past few weeks.

Becky glares at me. "Don't you try to change the subject."

"Me?" I ask innocently. "You can try all you want, but you can't keep avoiding this topic forever, you know."

"I can avoid it for as long as I can."

"You can certainly try." I turn back and give Penny's leg a little shake. "Hey, we're home."

Her eyes flutter open. Penny straightens in her seat, her hands patting around her as she tries to remember where we are.

"You fell asleep in Becky's car on the way home."

"Oh, okay."

I open the door and hop out. "See you in school, Becky?"

"Sure thing."

Penny and Henry get out, and I grab our bag.

"Thank you for inviting us today," I say, leaning against the door.

"Yeah, thank you, Becky," Penny chimes in as she stops by my side. "I had a lot of fun."

"Anytime, sweets. We'll have to do something fun again sometime soon."

My eyes meet Becky's sincere ones.

Thank you, I mouth. Becky just winks. With another good-bye, I close the door, and we move so Becky can pull her car out onto the street. She honks once as she drives away.

"She seems like a nice person," Penny says. "When she's not scary, that is."

"Yeah, she's pretty good."

Maybe Penny is right, and this will be good for both of us.

"Kate, wait!"

I look up at the sound of my name being called to find Emmett jogging toward me from the football field. Every now and again, he looks over his shoulder as if he's expecting somebody to run after him.

"Hi," he pants as he comes closer to the fence, his voice barely a whisper.

"Hey," I whisper back. He's in full football uniform, with shoulder pads widening his already big frame and a helmet on his head. "Shouldn't you be at practice?"

"Yeah, I guess." He takes a peek over his shoulder. "Miguel's covering for me, so I have a few minutes."

"What happens if you get caught?"

Emmett cringes. "Let's hope we don't find out, huh?"

I chuckle at that, which makes him smile too. For a while, we stay like that, just staring at each other and not saying anything.

Last night I couldn't fall asleep; my mind was too busy going over everything that had happened and everything Becky told me afterward.

"What are you doing here, Emmett?" I ask, first to break the silence.

"About yesterday..." He lifts his hand as if he's going to run it through his hair but then remembers he still has his helmet on. He curses silently.

"There is nothing to say…"

He shakes his head. "Rose was drunk. I just wanted to make sure she got home all right."

"Emmett, this really isn't nece—"

"There is nothing going on between us," he interrupts once again. He puts his hands on the fence between us, and I know if it weren't there, he'd be cupping my cheek instead.

"It didn't look like that," I repeat the words that I told Becky yesterday.

"Well, it's not. I just wanted you to know that."

"Okay."

Emmett nods. Once again, we fall into silence. I know he wants me to say something more, but I'm not sure what. He looks over his shoulder, sighing.

"I better get back to practice before Coach finds out and makes me run drills on the bleachers."

"That doesn't sound like fun."

"If you consider puking your guts out fun…" He shakes his head and takes a step back. "I guess I'll see you later?"

I want to reach out and tell him to wait, but I hold myself back.

"Yeah," I agree softly. "Later."

He nods, his eyes lingering on me a bit longer as he retreats. When he's halfway there, he turns around and jogs back to join his team. And I stand there, watching him leave, unable to look away.

Chapter 18

KATHERINE

"What are you doing this weekend?"

Startled, I jump in my seat before turning to look at Emmett over my shoulder. "You have to stop doing that."

"Sorry." He gives me a sheepish smile that doesn't look like he's sorry at all.

I glare at him, wanting him to know I've seen right through him, which in return only makes his grin widen.

I haven't seen Emmett much since the day at the pond. We still have lunch together, but the guys talk football even more than usual. Apparently, there's an important game with one of their biggest rivals coming up in a few weeks, so they're trying to get ready to kick their asses. Their words, not mine.

"Yeah, right." I start to turn around, but he pokes me in the back.

"So?"

Sighing, I turn back. "So what?"

"This weekend? Any plans?"

I push a strand of hair behind my ear. "I'm not sure. I'll probably do something with Penny."

Emmett smiles, big and genuine. The kind of smile that's designed to melt even the coldest of hearts. "How is she doing?"

"She's fine. Adjusting. We tried compensating before, but the thing is, going to a school that specializes in working with blind people is the right choice for her. They can help her so much more than I ever could."

"I'm glad to hear that. Maybe you should..."

But before he can say anything, Mrs. Burke comes rushing in, hair messy, cheeks pink. "Settle down, settle down," she pants slightly.

Emmett and I exchange a look. I turn around, facing the front of the classroom as the rest of the class settles down in their seats.

"Mr. Jenkins called in that he isn't feeling well, so y'all will have a free period." People start chatting excitedly before Mrs. Burke even finishes. "I know, I know, y'all have been excited to spend this class working on math, but oh, well, you'll have to make do." She puts her hands on her round hips and sweeps the classroom with her sternest look. "Just don't leave the school premises and don't do anything that will land you in my office, 'cause we'll have a problem then."

As quickly as she got here, she's out of the classroom, probably back to dealing with another problem that needs her attention.

Oh well, I guess I can get an early start on my homework.

I stack my books together and shove them into my backpack.

If only Becky were here now, we could have gone to the quad or something, but she has history.

"C'mon." Emmett throws the strap of his backpack over his shoulder and then grabs mine.

"What are you doing?" I ask, looking at him in confusion.

"We have a free period, right?"

"Um, yeah..."

Didn't Mrs. Burke just say so?

"Then let's go."

"Go where? I figured I'd go to the library and work on some homework," I say, but he isn't listening. Most people have already left the classroom, Emmett right behind them. "Emmett!" I hiss, hurrying after him. "Where are you going?"

He turns around, flashing me a grin, but doesn't stop walking. "Let's go do something fun."

"Fun? What fun?"

"Do you trust me, Kitty?"

"That's not the issue here." I sigh and glance over my shoulder. "Let's just go to the library and—"

"Kitty?" Emmett quirks a brow, waiting for me to look at him.

"I'm not sure that's the best idea."

He stops abruptly, and I crash into his chest. Placing his hands on my shoulders, he steadies me. I lift my head until our eyes meet.

"Do you trust me?" Emmett repeats slowly.

The heat in his dark irises makes me suck in a breath. There's an intensity in his gaze that is so big and overwhelming, much like him—like a wave that's going to crash over me and pull me under.

But the thing about Emmett? I don't want to resist the pull.

I graze my teeth over my bottom lip, letting it pop. "Yeah," I rasp finally. "I trust you."

The smile that spreads over Emmett's lips is blinding. His palm slides down my hand, fingers intertwining with mine. His touch is firm and strong as he pulls me after him. "Let's go then."

EMMETT

"Your truck?" Kate whisper-yells, looking around like she expects somebody to jump at us and demand an explanation. *Ha*, like that'll happen. "Are you crazy? Mrs. Burke told us, explicitly, not to leave the premises."

I chuckle at her nervousness. You'd think I was taking her to rob a bank or some shit. "We're not leaving the premises, Kate. Chill."

"Then where are we going?"

I lift my brows. "I thought you said you trusted me."

"I did," she says, then corrects quickly, "I do."

"I'm not going to get us in trouble."

She exhales slowly, relaxing a little. "Okay."

"C'mon." I tug her hand, pulling her after me. With my free hand, I grab my keys out of my pocket and unlock the truck.

"You can let go of my hand, you know. I'm not going to run. And even if I did, I don't think I'd get too far anyway."

I look down at our joined hands, tightening my grip for a second. It feels nice holding her hand like this. I don't think I've ever done it before, held a girl's hand just because I wanted to— not even with Becky, and we've been friends forever.

"I'm not afraid you'll run."

"Then why not let go?"

"Why should I?"

"Guys don't hold hands."

"And you know that how, exactly?" I ask slowly, not really knowing if I want to hear her answer.

Was there somebody else? Before? Is that the reason why she's so reluctant to give me a chance? Give anybody a chance really?

A hot wave of jealousy hits me out of nowhere, and holding

her hand is the only thing keeping me sane as my vision turns red.

Chill the fuck out. You don't even know if there was *somebody.*

"It's all the girls talk about," Kate says, shrugging.

"Oh really?"

"Don't be like that."

"Like what?"

She waves her free hand toward me. "That. Whatever that is."

"Let's be clear about one thing." Coming to a stop in front of my truck, I pull her closer to me. "You're not one of those girls, and I'm not one of those guys."

Kate tilts her head to the side. "Then what are we?"

"Just Katherine and Emmett. And whatever they say, it doesn't apply to us." I nod my head decisively. *There.*

Kate is quiet for a moment. She nibbles at the inside of her cheek as she thinks. "How can you be so sure?"

"Because I know. I know me, and I see you, Kitty."

Inhaling sharply, I take a step back. "Now, let's have some fun."

With my free hand, I pull the door to my truck open. My duffle bag is on the floor; I grab it and shut the door.

"You should really let me carry my bag."

"Not happening." I shake my head. Locking the truck once more, I pull her away. "Let's go. Time's a-wastin'."

"Why do you always have to be so stubborn?"

"Why do you always have to ask so many questions?" I shoot back instantly.

She groans. "You drive me mad, Emmett Santiago."

"The feeling's mutual, baby."

"I'm not your baby."

Glancing over my shoulder, I find her glaring at me, her lips pursed. "We'll see about that."

Kate harumphs but doesn't protest any longer as I lead her to the empty football field.

"You sure nobody is going to come here?" Kate asks as I let the bags fall to the ground on the sidelines. Crouching down, I open the duffle and take the football out of it.

"And do what?" I ask as I get back up, throwing the football up in the air and catching it.

"I don't know." She shrugs but still looks unsure. "Ask us what we're doing here?"

"Trust me, Coach is the first who'd have us here all day long if he could do that. We're good."

"If you say so." Kate turns her attention to me. "Shouldn't you have asked one of the guys to join you if you wanted to play?"

I keep leisurely throwing the ball while giving Kate all my attention. Today her dark hair is loose, falling over her shoulders. She's dressed in another simple top and a faded pair of jeans that fit her like a second skin.

"I want to play with you."

"Me?" Her mouth falls open in surprise, making me chuckle. "You want to play with *me*?"

"Yes, you. Why is that so surprising?"

"Because I don't play football?"

"Don't tell me you never played catch before."

"I don't think..."

"Didn't take you for a coward, Kitty," I sing-song, interrupting her before she gets a chance to finish her sentence.

Her eyes narrow at me like I expected they would. Katherine can't resist a challenge. "I'm not a coward."

"Then show me." I wiggle my brows, which only makes her scowl deepen.

Kate looks at me for a while. "Fine," she says finally, stomping toward me determinedly. "Let's see what you've got, big guy."

"Big guy, huh?" I ask, pulling away from her.

"How are we going to do this?"

"It's just a game of catch, Kitty, not the Super Bowl," I laugh. "I throw, you catch."

Happy with the distance, I extend my hand and let the ball fly. The pigskin lands softly in her outstretched hands.

"See? Easy. Now you tr—"

The words die on my lips as the air is kicked out of my lungs. I wrap my hands around the ball at the last second as it bounces off my chest.

"Like that?" Kate asks, innocently batting her eyelashes.

My fingers grip the ball as I face her, a grin spreading over my face. "Oh, it's on, Kitty."

I pull back, creating more distance between us, and this time when I throw the ball, I don't hold anything back. Okay, I hold back, just not as much as I did that first time around. For a while, we play catch, trash-talking one another.

For all her complaining, Kate is actually pretty good at this. Although she fumbles a little bit when it comes to catching, she has a pretty good arm on her and quick legs.

"Okay," she says, lifting her hands in the air. "I'm done."

"No," I protest, not ready to go back just yet. I didn't get nearly enough time with Kate in the last few days, and even the little we did get was with our friends, which is definitely not the same. How can a guy show a girl what she's missing when there are busybodies mingling around? He can't. "There's still time."

"I know, but I'm done." When I move closer, I can see that her chest is rising and falling rapidly and that her cheeks are bright red from the exercise. "I don't think I've exercised that much, like ever."

"Don't be a party pooper, Kitty."

"The only party pooper here is you." She points at me and starts walking backward. "Standing between me and doing nothing." Then she goes and pokes her tongue out at me before turning on the balls of her feet and running away.

"Oh, now you've gone and done it, Kitty," I yell after her, but of course, she ignores me. I throw the ball in the direction of our things and go into a full-on sprint, catching up to her in no time.

"What..."

But before she can even finish, I'm already tackling her to the ground. My hands wrap around her waist, pulling her closer to me as we both fall to the ground. I take the brunt of the fall, but as soon as we're down, I roll us so she's under me.

"You were saying?" I pant, looking down at her.

"Y-you're crazy!"

Crazy about you. The words are there before I can blink, but I hold them back. The last thing I want to do is scare Kate away. But it's hard. So fucking hard when she's lying down under me, looking at me with those big blue eyes of hers.

Slow the fuck down, dude. You need to think about the long game.

I softly push the hair out of her face, my heart doing a funny flip in my chest. "That's because you said I'm a party pooper," I say gently, my fingers skimming over her cheek.

God, she's beautiful. So fucking beautiful even when she scowls at me.

"Do you usually have a tendency to tackle everybody who doesn't agree with you?"

"Nah." I shake my head. "You're special."

The corner of her mouth lifts in a half-smile.

We stare at each other for a while. Her lips are parted slightly, and she's so close that all I have to do is lean down to kiss her. Not even a couple of inches separates us. It'd be so damn easy to lean down and close my mouth over hers. Her tongue peeks out, sliding over her lower lip.

Reluctantly, I lift my gaze from her mouth back to her wide eyes.

"Emmett," she breathes softly. Her eyes fall down to my lips and then come back up. She must have realized what's on my mind.

Kiss me, Kitty. Just one tiny little kiss.

It's a lie, and we both know it. There is no way I could ever stop at just one kiss. Not when it comes to her. And she's not ready for that.

Sighing, I pull back and offer her my hand.

"C'mon, let's get back."

This time, Kate doesn't protest me holding her hand or carrying her bag. I'm not sure if she's growing soft on me or if she's thinking about what just happened, but either way, I'm going to relish this moment.

Slowly, we get back to the school just as the bell rings.

I pull her hand, holding her back for a moment.

"About this weekend?" I ask, remembering the question I wanted to ask before Mrs. Burke interrupted us earlier.

"Yeah?"

"There is a fair coming to the next town over, and I thought we could go."

"As a d-date?" she asks, her voice stuttering on the last word.

"Do you want it to be?"

Her cheeks flush. "Oh, God, that's not—"

She starts fumbling, looking anywhere but at me. I move in closer, my finger slipping under her chin, and I lift it so she looks at me. "Because you just say the word, and I'm gonna date the hell out of you, Kitty."

Kate lifts her hands and covers her face, making the words come out stifled. "Can we forget this?"

"No way," I laugh, pulling her hands down. "But seriously, everybody's going. You should come."

She bites into her lip, thinking. "Who's everybody?"

"Becky, Miguel, some guys from the team." I shrug. "People."

"So it's like a group thing?" The idea of it perks her up a little.

"Yeah, you could say that." It should probably bother me that she wouldn't want to go if it's just the two of us, but I'll take her anyway I can get her.

"Over the weekend?"

"Yes, we have an away game on Friday, but Saturday afternoon is all free."

Kate nods.

"Is that a yes?" I ask, feeling hopeful.

"I guess so."

"You guess so?" I lift my brows.

"Fine, yes, I'd like to go with you guys."

"Great." I grin, letting my hand fall by my side. "I'll pick you up on Saturday, at five."

Pulling back, I continue walking towards the school, my mind already going through all the possibilities of getting Kate all on my own on Saturday, even if only for a little bit. Ride there included.

"You said it's not a date," Kate calls after me.

I look over my shoulder and find her still standing where I left her. "It's not."

"Then why are you picking me up? I'm sure Becky would be more—"

"Nope." This is definitely not up for discussion. "I'm picking you up for our group non-date date."

"That doesn't even make sense," she protests.

"It doesn't have to," I say, going back to her. When she's within arm's reach I slide my finger under her chin, lifting it so she looks at me, and then add more gently, "I'm not backing down on this, Kate. Might as well save your breath."

Kate nibbles at her lip, and I can practically see the wheels in her head turning as she debates what to do.

"Fine." She stabs her finger in my chest. "But I'm bringing Penny with me."

Slipping out of my reach, she walks around me and ascends the stairs. Chuckling, I follow after her. She pushes the door and enters, the door slamming in my face, but even that doesn't wipe the smile off my face. Because whatever she might think, I won this round, and I get to spend Saturday with her.

Chapter 19

KATHERINE

The sound of the doorbell echoes around the house.

"Oh my God, Emmett's here." I turn around in a panic, my eyes landing on Penny sitting on the edge of my bed, petting Henry who's resting by her side.

"Say what you want, but you can't fool me," Penny chuckles. "You like him."

"Oh, hush. I don't." My cheeks heat, and I'm grateful that she can't see my face right now. Not that she needs to see me to know the truth. The words sound like a lie even to my own ears.

"Then why are you so nervous?"

No, Penny can't see me, but she's awfully good at reading the tone of my voice and just the overall feeling in the room. Or maybe it's just me. Maybe I'm that obvious to her, like an open book. I'm not sure how I feel about that.

"I'm not nervous," I protest weakly.

Just jittery.

Overwhelmed.

Edgy.

Anxious.

But definitely not nervous.

"Right, you tell that to somebody else, maybe they'll believe you." Penelope stands up, and Henry follows suit. "I'm going to grab my jacket. See you downstairs in a few?"

"Sure thing, take your time."

I watch her as she walks out of the room. When we first got here, Penny had such a hard time adjusting to the new environment. She had to use the cane even inside the house and still managed to bump into things more often than not, but she's finally settling in, and I know a part of it is thanks to Henry. Even when he isn't officially working, like now, he never leaves her side, steering her in the right direction when necessary.

Closing my eyes for a moment, I utter a silent prayer.

"Katherine, company!" Aunt Mabel yells from downstairs.

Inhaling sharply, I open my eyes and look at my reflection in the mirror. After obsessing over it longer than I care to admit, I finally settled on a cute flower top, and a jeans overalls skirt combination with my red chucks. Okay, Penny decided it's the best option after I drove her crazy with all the possibilities in my humble closet.

"Coming!" I shout back, pushing my hair behind my ears.

You can do this, I tell myself as I descend the stairs. *Everybody is coming. It's not like it's a date.*

Keep telling yourself that, the other, more stubborn voice says, but I shove it back. I can't obsess about it because if I do, I'll start thinking about other things, like how it felt being tackled by him to the ground. The feel of his hard body hovering over mine. The way his warm breath touched my skin.

Yup, definitely *not* thinking about that.

I stop in the middle of the landing, my hands gripping the railing as my eyes fall on Emmett standing down in the foyer. He must have heard me coming because he lifts his head instantly, his eyes taking me in before they land on mine. His mouth hangs open as I tentatively descend the last few steps, stopping on the final one so we're on the same eye level.

"Not good? I knew I should have gone for the—"

I start to turn around, ready to dash back upstairs and change, but Emmett grabs my hand and holds me in place.

"You look perfect."

His words ring in the air, making a shiver run down my spine. I lick my lips, which suddenly feel dry. I know I need to say something, anything, but I'm left completely speechless by the intensity of his gaze. Those dark eyes of his hold me hostage as he swipes his thumb over the back of my hand, making my skin prickle.

"I told her that too, but she didn't want to listen."

From the corner of my eye, I see Henry move down the stairs, followed by Penny. Emmett and I pull back from one another instantly. I take the final step, leaving her enough space to get down safely herself.

Penelope was so excited when I told her about the county fair, but that excitement turned to wariness until I convinced her it's a group thing, and she won't be intruding on anything. Since then, she hasn't stopped talking about it. Not that I can blame her. We've never been to a fair before so it's a completely new experience for both of us.

"And she's not the only one." Emmett takes her hand in his as soon as she's safely on the floor and has her twirl around.

You see what I mean? Freaking charmer.

Emmett and Penny laugh at something, I'm not even sure what because I'm transfixed just watching the two of them interact.

How can a girl resist it when a guy is so freaking nice to her sister? He's killing all of my defenses, one smile at a time, and I'm not sure what to make of it. What to make of him.

Penny giggles as he pulls her into his side. "Between the two of you, I'll be the luckiest guy around."

Contrary to me, Penny didn't have a hard time picking out what she'd wear, choosing to go with her favorite pale pink dress with a delicate floral lace pattern on the hem. With her honey-blonde hair and blue eyes, it makes her look like a doll.

Penny shoves him away lightly. "That's assuming we let you be our date."

My heart aches as she giggles. I've never seen my sister so relaxed, so carefree, especially not around a boy. And that's exactly how she is when she's around Emmett. It's like he can pull out that other side of her—the side that she's afraid to show to the world—out into the light. He treats her like she's just any other teenager and lets her be who she wants to be.

"Oh, now you wound me, Little Adams." Emmett tightens his grip around her, playfully ruffling her hair. He looks up, his eyes finding mine, a playful smile on his mouth. "I wonder who taught you to be so ruthless."

"You call it being ruthless. I say you have to work to earn your place."

"Ruthless," he repeats, all the while chuckling. "But that's good. Once a guy comes sniffing around, and he will, be sure to make him work for it."

"Okay, okay. She's just thirteen." I move closer to them and lightly jab my finger in her shoulder. "No boys until you're twenty, you hear me, Pen? They just give you a headache anyway."

"Hey, now I feel offended," Emmett protests.

"Oh, please." Penny grabs my hand and pulls me toward the door. "Now are we going or what? I was promised I could go on *all* the rides I want."

"What about Henry?" Emmett asks, walking around us to pull the door open.

We yell our goodbye to Mabel and close the door on our way out. I already told her we're going to the county fair, and she was actually excited to see us making friends.

"He's not going." She lifts the folded cane that she's been holding in her hand. "But this is."

I watch Emmett for some kind of reaction, but there isn't any, just genuine interest.

"Why not?" Emmett asks as we go to his truck that's parked by the curb.

"It's harder for him to navigate in a bigger crowd," I explain. "Plus, people can be real dicks about it."

"How so?" A confused frown appears between his brows. I want to move closer and smooth the worry lines, but I hold myself back.

"People don't pay attention to the harness. They think he's just a regular dog, so they want to pet him."

"But he's working." He nods and looks at me expectantly. With those dark eyes and his hair peeking from underneath his ball cap, he reminds me of a puppy waiting to be praised. I bite the inside of my cheek to prevent a smile from forming.

"Yup, he's working. But there is also the fact that he *isn't* just a regular dog, which people don't understand."

"Or don't want to understand," I add dully. Penny puts too much trust in people. Way more than most of them deserve.

Emmett tries to open the passenger door, but I wave him away. He isn't happy but lets it go, walking around the car to the driver's side.

"Once we went to Walmart, but a lady exiting the store started yelling at us." Penny rolls her eyes, and in her most obnoxious voice says, "You kids, no respect for anybody or anything. Taking a dog to the place where people buy food? Are you crazy?"

I open the door and help Penny inside before sliding next to her and closing the door. Emmett does the same on the other side.

"Like I said, people can be real dicks."

Emmett blinks, truly looking stunned. "Are you for real?"

"I wish I was joking."

"But he's allowed to enter, right?"

"Yes, he's her guide dog. Which basically gives him the same rights as humans. Together they should be allowed to enter anywhere they want. Restaurants, public transportation, stores, you name it, he should be able to go."

"That's insane." Emmett shakes his head, then stops suddenly as if something came to mind. "That didn't happen here, right?" He turns in the driver's seat to look at me, his fingers wrapped around the key. "Right?"

He seems so appalled by the idea that I don't have the heart to tell him the truth. But he sees it regardless.

"Of course it was." He shakes his head and starts the car. "And I bet it was that old Mrs. Merrick. I'm telling you that lady is like a witch or some shit. When we were little trick-or-treating around town, it was always a challenge to see who'd go up and ring her doorbell."

"Did you ever do it?" Penny asks, laughing.

"I tried, but I always chickened out before pressing the bell. We all did."

We all burst into laughter.

"Hey," Emmett protests. "She's one scary lady. I'd love to see you try it."

"Excuses, excuses," I sing-song, happy for the change of subject.

"I'll give you excuses." He turns the key, firing the ignition. He lifts his head, that wicked grin of his lighting up his whole face. "You girls ready for some fun?"

EMMETT

"Let's do the roller coaster again." Miguel grins, his arm wrapping around Becky's shoulders and pulling her toward the line.

"No way." Becky shakes her head. "The last time I almost threw up."

"Don't be a Debbie Downer, Becs," Nico says, nudging her with an elbow.

Becky shakes her head. "No way, not happening."

She does still look a little green from the last ride.

Miguel pouts. "Fine, suit yourself."

Nico shrugs and turns to me. "Emmett? You coming?"

"Nah, man." I shake my head, throwing my arm over Penelope's shoulder. "I promised Penny here I'd get her something on one of the shooting ranges. You go ahead."

Nico makes a gagging sound, while Miguel gives me his *who're you trying to fool* look, but I ignore them both.

"Sure thing," Miguel drawls. "I guess we'll see you later."

The guys leave together toward the roller coaster, muttering something between themselves. I already know I'll never hear the end of it next time we hit the locker room, but ask me if I care. They're just jealous assholes, it's not my fault the ladies like me better.

"You could have gone with them, you know," Penny says quietly, those trusting blue eyes looking up at me.

"And miss a chance to be surrounded by beautiful ladies? No way." With her white cane in hand, slowly tapping the space in front of her, I help steer her toward the shooting booths, Kate and Becky following behind us. "Now tell me, which one do you want me to get you?" I scan the prizes put on the shelves. "There is one really ugly green frog, a tiger, a koala..." I recount all the things up there while a clerk behind the counter, an older guy with a beard that reaches halfway down his chest, gives us a curious look. "Oh, and a pink teddy bear."

"I want that one," she says instantly, her whole face lighting up.

"And I'll take the frog," Becky chimes in. "Kate, what do you want?"

"What's this?" I look over my shoulder at the two of them. "Are you trying to bankrupt me?"

"Hey, you wanted to have a harem, now you better pay up."

I turn to the guy managing the booth, looking for some male solidarity. "Can you believe this?"

He lifts his hands in surrender. "I'm not getting into this. Just manning the booth, but if you want to play, I can help you with that."

Sighing, I pull out a few five-dollar bills and give them to him. "A pink teddy, that ugly frog, not that I get why she wants it. That thing is scary as fuck."

"Hey," Becky protests, jabbing her finger in my side. "Don't insult George. He isn't ugly."

"And she named him too." I shake my head. "What is he then?"

"Misunderstood. You never know, I might kiss him and get a prince."

Becky nods her head, the serious look on her face making me crack up.

"Yeah, keep on dreaming, Becs. Keep on dreaming."

The guy puts five baseballs on the counter. "You have to hit all five targets in order to win," he warns, taking a step back so I can look at the targets.

Letting go of Penny, I grab one, weighing it in my hand. "Should be easy."

I squint at one of the targets, my fingers gripping the ball in my hand, and let the ball fly. A loud *bang* joins other noises at the fair as the ball connects with the target. Penny cheers happily, and the corner of my mouth lifts as I grab another one.

Fifteen minutes and twenty-five dollars later, we leave the booth with three stuffed animals in tow. Hey, even I'm not *that* good. Besides, can't shame all the guys who come after me trying to charm their girls, now can I?

"Let's do the Ferris wheel!" Becky shouts, pointing at the attraction we can see in the distance.

"I thought you don't like heights."

"I don't like all the twists and turns of roller coasters, they make me nauseous." Becky turns to Kate and Penelope. "Ferris wheel next?"

Kate nods, and together we move through the crowd. Now I can clearly see what they meant when they said this isn't a place for guide dogs. Since it's Saturday evening, there are a lot of people—teens like us, families with kids running around, couples... They're all walking around, laughing and talking, barely paying any attention to their surroundings. And while Penny's good with her cane, there is no help if somebody bumps into you and makes you lose your focus, so she usually holds onto one of us, Kate mostly, as we walk around the attractions.

I look at the girls, who are talking about something, I'm not even sure what, but Kate's head falls back, and she laughs.

The corner of my mouth twitches up. For all her protests, she seems to be having fun; they both do.

We get in line, chatting while we wait for our turn. Thankfully the line moves relatively quickly, so we don't have to wait too long.

"Next!" the guy yells, motioning us over. "When it gets here you have a few seconds to jump in, okay?" he explains, barely paying us any attention as he pushes Kate and me forward.

"Sure."

Kate looks behind her to see Becky and Penny whispering something between themselves.

"I should probably—"

"C'mon, kids." The guy pushes us toward the carriage as it comes to the platform.

"But..." Kate tries to protest, but the guy's already pulling the railing down, and we're off. Kate looks over her shoulder at Becky and Penny, who've taken our place. "Penny!"

Both girls look up at us, lift their hands and wave. "We'll be good," she shouts, making people turn their heads toward us to see what's going on. "You guys have fun!"

Becky winks just as their carriage arrives, and they too are ushered inside.

"But..." Kate looks down at them, and then she turns to me. She blinks as what just happened finally falls in place. "They tricked us."

"They totally did," I agree, laughing. I'm not the least bit sad at the turn of events.

"Oh, I'm going to kill them once I get down."

Kate pounds her fist against the railing, making the whole thing rattle. She inhales sharply as the carriage sways in the air. I grab her hand in mine as we wait, utterly still, for it to calm down.

"What? Is it that bad to have to spend the next twenty minutes in my company?" I try to laugh it off, not wanting to sound hurt, but it comes out that way anyway.

"No, of course not," Kate sighs, looking down at our joined hands. "I'm just worried about Penny, that's all."

"Becky's with her." I tighten my grip on hers, enjoying the feel of her warm hand in mine. "She won't let anything happen to her."

Kate looks up, her face softening. "I know. Doesn't ease my worries, though."

"I figured not," I sigh. Seriously, this girl will be the end of me. Just one soft, pleading look from her eyes, and I'm a goner for her. Falling deeper than before.

"Thanks for today, by the way. I don't remember when the last time was I saw Penny that happy. You're so good with her."

"Just her?" I wiggle my brows playfully.

Kate rolls her eyes. "I don't know what you're talking about."

"C'mon, Kitty. Give a guy a break, huh?"

She chuckles, shaking her head. Placing her hand on my chest, she shoves me away a bit, but sitting in the carriage, there isn't really anywhere to go. I put my hand on hers, twining our fingers together.

"So?" I urge, wanting to hear the words.

"Fine, I had fun too. Happy?"

Her eyes dance with amusement, and something in my chest twists, making it hard to breathe.

Unable to resist it any longer, I reach forward, my fingers tracing her cheek.

Kate sucks in a breath, her lips parting. She put something on them, that glossy thingy girls like to use because they've been shimmering all night long under the bright lights of the amusement park.

"You can't imagine. Seeing you happy and carefree like that is like a drug to me, and knowing I'm the one who put that smile on your face." I swipe my thumb just below her lower lip. Her fingers grip mine, and it takes everything in me not to lean down and kiss her. "You know I'd do anything to see you happy, right?"

"Even bring my little sister to our group non-date?" she asks, her voice shaking slightly.

"Sorry to disappoint, but allowing Penny to come to our non-date has nothing to do with you."

"Oh?"

My fingers skim over her face, my hand cupping her cheek. "I'm not sure what it is about you Adams girls that draws people in and makes them fall for you."

"Emmett..."

My name is a soft sigh falling off her lips. She tilts her head back to look at me, her dark eyes zeroing in on my face.

"Shh." I press my finger over her lips to stop her from saying whatever she wanted to say. I know that tone all too well, and it's usually followed by words I don't want to hear. Leaning forward, I press my forehead into hers. "Not now, okay? Whatever you want to say, it can wait."

A heartbeat passes in silence, then she nods slowly in agreement.

We stay like that for a few minutes, watching one another like there is nothing and nobody around us. Because there isn't. Just a vast sky full of possibilities.

Letting out a shaky breath, I pull back, lean into my seat, and throw my arm around Kate's shoulders, pulling her near. She doesn't resist me, instead snuggling closer, placing her head on my chest.

That's how we stay for the rest of the ride, with her by my side, watching the stars. There aren't that many since the lights of the amusement park are bright, but Kate doesn't seem to mind.

Once we start our descent, Kate pulls back so we can jump out on time. When we're safely on the ground, I take Kate's hand in mine, and she doesn't protest.

We don't say anything as we wait for Penny and Becs to join us. I expect Kate to bite into them as soon as they touch the ground, but instead, she wraps Penny into a hug.

"Did you have fun?"

"Yes, Becky told me everything that you can see from the top."

Penny continues talking Kate's ear off as we get away from the line so we don't get in people's way.

Becky joins me, looping her arm through mine. We exchange a glance, a silent conversation passing between us as we listen to the two sisters talk.

It's fascinating the way Penny can find beauty in little things. How she opens up to the world in her own way and takes it all in, enjoying every moment to the fullest while most people let it pass by them without even noticing. We all should be more like her.

Becky shrugs helplessly, holding that ugly frog close to her chest.

"C'mon, let's go and find the guys."

Together we move around, looking for our friends. Becky sees a stand with cotton candy, and the girls decide to buy one to share.

I snap some photos as they get their faces all covered in candy, which results in Becky chasing after me to get my phone.

You'd think after seventeen years of friendship, she'd be better at this by now, but she's still the least athletic person I know. Becky trips twice, almost falling face first, when Miguel appears and catches her before she breaks her nose.

"I think that's our cue to go." Miguel laughs as he helps steady her. He looks down at the ugly frog she's still clutching tightly. "What's that thing?"

I pat him on the shoulder as I pass them by on my way back to Kate and Penny. "Her Prince Charming. Good luck with that."

Kate and Penny are still standing where we left them, munching on the candy.

"You have something..." I swipe my finger over the tip of

Kate's nose. "There, that's better." I look between the two girls. "You ladies ready to go home?"

"Yup."

The rest of the crew joins us on our way out. There are fewer people now than there were when we got here, so we get back to the parking lot in no time. Becky, Nico, and Miguel huddle in Miguel's truck, waving their goodbyes.

The drive back is quiet. The radio is playing softly in the background, and Penny is sitting between the two of us, dozing off. Kate and I share occasional glances, but neither of us says anything.

Just as I'm pulling onto their street, Kate shakes Penny awake. "We're home."

"Oh, okay."

Penny rubs at her eyes sleepily as I park in their driveway. I get out and meet them on the passenger side, just as Kate helps Penny out.

Penny looks up, her eyes almost meeting mine. "Thank you for today, Emmett. I had so much fun."

"C'mere." I offer her my hand, which she takes, coming into my arms and hugging me, squishing the pink teddy between us in the process.

"And thank you for Pinky."

"It was my pleasure."

Giving me one final squeeze, she pulls back. "I'm going inside. I'll see you soon, Emmett."

We watch her as she gets to the door. As soon as she pulls it open, she's assaulted by Henry's slobbery tongue. Giggling softly, she pushes the dog inside so she can enter.

"Next time, we should take the dog too. I think you broke the poor pup's heart."

Kate turns toward me, observing me silently for a moment. Her face is unreadable, making me nervous. Lifting my ball cap off my head, I ruffle my hair before putting it back.

"You're something else, Emmett Santiago," Kate says finally, after what feels like forever.

"Is that a good thing?"

There is another pause where she just looks at me. I'm not sure what to make of it.

After what seems like an eternity, she nods. "Yeah, it's a good thing."

Lifting on the tips of her toes, she presses her mouth against my cheek. It's soft. So soft I can barely feel it. Just a brush of her mouth against my cheek, and then she's pulling back, and I have to convince myself I didn't imagine it.

"Thank you for today. I really had fun."

Kate smiles at me while I stand there, dumbfounded. My heart is thundering in my chest so loudly I can barely decipher her words. Blood rushing through my veins. It's like lightning has struck me, and I can't breathe, can't think, can't—

"Emmett?"

"Hmmm?" I blink, trying to focus on her instead of the tingling sensation her lips left on my skin.

"I kissed you first," she says, as if I need to hear that to know what just happened.

She kissed me.

Katherine kissed me first.

It wasn't the kiss I had imagined for weeks. No, in a way, it was even better.

With one final smile, Kate turns around to walk away, but before she can slip out of my reach, I wrap my hand around her wrist and pull her back to me. She crashes into my chest, sucking in a breath, but before she can say anything, I bend down and place my mouth on hers.

I can hear her soft inhale as I kiss her gently, swiping my

mouth over hers slowly so I can prolong this moment as much as possible.

Her mouth is lush under mine as she returns my kiss. My tongue slides over her lips, seeking entrance, and a soft moan rips from her lungs as her tongue tangles with mine. Swirling. Sucking. Tasting.

Kate wraps her arms around my neck, her fingers running through the hair at the back of my neck as I give one final sweep of my mouth before pulling back.

"Kitty?"

She blinks her eyes open, dazed like I was just moments ago. "Hmm?"

Her cheeks are pink, mouth swollen from our kiss. I swipe my thumb over her lower lip, enjoying the softness of her skin.

"I kissed you back."

"Yeah," she sighs. "Yeah, you did."

I grin at her. "You know what that means, don't you?"

"That you liked tonight as much as I did?"

"That too, but also..." I press my mouth against hers once more. Just a quick peck on the lips before pulling back. "You're mine now."

Chapter 20

KATHERINE

"That was brutal," I groan as we exit the classroom.

"Tell me about it. There is no way I'll pass." Becky shakes her head. "And my momma will kill me."

"Like, seriously, who thought pop quizzes were a good way to measure somebody's knowledge?"

"Beats me." Becky rubs her temples. "The only thing they give me is a premature heart attack." She looks at me. "How did you do?"

"No idea." I shrug. Maybe if I'd spent more of the weekend studying and less thinking about a certain boy, and the way his eyes darkened as he kissed me. Yeah, better not to go there. "I figured if I write something, at least it'll look like I was paying attention, you know?"

"You know what? Who cares? What's done is done. But they better have some mac and cheese in the cafeteria because I'm starving from all this stress."

"Priorities," I chuckle, my own stomach growling in agreement.

"Damn right."

We chat the rest of the way to the cafeteria about the rest of our classes. Becky had Mrs. Marty last year, and she's telling me all about the class as we grab our lunch and pay.

Becky looks up, eyes scanning the crowd until they land on our table. It's funny—if you asked me last week, I'd have told you it's *their* table, but not today.

Is it because of the kiss? No, I don't think so. It was a nice kiss, don't get me wrong, better than nice, really, but little by little, these people started to sneak under my skin, making me feel accepted into their group.

"You can always rely on that they'll be here, eating as soon as the bell rings," she says, shaking her head.

My eyes fall on the table in the middle of the room that's filled with Emmett and his teammates, my stomach doing a somersault as he laughs at something Nico said.

This is the first time I've seen him since the weekend.

Since the kiss.

Oh, God.

If my hands were free, I'd burrow my face in my palms, but this way I'll have to be content with gripping the tray so hard my knuckles turn white.

It felt surreal.

The kiss.

The whole night really.

As if he can feel my eyes on him, Emmett lifts his head and looks right at me. His smile falls as his intense gaze zeroes in on me, making my whole body shiver.

I'm not sure what to expect or how to act. We texted a little on Sunday, but he told me he had to help his dad on the ranch and catch up on some homework afterward, and we never really discussed what comes next.

"Girl," Becky drawls quietly. "I can feel the heat all the way over here."

"You and me both," I agree, sucking my lower lip between my teeth.

"Wait." Becky stops and turns to look at me. Her eyes are so wide I'm surprised they don't fall out of her eye sockets. "Did I miss something?"

I look away, feeling my cheeks heat.

"Oh, my God! I did miss something!"

"Shh, not so loud." I look around and already find some people giving us curious glances, Rose and her friends included. "And definitely not here."

"What happened?" Becky whisper-yells. She grabs my upper arm, her fingers digging into my skin. "I want to know. Now."

"Becky," I groan, my head falling back.

"Don't you *Becky* me. The suspense is killing me." She gives me a little shake. "Now spill."

"We kissed," I admit, my voice barely a whisper. "Teeny-tiny kiss. That's it."

There was nothing teeny-tiny about that kiss. I can still feel Emmett's mouth on mine. The warmth of his body, the feel of his hands as he cradled my face, and his citrusy scent surrounding me.

I dreamed about kissing him, but nothing even came close to the real deal, and now that he kissed me, I can't stop obsessing about it.

"Oh my God, oh my God, oh my God!" Becky squeals excitedly. "I knew it. I just knew it."

I shush her once again. "You're crazy, you know that?"

"Say what you want, but I called it!"

Her grin is so wide you'd think she won the lottery.

My gaze darts over her shoulder to Emmett. He's leaning back in his chair, still watching us.

Watching *me*.

187

Maybe *I* won the lottery after all.

I shake my head to clear my mind and turn my attention to Becky. "Just stop it. Let's not make it a bigger deal than it has to be." I walk around her. "I'm hungry. Let's go eat."

Becky falls in step with me. "Mm-hmm, hungry, right. So, that's what the kids call it these days."

I glare at her over my shoulder. "Stop it," I hiss quietly as she just grins. "God, why are we even friends?"

"Because I'm irresistible, and you love me." She blows me a kiss as she takes her seat between Miguel and Nico.

"What were you guys talking about for so long?" Nico asks between bites.

"Girl stuff."

Becky looks at me across the table, her brows lifted. *See?*

"What kind of girl stuff?" He frowns.

"Dude, do you seriously want to know?" Miguel asks, his mouth full.

Shaking my head, I walk around to the only available chair left that has somehow turned into my space. Right next to Emmett.

Warmth spreads through my cheeks as I walk right past him. "Hey," I say softly.

"Hey back."

I put my tray on the table, and I'm just about to sit down when hands sneak around my waist. I inhale sharply, and before I can blink, I'm sitting in Emmett's lap, my back pressed to his chest.

"Emmett!" I protest, giggling as his mouth lands on my neck.

"That's no way to greet your bae."

"Bae?" I laugh and look over my shoulder at him. "Are you serious?"

"You're damn right I'm serious." His eyes fall down to my

lips, staying there for a moment longer than necessary before looking back up. "I'm always serious when it comes to you, don't you already know that?"

My tongue darts out, sliding over my lower lip. I want to feel his mouth on mine so badly it hurts.

"I think I'm starting to realize that," I whisper back so only he can hear me.

This time, Emmett leans down, his mouth pressing against mine.

"Oh good," John says dryly. "Now they're finally together, and we won't need to look at them throwing each other longing glances across the table. Instead, we get to look at them make out. No biggie, guys, you just carry on."

Emmett pulls back, breaking the kiss. "Shut up, John," he says, not moving his eyes from me.

The rest of lunch passes as it does every day. Well, except the fact that Emmett doesn't let me take my chair, insisting I stay where I am—in his lap. The guys talk football, and Becky tells me how her mom wants them to go and buy a dress for homecoming, which she refuses since she doesn't have a date.

When we're done, we take our stuff and get out. Emmett grabs my hand as we walk together to our next class.

"I was thinking..." His voice trails off as he looks around. Then he pulls us under the stairs and away from the rest of the people still lingering in the hallways.

"About?"

"How about you come to my place tomorrow?"

I tilt my head back to look at him. "What for?"

"So, I can make good on my promise."

"What..." I remember our conversation at the pond. "Ah. I'm not sure if that's..."

"It'd be just the two of us," he rushes out before I can

protest. "I have the afternoon off, and this will probably be our last chance to do it before it gets too cold to swim."

"You just want to get me out of my clothes."

He grins unapologetically. "And if that's the case?"

"I'll think about it." I shove him a little and continue to the classroom, but Emmett just laughs and falls in step with me soon enough.

"Always trying to keep me on my toes."

"Not sure what you're talking about."

Emmett pulls me into his side just as we enter the classroom. "No worries, I like a good challenge."

Chapter 21

EMMETT

"Isn't the pond in that direction?" Kate asks, looking out the window as we pass by the narrow dirt road, that indeed, leads to the pond.

I give it a quick glance but don't bother slowing down. "Sure is."

"Aren't we going there?"

"We are, but first we have to leave the truck at the house and change."

"Oh." Her cheeks redden. "Change. Right. I didn't think about that."

"What did you think? That we'd go skinny dipping?" I ask, grinning. I can't help myself; I have to tease her. I love seeing her react. Her cheeks turn pink, lips parting slightly as her eyes grow wide.

"N-no," she stutters.

"Relax, I'm only kidding." I place my hand on her thigh, giving her a reassuring squeeze. She's wearing another pair of shorts which leave her skin bare to my touch. It's soft and smooth, like silk under my fingertips. "As much as I wouldn't mind that, it's still early, and my dad or any of his workers could stumble upon us, and there is no way I'm letting them see you like that."

Just the thought makes me want to punch somebody. But that's not what grabs Kate's mind.

"Your family's home?"

I nod as we near the house. "Dad's out on the ranch, and Mom's around somewhere." I park the truck in the driveway, kill the engine and turn to look at her. "They don't bite, you know."

"I know." Kate looks down and fumbles with her fingers in her lap until I place my hand over hers to stop her from fidgeting.

"Kate?" Slowly, she lifts her head until her eyes meet mine. "They're going to love you."

Her throat bobs as she swallows, but she nods regardless. I get out, and she meets me at the front of the truck. Grabbing her hand in mine, I take her backpack and pull her toward the house.

Turns out she worried for nothing because the house is quiet when we get inside. I lead her upstairs to my room. Kate follows me inside with wide eyes, taking everything in.

I look around, trying to see my room through her eyes.

The light green walls are covered in posters of my favorite players, shelves hoist trophies that go all the way back to pee-wee league, and an unmade bed and scattered clothes lurk in the corner where I left them last night.

"You want to stay here or take the bathroom?"

Kate spins around to face me. "Here's fine."

"Okay." I sway on my feet. "I guess I'll see you in five?"

She nods. "Sounds good."

Grabbing my swimming trunks and tee, I get out of the room in a hurry before I do something stupid. Something like grab Kate, throw her on my bed, and then kiss the hell out of her.

Focus, Santiago. Focus.

"How are we going to do this?" Kate asks a little while later when we get to the pond. I tried to convince her that we should take Thunder for a quick ride instead of walking here, but she didn't want to hear about it.

"We jump right in," I say, pulling off my shirt and throwing it on the dock next to our towels.

"Did you forget that little tidbit when I told you I don't actually know how to do this?"

I turn around to find her nervously watching the water. "Oh, you were serious? I thought you just wanted to get me all on your own so you could grope me." I wiggle my brows playfully, hoping to ease the tension.

It works because Kate narrows her eyes at me. "You just keep on dreaming, big guy."

"It would be one sweet, sweet dream; you've got to admit it."

Her cheeks turn deep red, making me wonder if she ever dreamed about me, and if so, what kind of dream it was. Sexy? Sweet? Either way, I'd be happy just having her think of me half as much as I think about her.

"You're not going to let me drown?" Kate's hesitant tone brings me out of my thoughts.

I step closer and put my hands on her shoulders. The scent of apples surrounds me almost instantly; the need to burrow my head in her neck and inhale deeply almost overwhelming. My thumb rubs her skin as I wait for her to lift her head and look at me before making a promise. "No way in hell is anything happening to you on my watch."

Kate's throat bobs as she swallows, but she nods. "Turn around?"

"I'll do you one better, but you better be quick."

Turning my back to her, I sprint down the dock and jump.

The water is cool when I sink into the pond, leaving me breathless for a moment. Reaching the muddy ground, I push against it to get back up. Once I break through the surface, I shake my head to get the water out of my face.

"You look like a dog when you do that."

When I open my eyes, I see Kate sitting on the dock, her legs dangling off the edge. She took off her clothes, staying only in a red one-piece swimsuit.

I swim closer until I'm standing just in front of her. "C'mere."

"You're so wet!" Kate shrieks as I wrap my arms around her, pulling her to my chest.

"If you keep wiggling, I'm going to drop you," I warn her.

"Holy shit," she hisses as I pull her into the water. Instinctively she wraps herself around me like a little monkey. Freaking cutest monkey ever. "That's so damn cold."

"You just had your toes dipped in, how did you not notice?"

"Those were my toes!"

"How is that different?"

"It just is! Oh my God!" Kate's grip around me tightens as I start swimming away from the dock. "You better not let go, Emmett."

"Or what?"

Her fingers dig into my skin. "Or I'm going to kill you, that's what."

"So bloodthirsty," I tsk. "You know what? I changed my mind."

"About?"

"I'm not going to teach you how to swim."

I stop when my feet can still touch the ground, and the water reaches just under my collarbone.

"What?" Kate pulls back so she can look me in the face, her whole body still clutching onto me for dear life. "You better be joking right now, Emmett Santiago, or I swear—"

Sliding my hand behind her neck, I pull her in for a kiss. Kate sighs, her body relaxing against mine as my mouth devours hers, stopping her from whatever she wanted to say.

I slide my other hand down her back, loving the feel of all that skin under my fingertips. Kate's tongue slides into my mouth, our tongues melting together just as my hand dips lower, over the curve of her back and onto her ass, giving it a firm squeeze.

"I thought you'd teach me how to swim," Kate pants as we break the kiss.

"I thought so too, but this is better."

"Way, way better," she agrees, and then she kisses me again.

I'm not sure how long we stay just like that, Kate holding onto me as I keep us afloat, our mouths pressed together.

We make out for what feels like hours, and I enjoy every freaking second of it. My hands glide over Kate's body, learning every dip and curve.

"Emmett," Kate whispers, her head falling back. I lean forward, my mouth tracing the side of her neck with kisses. Her fingers slide through my hair, and she tugs my head closer.

"Yeah, Kitty?"

Her blue eyes are so dark they almost appear black. Her mouth is slightly parted, lips pink from our kisses.

"Kiss me."

So I do, teasingly at first, little brushes of my mouth over hers. Until she pulls me to her, attacking my mouth with hers. A groan rips from my throat as her tongue slides and tangles with mine.

A shiver shakes Kate's body, goosebumps rising on her flesh.

Breaking the kiss, I run the back of my hand over her cheek. "We should get out."

Wrapping my hand around her waist, I start swimming back toward the dock.

"No."

"No?" I ask, surprised.

"No, you promised you'd teach me how to swim. Teach me," she demands, her hands clenching around my neck.

"And you want to do that now?"

I figured I'd get her out on the dock and wrap her in a towel. Maybe sneak in a few more kisses before I take her back home, but apparently, she has other ideas.

"Yes." She nods decisively and then jabs her finger into my chest. "And no more funny business."

"Okay," I chuckle. "Let's start with something small."

"Small?" Kate thinks about it for a moment. "I can do small."

"You should probably let go of me, though."

"Oh, right."

She loosens her grip reluctantly but doesn't let go completely.

"I have you, Kitty." I slip my hands, so one is around her waist while the other is under her knees. Then I push her upwards, so her body is floating on the surface. "I've gotcha."

"Don't let me go," she pleads, her hands going back around my neck.

"I'm not letting go, Kitty."

I don't have it in me to tell her to let go. I wasn't joking when I said I'd keep her like this forever. Kate is so strong and independent on her own, but I like knowing that she needs me, even if it's for something as silly as this. She needs me, and she trusts me to keep her safe.

"Okay, now start working your legs." I look down as her legs start threading through the water. "Just like that."

"Why do you keep calling me that?" Kate asks after a moment.

"What?"

"Kitty."

"It suits you." I shrug. "Now, hands too, spread them out."

Kate does as I say, but her mind is still on our conversation. "It doesn't," she protests.

"Does too."

"I don't even like cats."

"Well, you're like one. All hissing on the outside, but when someone finds the right spot to scratch, you start to purr."

"I don't think I like that analogy."

"Okay," I chuckle. I can see why she wouldn't like it. "You're fierce and protective, too, especially when it comes to people you love."

"That's true," she agrees.

"See? I'm always right."

"That's what you'd like to think." She tries to swat me on the head, which makes her lose her balance. "Emmett!"

"I've got you." I wrap my arms around her body, pulling her flush against me. "Enough swimming for today."

With my arms wrapped firmly around Kate, I walk us to the dock and sit her on the wooden boards. Stepping between her spread thighs, I brush a strand of hair behind her ear and lean forward, placing my mouth against her forehead for a chaste kiss. "You did good until you tried to smack me. I guess that's karma at its finest."

"You're the worst."

Kate shoves me away, but I don't move an inch.

"You'll have to work on those muscles, Kitty."

Her hand sneaks behind my neck, and she pulls me closer.

Her mouth hovers over mine, her tongue sliding out and over my lower lip, making me groan. I try to capture her mouth with mine, but the little minx puts her hand on my chest.

"Why would I?" she whispers, her lips brushing against mine. "When I can tease you and still win."

Then she pushes me away. I don't resist gravity as it pulls me underwater, needing the water to cool me off.

She's right though, no need to have muscles when she has me all wrapped up around her little finger. And I don't mind it one fucking bit.

Chapter 22

KATHERINE

"You wanna change before I take you home?" Emmett asks as we come closer to the big, two-story farmhouse. The white house is huge, one of the biggest I've seen in Bluebonnet, and honestly, slightly intimidating. The doors and shutters are colored cherry red, and out on the front porch, there are different potted plants and a swing with mismatched throw pillows on it, giving it a homey feel.

"I think I'm go—"

"Emmett?"

We turn around at the sound of a soft voice and come face to face with an older woman, probably around my mom's age. She's short, even shorter than me, and has wild, curly red hair that she tried to—unsuccessfully—tame in a bun. There is a dusting of freckles covering the bridge of her nose and her cheeks. "I've been looking for you!" She looks over her shoulder. "Brad, he's here!"

"Hey, Ma. Sorry about that." Emmett grins sheepishly as my whole body goes rigid. *That's his mother?* "We were at the pond."

The woman's curious eyes land on me as she takes me in. "I didn't realize we had company."

"Nobody was home when we got here earlier," Emmett explains, pulling me closer into his embrace. The woman's eyes dart to Emmett's hand, which is curled around my shoulders, before returning to us.

"Hi!" I say, my voice coming out more high-pitched than normal.

"Oh, right!" Emmett slaps himself on the forehead and nudges me forward. "Mom, this is Katherine, my girlfriend. Kate, this is my mom, Olivia."

Mrs. Santiago's eyes widen at the word girlfriend, but she schools her face quickly. "A girlfriend, huh?" She shakes her head and crosses the distance between us. Pushing Emmett's hands away, she pulls me in for a hug. "It's so nice to meet you, honey. That boy never tells us anything any longer. And to think once he needed to tell us every single detail that had happened to him, including when he—"

"Mom," Emmett groans loudly.

"What?" She pulls back as she faces her son. "I'm just telling the truth."

"You're trying to embarrass me in front of Kate, that's what you're trying to do." He wraps his arms around my middle and pulls me into his chest. "Don't listen to her, Kitty."

"Oh, I find this really interesting," I tease, giving him a small jab in the side. "It's nice to meet you, Mrs. Santiago. So sorry for keeping Emmett away."

"Oh, nonsense." She waves me off. "That boy is always doing something. And please, call me Olivia."

Yeah, no way of that happening. Like ever.

There is a movement behind her that catches my attention, and then a man comes out of the stables, wiping his hands.

"Oh, there you are. You had your momma worried, Emmett."

He moves closer, one of those dark brown cowboy hats obscuring his face, but there is something about him...

"Yeah, I heard that. If I knew y'all would miss me so much, I'd have left a note." Emmett extends one of his hands toward the guy for a handshake. "I took my girl here, out to the pond, since apparently, she doesn't know how to swim."

"Emmett!" I protest, my cheeks heating in embarrassment.

"What? They won't tell. Right, Brad?"

I look at the guy and inhale sharply when recognition sets in.

"It is you! I thought the voice sounded familiar, but I couldn't tell for sure." I wave in his direction. "The hat and all."

"You know each other?" Emmett asks, looking between the two of us, a furrow between his brows.

"We've met before." Bradley nods in my direction. "Kate likes her coffee."

"I usually stop at the diner to get some before school."

A half-smile plays at his lips. "And occasionally in the afternoons too."

"What can I say?" I shrug helplessly. "It's good coffee, and this is one really small town."

"Miss Letty is the best," Emmett and Bradley say in unison and then chuckle.

"So, what are you guys planning to do now?" Mrs. Santiago asks.

Emmett smiles down at me. "I was just about to drive Kate home."

"What?" Mrs. Santiago puts her hands on her hips and stares her son down. "Emmett Santiago, where are your manners?" She shakes her head, turning her attention to me.

"You have to stay for dinner; it's practically done. That's why I was looking for this little hooligan."

"Oh, no." I shake my head. "I don't want to impo—"

"You won't be imposing. There's always somebody at the house, so I make sure to prepare extra. Bradley, do you want to join us?"

Bradley looks at me for a moment, his face serious. I'm not sure how to interpret it or what to make of him since I don't know him that well. Aunt Mabel likes him, and he seems to be a nice guy. Finally, he shakes his head. "You go ahead. I have to finish something in the stables, and then I'm meeting some guys in town."

"Are you sure?"

"Sure thing, thanks, Olivia. I'll see you guys tomorrow morning."

Bradley's eyes meet mine, and he gives me a slight nod.

"Okay, until tomorrow then." Mrs. Santiago wraps her hand around mine. "C'mere, honey. Let's go inside."

I tilt my head back to look at Emmett. I'm sure I have to look like a deer caught in the headlights, but he just shrugs.

"Emmett, take the girl's bag. Seriously, I raised you better than that, young man. Kate, you should call your parents, let them know you'll be home late." She frowns. "Are you new in town? I'm not..."

"I just moved here," I explain. "Well, my sister and I. We're living with our aunt, Mabel Adams?"

"Mabel Adams! Lovely lady. How is she doing?"

Mrs. Santiago pulls me toward the house, Emmett walking behind us quietly.

"She's fine, busy with work."

"She still works in that accounting office next town over, does she?"

"Yes, ma'am. She does."

"She's always been such a hard-working woman. Did you know we actually went to school together? She was a couple of years older than me, but still..."

Emmett's mom continues chatting away as we enter the house, telling me all about her school years at Bluebonnet High. I try my best to keep up, but it's completely hopeless. Still, I do my best to nod at the right moment and murmur something every now and then that seems like I'm following.

"Emmett, go and wash up before dinner," Mrs. Santiago throws over her shoulder as she pulls me into the kitchen. He mutters something under his breath but turns to do as his mother said. If I weren't slightly freaked out by staying alone with her, *my boyfriend's mother*, I might have thought it funny. Okay, I still think it's funny.

Something is simmering on the stove in the kitchen, the smell of tomato and spices filling the air. Letting go of my arm, Mrs. Santiago goes straight to check it, stirring whatever's inside.

"Can I help you somehow?" I ask, looking around the kitchen.

"Thank you, but I'm almost done. You go on and take a seat."

Although she can't see me, I nod and look around.

Like the rest of the house, this room is equally as homey. The space is huge, serving as both the kitchen and the dining area; the only thing separating them is a counter.

All the furniture is built from dark, cherry wood and has that old school look to it without making it look shabby. This room, hell this whole house, has a story to tell, the story of different generations of this family that have gone through it.

I can see it clearly in my mind. A big family gathering for holidays or just weekly family dinners. Children running through the halls, their laughter echoing inside the space.

They lived, they laughed, they cried together.

The dining area overlooks the back terrace, and you can see the sunset over the green fields through the big windows. A huge table that seats twelve people easily, if not more, is already set for dinner.

There is a pang of guilt squeezing at my chest for interrupting a family moment.

I should have called Mabel to see if she could pick me up. Or walked home, but there is no way I can leave now.

"We usually have ranch hands join us for breakfast early in the mornings so we need all the space we can get," Mrs. Santiago explains as she passes by me, a plate and utensil in her hands.

"All of them?" I ask, surprised. Becky mentioned this is a big ranch, so I guess it's only natural they need a lot of help to keep it running smoothly. Still, it seems like an awfully big number of people to cook for.

"Yes, they're like a family to us. Besides, working on a ranch is hard work, and the hours are long. The boys need all the strength they can get."

The boys.

If all the boys are Bradley Jones's age, I wonder what they'd say to the nickname. Bradley Jones. I didn't expect to see him today; then again, he always seems to appear when I least expect him.

Before I can think too much about it, the back door opens, and a man enters. "What smells so good?" he asks, pulling off his cowboy hat to reveal neatly cut light brown hair peppered with gray.

"Tacos," Mrs. Santiago says, beaming. "Your favorite. Plus, we have company." She puts her hands on my shoulders as her husband notices me for the first time.

While Emmett looks almost nothing like his mother, he's a

carbon copy of his father. They're both tall and wide-shoul-dered, with dark hair and eyes.

I nervously shift my weight from one leg to the other and urge the corners of my mouth to lift.

I'm going to kill Emmett. Once he shows up, that is.

"Honey, this is Katherine." There is a slight pause. "Emmett's girlfriend."

I wipe my hand against my jeans before extending it for a handshake. "It's so nice to meet you, Mr. Santiago."

He looks at his wife before returning his attention to me. A bright smile, the same one his son has, spreads over his mouths.

"The pleasure's all mine, Katherine." He takes my hand in his and gives it a firm shake. "Well, I'll be damned."

"What?" Emmett asks as he enters the kitchen and spots us all standing next to the table.

"Just trying to figure out how you got such a sweet girl to be your girlfriend, that's all," his dad says and winks at me.

Yup, definitely Santiago charm.

"Hey, what's this?" Emmett protests, wrapping his arms around me and pulling me into his chest. "My own family is trying to sabotage me."

"Just callin' it as I see it."

"C'mon you two. Settle down," Mrs. Santiago chastises them as she leaves us to go back to the stove. "Keith, go wash up; dinner will be ready in a few minutes."

"This was..." I shake my head, not even knowing what to say.

"That bad?" Emmett chuckles as he leads me up to my front porch, hand in hand.

At first, I wasn't sure what it was about him and touching people. But after meeting his parents, I see where he got it from.

Both his parents embraced me with open arms, and the way they interacted throughout dinner was mesmerizing to watch. I've never seen anything like it before. The little looks they shared when they thought nobody was watching, the way his dad always seems to find a way to put his hands on Mrs. Santiago, and not in a sleazy way. It was the little things. His hand on her waist as he was passing her by, a kiss on the top of her head, his fingers touching hers as they exchanged the bowls with food across the table.

Yes, I could totally see where Emmett got it from.

His hand is warm and steady, holding onto mine tightly. Our fingers are intertwined, and the way he rubs his thumb over the back of my hand has tingles pricking my skin.

"Not bad," I protest instantly, not wanting to give him the wrong impression. "Your parents seem really nice."

Since my interactions with parents were close to none, I wasn't really sure what to expect, but they were both really welcoming. I expected them to protest that we were alone at the pond earlier, but they barely mentioned it. Instead, they spent the whole evening getting to know me, all the while teasing Emmett.

"They're the best," he agrees. "And they loved you. I knew they would."

Emmett pulls me to a stop before we get to the stairs that lead to the porch. Just out of the reach of the sensors, which I'm grateful for since my cheeks are burning.

"You think?" I look down, unsure. I thought I wouldn't care, but I realized that I do. Emmett loves and respects his parents a lot, and I want them to like me.

"I *know*." He tucks a strand of my hair behind my ear. "Come to my next game."

"I already saw you play," I point out, looking up at him.

"Not as my girlfriend, you haven't."

His words make a chill of excitement run down my back. There is that word again.

Girlfriend.

I've never been anybody's girlfriend before. Oh, I kissed a few boys here and there. I wanted to know what it was about them that made girls go all crazy. What I found were slobbery kisses, wandering hands, and lines that made me roll my eyes.

Not Emmett, though. He can get cheesy too, but he's also fun and caring and kind. And the way he kisses me takes my breath away. Emmett's kisses leave me wanting more, and when he touches me, all I want to do is curl my body around his and never let go.

"C'mon." He nudges me. "Say you'll come. Bring Penny with you, too."

I chuckle at his boyish excitement. "You know she can't actually see you play, right?"

He shrugs. "No reason not to tell her how freaking amazing I am out there on the field."

I shove him away lightly. "You're incorrigible."

"Charming," he counters instantly.

"Insufferable."

"The word you're looking for is irresistible." He grins, moving closer.

"Ugh, you drive me crazy."

He leans down, placing his mouth on mine. The kiss is short, so damn short it shouldn't be legal, giving me just a tease and leaving me wanting more. So. Much. More. Maybe that's his plan, to drive me crazy with want for him.

"But you like it."

Yeah, yeah, I do. There is no sense denying it.

"I'll come. And I'll talk to Penny, too. See if she wants to come."

"Great, now that's settled, there is another thing..."

Emmett takes a strand of my hair and twirls it around his finger.

"Another thing?" I ask, suddenly wary of his tone and the way he avoids making eye contact.

"The next game?"

"Yeah?"

"That's rivalry week."

"Okay..." I say slowly, not knowing where he's going with this. What the hell is rivalry week anyway? And what does it have to do with anything?

"Rivalry week?" He repeats as if that should mean something to me. When he realizes I still don't get it, he just shakes his head. "We're playing against our rival on our home turf. Homecoming?"

"Oh."

Homecoming, right.

His brows furrow. "You don't seem excited."

"I'm not really sure what to tell you."

Emmett shakes his head. "Any other girl, and she'd be jumping in my arms right now."

"I think we established I'm not like any other girl." I quirk my brow at him, biting down the words I want to say.

Just the idea of Emmett with another girl has my stomach rolling uncomfortably.

His tongue peeks out, sliding over his lower lip. "No, you're way better."

This time when he kisses me, his mouth lingers. My lips part under his assault, our tongues tangling in a dance that melts me from the inside out. My hands wrap around his shoulders, and I lift to the tips of my toes to deepen the kiss.

"Say you'll be my date, Kitty," he whispers as he breaks our kiss, his forehead pressing into mine. "Say yes."

"You don't play fair," I moan in protest, my fingers clenching his shoulders.

"I warned you," Emmett chuckles, his fingers skimming over my cheek. "I play to win."

Did I even have a chance?

No, definitely not.

"Fine," I whisper my surrender.

"Fine, what?" His finger slips under my chin, lifting my head so I look him in the eyes.

"Fine." I glare at him. *Smug asshole.* "I'll be your date, but only if you kiss me again."

"My pleasure," he says, his grinning mouth covering mine.

After a few more long kisses that are not nearly enough, Emmett lets go of me and pushes me up the stairs. He waits as I get my key out and unlock the door.

"Get inside, Kitty," Emmett says when I give him one final look over my shoulder. His arms are crossed over his chest as if he's trying to hold himself from coming closer.

I bite the inside of my cheek to prevent a smile from forming. With one final wave, I step inside and close the door behind me.

As the bolt clicks in place, I lean my back against the door. My heart is beating rapidly against my ribcage, and I know I have a goofy smile on my lips. But I can't help it. Emmett just has that effect on me.

Sighing, I push away from the door. The light is on in the hallway, and I can hear the sound of TV coming from the living room.

"I'm home," I say as I slip out of my shoes and go to look for Penny and Mabel. I texted Mabel that I'd be staying at Emmett's for dinner, and she just texted back with a quick okay.

Penny laughs, and my smile instantly widens.

I stop in my tracks when I get to the doorway and see people sitting on the couch. Mabel is in her old, trusty armchair that's probably seen better days, and on the couch opposite her is Penelope and my—

"Mom?" I ask, completely confused.

Mary Adams lifts her head, her eyes falling onto mine. Her platinum blonde hair is styled to perfection, her makeup impeccable as always. Dressed in a tight red number and high heels, she looks completely overdressed for this place.

"Hey, baby!" she says cheerily. She jumps to her feet and crosses the room, pulling me in for a hug.

Stupefied, I stand there not knowing what to do.

What is she doing here?

She should be back in California, preparing for her next audition or spending time with her latest boy-toy.

"Kate, darlin', just look at you!" She puts her hands on my shoulders and pushes me away a bit so she can take me in. "You've turned so beautiful."

"It's barely been a few weeks," I comment dryly, finally snapping out of the daze I've been in. "What are you doing here, Mom?" I pull out of her reach, crossing my arms over my chest. "Shouldn't you be in Hollywood, filming your next movie or show or whatever?"

Mom's smile falls, replaced by a deep scowl. "Well, they decided to go with somebody else." She shakes her head. "The next one is surely mine. I can feel it."

Yeah, that's what she's been telling us for years. Occasionally, she'd get a smaller role here or there but not even close to what she craves—the main lead in a blockbuster movie.

"So, what? You just decided to show up?"

Mom's eyes narrow at my cold tone. "I wanted to see my girls. Is that too hard to believe? Seriously, Katherine, it was you who decided to leave California, not the other way around."

"You know why we left! It wasn't—"

She flips her hair. "Oh, please! You're just like your father, always thinking there's something better out there for you."

"Well, I wouldn't know, now would I? Since I don't even know his name."

Mom scoffs. "Trust me. I'm doing you a favor. It's not like you're missing much."

"Mary!" Aunt Mabel chastises her, but Mom's on a roll, and when she gets like that, there is no stopping her.

"What? I'm just telling the truth!"

I press my lips in a tight line, all the happiness I've been feeling leaving my body.

Mabel stands up and wraps her hand around mine. "Don't yell at her, she just got home, and she's surprised to find you here. After you've been gone for *eighteen years*."

Mom glares at her sister. "I left so I could work."

"*Exactly*," Mabel drawls slowly, but Mom misses the point, instead turning her scowl on me.

"Where were you, anyway?"

Now she asks that?

"It's none of your business," I mutter, gripping the strap of my backpack tighter. "If you'll excuse me, I'm going to go upstairs to take a shower and finish my homework."

"Sure thing, honey," Mabel says kindly, giving me one last squeeze before letting go.

"Kate, answer my—" Mom starts to protest, but I turn on the balls of my feet and leave the room. I can hear her shouting after me, but I don't bother slowing down or turning back. If I do, I might say things I won't be able to take back.

Chapter 23

EMMETT

"Why are you all grinning like that?" Miguel grumbles, giving me the side-eye.

I grab a clean shirt from my duffle bag. "What? Can't a guy just be happy?"

"After the torture, Coach just put us through, out on the field?"

"It wasn't that bad." I shrug and pull the shirt over my head, ready to get out of here. I'm hoping that if I hurry up, I might get a chance to catch up with Kate before we go to our morning classes. Last night I texted her when I got home, but she said she had to finish some homework before going to bed, so I let her be. If anybody understands how it is to have a full schedule, it's me.

"Not that bad?" Miguel's brows rise. "John legit puked."

"That's because the idiot stuffed himself with breakfast burritos before coming to practice."

Seriously, what dumbass does that? John, that's who.

"Hey, I heard that!" John groans from the other side of the locker room, where he's still sitting in his practice clothes, his face this weird combination of pale with a greenish undertone.

"Good, maybe next time you'll remember not to stuff yourself before practice. You're not the only one who has to work out next to that stink."

"Fuck off, Santiago," John huffs.

"Gladly." I grab my duffle and backpack and throw both over my shoulder. "Later, boys!"

"Wait for me!" Miguel yells as I head out of the locker room.

"Hurry up, 'cause I'm not sticking around."

"What has you all in a hurry?" he asks as he gets in step beside me.

"I want to catch Kate before the first class."

"Kate, of course. How's that going?"

"Good," I say, a smile curling my lips at the memories of last night. "Better than good. I took her to the pond yesterday after school, and then she stayed for dinner."

My best friend looks at me with wide eyes. "No shit."

"Shit, man," I say and grin. I tell him everything that happened yesterday—well, *almost* everything. There is no way I'm sharing some details with anybody, my best friend included.

"So, you two are like serious?"

"I've been serious about her from the start."

And ain't that the truth.

"It just seems too soon, and she's been here for like, what? A few weeks?"

I can see how he might think it's too soon, like an obsession. It all just happened so fast, but I couldn't get Katherine out of my head since that first day. That instant attraction I felt then only grew the more I got to know her and see all the things that have been hiding under the surface.

The shyness hidden underneath that sharp tongue of hers. Her big, kind heart. The way she protects the ones she loves. Her wit.

There are just so many layers that make her the person she is, and I want to know every single one.

"My mom and dad got together when they were freshmen in high school and haven't looked back since." I shrug, my voice sounding hard and defensive even to my own ears.

For a while, we walk in silence, my mind already on Kate and how I can't wait to see her. We're almost at the school door when Miguel calls my name.

I turn around, surprised to see him standing a few feet behind me.

"What are you doing?"

"I think I'm going to ask Becky to homecoming," Miguel blurts out so fast I'm surprised his tongue doesn't tangle.

"What?" I stop in my tracks and turn around to face my best friend. He pulls off his bandana and runs his fingers through his curly hair.

"What, what?"

"I don't think I heard you correctly. You're going to ask Becky to homecoming?"

Becky? As in our Becky?

"Yeah, so?"

"As a friend?" I ask to clarify. He can't possibly mean...

"No, dumbass, as my *date*," he whisper-yells the last word, his whole face turning beet red. He looks around to see if anybody is watching us, but surprisingly we're alone.

"Oh." *Well, shit, so much for that.* "Are you sure you want to do that?"

I have to ask. Both of them are my best friends, and I don't want to see either of them getting hurt, especially not by the other. And with how things have been going lately, it's a logical possibility.

"Would I say it if I wasn't sure?"

"You don't look sure."

"Fuck you, Santiago."

"Well, you better get in line. But seriously, *Becky*?"

"What's wrong with that?" he asks, crossing his arms defensively over his chest.

"Nothing's wrong with that. Becky's amazing, it's just..." I scratch the back of my head, unsure of how to word it.

"It's just..." He waves his hand, prompting me to finish.

"She's like our sister, dude." I scratch the bridge of my nose.

"Not to me." His answer is instant, and from the determined set of his jaw, I know he's not joking.

"Well, shit."

If anybody asked me if I could see Becky and Miguel together, I'd brush it off. Apart from the obvious fact that we've been best friends, almost *siblings*, since we were in diapers, they've been at each other's throats for the better part of the last couple of years.

"Well, shit," he echoes.

"But all the fighting recently?"

It just doesn't make any sense.

Miguel sighs. "I said I like her, not that she doesn't drive me crazy, occasionally."

"If you say so." I look up, and we both chuckle. "But why come to me?"

"Like you said." He shrugs. "She's like a sister to you. She's been our best friend for years."

"Damn straight. So you better watch out, Fernandez," I say, punching him in the shoulder, "because if you break her heart, I'm going to break your face."

"I wouldn't expect otherwise."

The warning bell rings.

"Shit, we better get going."

Together, we rush for the door.

"Sorry you missed Kate."

"Nah, it's okay. I'll get to her eventually."

"All I'm saying is the guys on the offense have to make sure to attack hard. Crush them like bugs, so they don't know what hit them," John says, taking a huge bite of pizza and chewing loudly.

You'd think he wouldn't be able to eat after puking his guts out earlier today, but you'd be wrong.

"Can you be less gross? Seriously, people are trying to eat here."

I look up just in time to see Becky put her tray on the table, her nose scrunched as she takes her seat.

"Fuck off, Becky," John grumbles. "Nobody's making you—" There is a loud *thud* under the table. "Hey, what was that for?"

"Eat your lunch, dumbass," Miguel growls from next to me.

"Hey, Becs." I look over her shoulder, hoping to see Kate, but she's nowhere in sight. "Did you see Kate?"

She tilts her head to the side, thinking. "We had a class together but didn't get a chance to talk much. Why?"

"I haven't seen her, that's all."

I pull out my phone, but there is nothing there either.

Me: Hey, where are you?

"Look at you, Santiago, getting all mushy because you haven't seen your girlfriend for all of five minutes."

This time it's me who's kicking John under the table. He sits upright and glares at me.

"Ouch, will you fucking stop?"

"As soon as you stop talking shit."

For a while, we just glare at one another, but then, Becky puts her hand over mine, drawing my attention to her.

"Maybe she got held up in her last class?"

"Yeah, maybe," I agree, shoving the food around on my plate.

It's not unusual that she's not here yet, but I'm getting a little bit antsy since I haven't seen her all day. I wanted to make sure we're still good after everything that happened yesterday.

But when, even after ten minutes, she doesn't appear, I give up all pretense of eating. Shoving away from the table, I stand up. "I'll go look for her."

"Do you want me to come with you?" Becky asks, already putting her fork down. From the corner of my eye, I see Miguel shifting in his seat. I remember our earlier conversation about how he wanted to ask her to homecoming. I'm not sure when he planned to do that, but I'm not about to get in his way.

"Nah, I'm good. You guys stay and finish."

Not wanting to give her a chance to protest, I turn around and leave the cafeteria. Since most people are eating lunch by now, the hallways are almost empty. I pull out my phone to see if Kate got back to me, but the message is still unread.

Where is she?

I decide to go and check the classroom where she had her last class, although, I seriously doubt that anybody would hold a student up that much, especially during the lunch break.

Maybe she's in our next class already? It's something she used to do that first week when she needed some space from everybody and everything.

Maybe I should check both, just in case.

Just as I'm turning the corner, I almost slam into somebody. No, not somebody.

"Kate?"

My hands fall on her shoulders to steady her.

She lifts her head and looks at me, her dark hair hanging around her like a curtain. "Hey, what are you doing here? Shouldn't you be at lunch?"

"I was looking for you." I narrow my eyes at her. "Are you okay?"

She seems a bit off; her eyes are distant with a dark shadow beneath them, her cheeks pale. Kate pushes a strand of hair behind her ear.

"Yeah, just a shitty day, that's all." She smiles, but it doesn't reach her eyes. "C'mon, let's get back, I'm su—"

"Hey." I step in her way, stopping her from going anywhere. I cup her cheek, lifting her head to face me. "What happened?"

Her smile falls, and she sighs, looking down at the floor.

"My mom's back," she whispers so quietly I can barely hear her.

"Back? As in back in Bluebonnet?"

But her mother stayed in California.

"Yup." Kate wraps her arms around herself defensively, rubbing at her forearms. "She decided to surprise us. At least that's the story she came up with when I got home last night."

Fuck.

I don't know the whole story behind what caused Kate and Penny to come and live here with their aunt, but this couldn't be good.

I catch sight of Kate's tired face.

No, this definitely can't be good.

My fingers clench, making me realize I'm still holding onto my phone. I turn it around and check the time. We have barely ten minutes left before we have to head off to our next class.

"C'mon, let's go."

"What?" Kate looks up. "Go where?"

Intertwining our fingers, I pull Kate with me down the hallway. I'm not really sure where we're going, I just know that I need to get her alone, if only for a little while.

We climb the staircase, and I peek into every classroom we pass by. Most of them either already have people inside or will have pretty soon, but when we come to the end of the hallway, I see the door that leads to the rooftop.

Bingo.

Looking around to make sure nobody's watching, I push the door open. The door's rusty, and I have to put in more strength, but it finally gives, opening with a loud squeak.

"Where are we going?" Kate asks, looking around curiously.

"Rooftop."

We slip inside the narrow, dark hallway and slowly start climbing up.

"Are we even allowed to go up there?"

"Not really." I grin at her.

"Emmett Santiago, you're going to get us into so much trouble."

"Only if we're caught."

When we get to the top, there is another door. Praying that it, too, is open, I push the doorknob and sigh in relief when the door swings open.

Looking over my shoulder at Kate, I wink. "C'mon. We don't have too long."

Turning around, I twirl Kate into my arms. Her body collides with mine, and I have to place my hands on her shoulders to steady her.

"You know, this reminds me of that scene in one of the *High School Musical* movies."

I frown, trying to remember which one she's talking about. "Wait, that lanky dude with long hair?"

I'd like to say I haven't watched them, but during the winter Miguel, Becky, and I usually have movie nights. Each one of us gets to pick a movie on rotation, and Becky takes immense pleasure in forcing us to sit through every single girly movie she can find.

Kate giggles. "Don't be mean."

"I'm not mean, I just call it as I see it."

"I find the fact that you know just who I'm talking about amusing."

"Don't get too excited. When we were younger, Becs made us watch all kinds of crap."

She glides her hand over my chest, brushing away some nonexistent lint.

"Oh, really? I guess I'll have to ask her more about those days. What else did she make you guys do?"

"Not if I get to her first."

"What are you going to do? Get rid of her so she can't tell?"

"The idea might have crossed my mind." I place my palm over hers, stopping it from moving. As much as I love to see a real smile back on her face, I know we have to talk about the real reason we came up here in the first place. "What happened with your mom, Kate?"

Her mood falls like a deflated balloon.

"I told you, she just showed up here yesterday. Out of the blue, which is nothing new, really."

Kate shrugs and turns her back to me. I let her go, seeing that she needs her space. She goes to the edge of the rooftop, her hands leaning against the metal fence as she looks at the sky.

"Why didn't she come here with you guys in the first place?"

"Work."

Her answer is flippant, but something about the whole situation keeps bugging me. I move closer, standing just behind her, able to feel her warmth but not touching her.

"Why did *you* come here?"

Kate's body turns rigid, and I know I've asked the right question. Something about the way they came here in the first place kept nagging at my mind, but I always brushed it away because I just wanted to get to know her. Have her know me.

It takes everything in me not to place my hands on her and pull her in for a hug.

"If you don't want to tell me..." I start slowly, wanting to give her a way out, but more than that, wanting her to share this with me. I want her to trust me as much as I trust her.

"No, it's okay. It's just..." Kate sighs and runs her fingers through her hair. "There was an incident. Back in our old school."

Her throat bobs as she swallows, her tongue darting out and sliding over her lips.

"What kind of incident?" I ask slowly, unsure if I want to know because there is something in her tone... Whatever she's about to tell me, it won't be pretty, and I'm not sure if I'm ready for that.

"Our mom, she's, well... self-centered. Reckless. Selfish. Take your pick." She shrugs. "The fact is, she always puts herself and her dreams over everything and everybody else—Penny and I included. She never could accept that Penny is blind. She just ignored it. As if her blindness would disappear if she didn't address it."

The more she speaks, the tighter the knot in my throat becomes, and this is just the beginning.

"Anyway, I always made sure to take care of Penny. Help her the best way I knew how, which wasn't much, but still. We tried our best."

"Didn't somebody notice?"

Did somebody ask if they needed help? Anything?

"They did, but there was little they could do about it. She wasn't a bad mother, she just was never meant to be one."

Silence falls over us. I'm not sure what to say, how to take this pain she's feeling away. But before I can even try, Kate continues.

"And all was well, as long as we went to the same school. I

made sure to take care of Penny, kept her under my wing, you know? But then I went to high school..."

Her voice trails off, and I can feel the hairs at the back of my neck rise.

"Kate, you don't have to..." I step closer, putting my hands on her shoulders, unable to hold myself back any longer. I have to touch her. Have to do *something*.

I have a feeling I know where this is heading, and I know I won't like it one bit.

Kate shakes her head but doesn't push me away.

"I'm not sure when the bullying started. Not sure how I hadn't seen it before." She shakes her head. "I was so damn stupid. Clueless."

"Don't say that."

"How can I not?" She turns around to face me. Her hair is a mess, and her voice starts to rise as tears fill her eyes. "I got caught up in my own things. My friends. A cute boy in my class. The schoolwork. Me, me, me. I'd become just like our mother, without even realizing it.

"I didn't see that the girl that had been my friend, *our* friend, had decided she was better than us and turned her back on my sister because her new friends didn't like Penny. They were the 'in' crowd, and Penny was just... good ol' Penny." Her hands ball into fists as tears stream down her cheeks. "The worst part? Penny never said anything. Not a fucking thing, for God only knows how long. She kept quiet while we still hung out with her at our building complex; when we invited her into our *home*. Days? Weeks? Months? I don't even know because I never saw it." She sucks in a deep breath and closes her eyes. "Not until I found Penny in our bathroom, holding a razor to her wrists while bawling her eyes out."

"Oh, Katherine..."

Fuck staying away.

I pull her into me, wrapping my arms around her and squeezing tightly. At first, she is limp in my arms, but then she slides her hands around my waist, her fingers holding on to my shirt as she starts to sob in earnest.

"That's not your fault."

She shakes her head. "I should have seen it. Seen the signs. I should have been there to help her!"

"There is nothing you could have done. If she didn't tell you, how were you supposed to have known?"

"I'm her sister. I practically raised her. I should have seen something."

I push her away so I can look down at her face. Cradling her cheeks, I swipe my thumbs over them. "You did; you must have because you got there in time."

"But not soon enough to save her."

"You saved her, Kitty. You saved her. But you can't protect her from everything."

There is so much sadness in her gaze that it makes my chest ache. I want to protect her from this pain that's long gone. I can understand now, her need to protect Penny above all else—to shield her from all the bad people in this world.

She clenches her hands into fists and pounds them against my chest. "It's not fair."

"I know. I know," I whisper, my hand soothing her hair.

She punches me a few more times, and I let her, not loosening my hold in the slightest. Once she's done, she places her head on my chest, and I can hear her sniffle softly. I let my hand slowly graze up and down her back.

"What happened? After you found her?"

"Besides almost killing her myself?" She chuckles, but there is no humor in the sound. "I hugged her, forced her to tell me what the hell had been going on and what she'd been thinking, and then I promised her I *will* kill her if she attempts that ever again. Then I got into a fight with Mom. A lot was said that day, but the only thing that matters is that I won, and she agreed to let us move here."

To me, I finish silently. And that's the story of how she came to me.

I wish I could feel sorry, and I am, I'm sorry they had to go through all of that to come here, but I can't say I'm sorry to have her in my arms here and now. I'll never be sorry about that.

"Why do you think she's here now? If she was so against you coming here in the first place?"

Maybe if things were different, if her mom didn't have some kind of grudge against this town, she'd have been here sooner. Maybe we'd have spent summers together. Maybe...

"I wish I knew, but Mary Adams is too fickle, too unpredictable."

"Do you think..." My throat feels thick, so I force myself to swallow before attempting to get the words out. "Do you think she'll want to take you back? To California?"

My whole body revolts at the idea, but if Kate is right and her mother is that unpredictable, it's a possibility. And I need to know about all the possible routes to make sure my defense is perfect.

"Honestly, I don't know. But she better not. Penny is finally settling in, she's happy and smiling again. She loves her new school and is finally getting the hang of Henry. I don't want..."

"What about you?"

Kate blinks, surprised at the sudden interruption. "What?"

"Penny's happy here, but what about you? Are you happy?"

Do you want to stay?

The words are out there, between us, although I haven't voiced them out loud.

"I—" Kate starts but stops almost instantly. Her throat bobs, tongue flicking over her lower lips.

I extend my hand, brushing her cheek with the tips of my fingers.

"Because I'm falling for you," I confess softly.

My heart thunders in my chest as the words slip out, my palms turning sweaty with nerves. This is probably the shittiest moment to put this on her, but after everything she's shared with me, I need her to know this. I need her to know how much she means to me and not some half-hearted bullshit. *Screw that.*

"No, I *have* fallen for you." I look into her eyes, those deep, deep blues that rock me to my very core. "I have fallen for you, Katherine Adams, and I don't think I'd be able to watch you leave."

Kate's mouth falls open as she sucks in a breath, her eyes widening in surprise.

For a moment, time seems to have stopped as my words, my confession, hang in the air between us.

"We're not leaving." Kate shakes her head, desperation in her voice. She looks down, her eyes fixed on my chest. "She didn't say anything. She's probably grown bored and just came for a short visit, and she'll be back on her way soon enough because God knows there isn't anything that can hold her attention here."

"But—"

The bell rings, stopping me before I can finish.

Kate gives me a small, pleading smile. "C'mon, you can't be late for class and risk being benched because the coach will kill you."

Disentangling from my arms, she grabs my hand and pulls me toward the door. For a moment, I wish it would be stuck so we can stay here and finish this conversation.

But it gives in without much trouble, killing any hope that I might get to hear her say those words back.

Chapter 24

KATHERINE

Because I'm falling for you. I have fallen for you, Katherine Adams, and I don't think I'd be able to watch you leave.

Why didn't I say anything back yesterday?

Stupid. Stupid. Stupid.

The disappointment was evident on his face, but as always, Emmett didn't push me; instead, we went to our class and continued with our day like nothing had happened.

Only it has.

I have fallen for you.

My whole body shivers as his words ring in my mind. My heart has been beating so hard; it's a surprise it hasn't given up on me yet.

I look down and see a squished to-go cup in my hands. I definitely didn't need more caffeine today, but I was nervous and needed something to occupy my hands.

But seriously, what am I going to do?

I should say it back, right? I mean, I want to, because the truth is, although I tried my hardest to resist him, I've been falling for Emmett too. Desperately, head-over-heels in love.

I burrow my head in my hands and sigh.

This is so freaking complicated.

But before I can think too much about it, there is a high-pitched squeal, and then hands wrap around my neck tightly.

I stumble, almost falling face first, but somehow, God only knows how really, I manage to regain my footing.

"Miguel asked me to homecoming!" Becky says breathlessly and jumps down to the ground.

"What?" I chuckle and turn around to face her. That girl seriously needs to slow down before she kills somebody.

Becky sucks in a breath, but there is no hiding her excitement. "Homecoming. Miguel asked me."

I can feel my eyes bug out. "As his date?" I ask slowly, not wanting to come to the wrong conclusion.

Becky nods her head yes. Her eyes are huge, and there is no stopping the smile that spreads over her lips.

"When?"

"Yesterday!" She loops her arm through mine and pulls me toward the school. "After lunch, he told me he needed to talk to me and to wait for him after the last class because he'd take me home."

"And?" I prompt, the suspense killing me.

I mean, I could totally see that Becky had a thing for Miguel, but I was never sure what to make of him. I know she can hold her own, have seen it on more than one occasion, but Becky is such a sweet person, and I didn't want to see her get hurt. And falling for your best friend has heartache written all over it.

"So we're driving back home, and he's mostly quiet, so I figured maybe he forgot, you know? And then suddenly, out of nowhere, he just blurts it out. I might have screamed, and he might have stomped on the brake suddenly."

"Oh my God!" I can totally picture it. Nobody could say these two are subtle.

"Good thing we live in the middle of nowhere."

"At least nobody got hurt," I agree.

"True. Anyway, at first, I thought he was joking with me, asking me to go as a friend or something, and I'm taking nobody's pity."

"Of course not. You deserve a guy who'll pull out all the stops."

"Damn right. Every girl deserves only the best!" She nods her head. "At first, I got pissed off, because how dare he tease me like that, you know? So I was yelling at him, all in his face, when he pulled onto the side of the road and kissed me."

"Whaaat?" I squeal so loudly that people start turning heads in our direction.

"Shhh!" Becky hisses, covering my mouth with her hand. I push it away.

"How was it?"

"It was... nice." Becky sighs, a dreamy expression on her face.

"Just nice?" I ask, wiggling my brows.

"Oh, hush, it was amazing, dreamy, earth-shattering. Just... perfect."

Yeah, I bet it was.

"So, did you say yes?"

"Once I found my voice again, sure."

"Oh, Becky," I laugh. She's too funny for her own good.

"But now we have a problem."

"What problem?" I ask, completely confused. Shouldn't she be happy about this whole situation? Isn't this what she wanted?

"Homecoming is next week, and I have nothing to wear. You know what that means, right?"

"That you'll go through your closet and try to find something?" I offer. But I might as well suggest she go around digging through the dumpsters if it's to be judged by the look on her face.

"No, missy. That means that you and I are going shopping."

Becky: Be there in five.

I type a quick okay back and lock my phone. Grabbing a few bills from my money stash that's growing thinner by the day— I'll seriously have to look for a job—and together with my phone, I slide them into my pocket.

Although I could probably find something in my closet to wear to the dance, I don't want to disappoint Becs. Besides, it's also an excuse to get my ass out of the house. Which is for the best since Mom has been around since she got here a few days ago.

She still hasn't mentioned the reason for her being here, and I still can't decide what her end goal is, but for today I'm going to push it to the back of my head.

Penny's out, having her piano class, and I'm going to help my friend find a dress that will make Miguel sorry he waited so long to ask her out on a date.

Seriously, boys.

Shaking my head, I walk out of my room and descend the stairs as quietly as possible. But apparently not quietly enough, because as I'm putting on my shoes, Mom appears from the living room.

"Going somewhere?" she asks, her brows raised as she looks down at me.

Tying my shoes, I get to my feet and dust my butt. "I'm going out."

"I can see that. Anywhere in particular?"

"Why?" I cross my arms over my chest and turn to look at her. "Since when do you care?"

She has the audacity to look actually hurt. "I've always cared, Katherine."

"Well, you have a funny way of showing it."

I turn around and dash for the door. For all her words, she doesn't even try to stop me. Surprising, I think not.

Becky is already parked in the driveway when I come out, so I hurry up and get into the passenger seat.

"Ready?"

I look toward the house, but it looks empty. "Yeah."

As we drive to the nearest mall, which is half an hour away, Becky tells me all about the dresses she saw online and what she thinks would work best.

"Mom wanted to come." She rolls her eyes. "But thankfully, my little brother was an ass, so she stayed home to deal with him." The door to the mall slides open, and we enter the cool interior. "Like, don't get me wrong, I love my mom, but she can be so old-fashioned sometimes."

"Right. So anywhere, in particular, you want to go?"

"Oh, no, honey, we're seeing it *all*."

Looping her hand through mine, Becky leads me into every single shop. She has this idea that she has to first *see* everything in the first walk around, and then she'll actually go and try something she likes.

According to her, it's a *process*.

If you ask me, it's exhausting.

But I follow after her like the good friend that I am, as we enter store after store.

"I still think that dark pink one looked awesome," I tell her through the curtain.

There is rustling on the other side as she changes, yet, again. I stopped counting the number of times she did it. You'd think the earlier process would help her narrow down her choices. You'd be wrong.

"Oh..."

"Oh, what?" I turn around and peek behind the curtain. "*Oh*. Becs, that looks..."

I shake my head slightly, at a loss for words. She looks stunning, the emerald dress hugging her in all the right places, making the red tones in her hair stand out. Ultra-thin straps cover her shoulders. The dress dips into a deep V, but there is a little wavy overlay that makes it look flirty. The dress fits like a second skin, reaching mid-calf with a slit on the side.

Her eyes meet mine in the reflection in the mirror. "Do you think he'll like it?"

"He'll love it."

"He better because I love it." She chuckles. "I'm taking it."

"Great, you change, and I'll wait outside."

Closing the curtain so she can change, I exit the dressing room and go back into the store. I'm strolling around the shop when my phone vibrates.

Emmett: What are you up to?

Me: Shopping with B.

Emmett: :O :O

Emmett: What about me?

Me: You were at practice.

Me: Besides, do you really want to go shopping?

Emmett: You're there. I think that answers it.

My heart skips a beat as I read the words on the screen.

"What are you blushing at?" Becky asks, looking over my shoulder so she can read the message herself.

I pull the phone to my chest, shielding it from her. "Just talking to Emmett."

She rolls her eyes. "I should have known. You always get that look on your face when you talk to him."

"What look?" I ask, pulling a dress out of the rack.

"That dreamy, I'm-hopelessly-in-love look." Her eyes fall on the dress that I pulled out. "Hey, what are *you* wearing to homecoming?"

I return the dress back where it belongs. "What do you mean? I'll find something." I shrug.

"Find something?" Becky blinks, and then repeats, "You'll *find* something?"

"Umm... Yeah? I'm sure I brought a dress from California."

"No, you're not." She grabs my hands and pulls me through the store. "How many homecomings do you think you'll get, huh?" Becky doesn't wait for my answer. "Two. This year and next. And who knows what will happen next year."

"Becky, I—" I start, but she doesn't let me finish.

"Hmmm..." She purses her lips, thinking. "I remember one dress that you might like."

"It's really not necessary."

"Of course, it's—" She stops suddenly and lets my hand drop. "This one."

Becky pulls the dress out and shows it to me. I suck in a breath as my eyes land on the dress, taking it in. The cut, the color, the lace—it's breathtaking.

"Right?" A smug smile curls her lips as she wiggles her brows playfully. "You know I'm right."

My teeth graze over my lower lip. "I'm not sure, Becs."

My protest is weak, and we both know it. The dress is beautiful, one of the rare ones I noticed before, and held just a few seconds longer so I could enjoy imagining how it would be to wear it for Emmett.

"Try it," she insists, shoving the hanger into my hands. "C'mon, time's a wastin'."

I look down at the soft material in my hands.

I could try it, doesn't mean I have to buy it, right?

Right?

Turns out, you have to buy it. Not even I'm strong enough to resist the perfect dress. Especially, not when I could imagine Emmett's face light up when he sees me.

"I'm going to kill you," I say as we exit the store, each of us carrying a bag in our hand. Okay, Becky is carrying a few because she got a new pair of shoes and a bag to match too.

"No, you won't. What you will do is thank me once Emmett starts—"

"Once Emmett starts what?" a voice asks.

I turn around and come face to face with the guy himself.

"What are you doing here?" I ask as Emmett pulls me into his arms, his mouth brushing against mine. He smells heavenly, like citrus and sandalwood and all Emmett.

"We finished with practice so we figured we might join you guys," Miguel explains, his arm thrown casually over Becky's shoulder.

She looks up at him. "You were just hungry?"

He makes a guilty face at which Becky rolls her eyes. "I know you too well, Miguel."

"Whatcha got there?" Emmett asks, peeking into the bag.

"Don't you dare, Emmett!" Becky shrieks just as I pull the bag out of his reach.

"What?" He looks between the two of us, completely baffled.

"You're not seeing that before homecoming. So you better keep your fingers in check so I don't have to chop them off."

"Vicious."

"That goes for you too, mister." She turns around and stabs her finger in Miguel's chest.

He lifts his hand in the air defensively. "I wasn't even gonna try."

"Yeah, right. C'mon, since you're here we might as well have something to eat."

Chapter 25

EMMETT

"I'm done," Miguel groans as he falls into the passenger seat of my truck.

"I feel you," I mutter, tossing my duffle on the floor and starting the engine. I look at the clock on the dashboard. It's a little after nine. The coach asked us to stay after practice to watch some film together, which dragged on for way too long.

"You mind if we stop somewhere?"

Miguel gives me a side glance. "Anywhere in particular?"

"Yup. I have something I want to give to Kate."

"And you couldn't have done it in school?"

I pull out of the parking space. "What fun would that be?"

The drive doesn't take long since the streets are mostly empty. Gotta love small-town life. Not ten minutes later, I'm parking in front of Kate's house. Light is shining through the windows, illuminating the darkness.

"Just don't go making out with her on the front porch," Miguel grumbles from his seat.

I slap him over the head. "Don't be a dick. This will only take a few minutes."

I unbuckle my seatbelt and hop out of the car, grabbing the bag I stashed under my seat.

"That's not something to be proud of, you know?!" he yells after me, laughing his ass off.

Dickhead.

I give him the finger before pulling my phone out of my bag and dialing Kate's number. It rings a few times before she finally picks up. "Hey, you," she says, sounding distracted.

"Hey, babe. Whatcha up to?"

"Just finishing some homework."

I can hear papers rustling in the background.

"Come out."

"What?"

"Come out," I repeat.

"Like, now?" But even before she finishes, the bed squeaks.

"Yes, now."

"Emmett, what are you..." The words die on her lips as she peeks from behind the curtain, and even from down here, I can see her eyes widen when she sees me. "What are you doing here?"

She pulls open the window and pushes her head out.

"We can do it this way too." I grin, knowing I probably look like a lunatic, but not caring because I finally get to see her.

This last week has been crazy, and I barely got to see her. If it weren't for lunch and that one class we share together, I probably wouldn't.

Then there was that day. We haven't talked more about her mom being here, or the fact that I basically told her I loved her, and she didn't say it back. It bugged me at first, but then I reminded myself that I could see it. I could see she loved me back with every look she directed at me, with every smile, every kiss, every caress. It'll have to be enough until she's ready to say the words out loud. God knows she didn't have much of an example growing up. Besides, I'm a patient man, and as I told her before, she's worth waiting for.

"Are you crazy? What are you doing?"

"Can't I just come to see my girl?"

"Of course, you can," she says softly, her teeth grazing over her lower lip, making me wish she'd come down so I could do it instead.

"I've missed you."

"So, you decided to stop by and play Romeo?"

"Fuck, no, I don't have any intention of dying." I move closer, standing just under her window. "You wanted to play it this way. I'd much rather put my hands on you."

"Emmett..." she sighs, her cheeks flushing slightly. "I missed you too."

"I missed you more." I grin, and she rolls her eyes.

"Are we going to play that game?"

"Actually, I have a present for you."

Her brows furrow. "A present?"

I lift the bag I've been carrying, letting it sway on the tip of my finger.

"What's inside?"

"You'll have to wait to find out."

"You're not playing fair," Kate protests, pouting. Does she really have to tempt me like that?

"You're the one who's not playing fair. I just follow your lead."

The front door creaks open. I hold Katherine's gaze for a heartbeat longer, before forcing myself to turn around and face whoever's at the door.

"Emmett?" Ms. Adams squints at me from the front door.

"Evening, Ms. Adams!" I call out, moving closer.

"Good evening." She looks at me and then up to the

window. "I figured I heard something. You could have come inside, you know?"

"I know," I try to reassure her. "Kate wanted me to profess my undying love the old-fashioned way."

"I did not!" she yells from the window.

Ms. Adams's brows shoot up as she observes us with amusement in her eyes.

"I love to tease her." I lean closer, but don't bother lowering my tone. "I'd have come inside, but it's getting late, and I have to get going. Miguel's waiting in the car. But could you please give this to Kate?"

"I'm not accepting it until I know what's inside!" Kate yells from upstairs, leaning out the window so she can see us.

"You don't have to, but your aunt is." I give Ms. Adams my most charming smile as I hand her the bag. "Make sure she wears it tomorrow?" I say in a hushed voice so Kate can't hear us.

"Hey! You can't do that," Kate huffs. There is rustling coming from above as she pulls back inside. "I'm coming down."

"I'm leaving!" No matter how much I want to see her open it, I know if I stay, I won't leave anytime soon. "Can you do that?" I ask Kate's aunt.

"Sure thing, hun."

"You're the best, Ms. Adams." With one final smile, I pull back. "Good night."

"Night, Emmett."

When I look up, hoping to catch one final glimpse of Katherine, I see a shadow standing in the doorway. I watch it, expecting the person standing behind the door to come out, but it doesn't happen, so I turn around and walk back to my car.

KATHERINE

"Did he leave already?" I ask, slightly winded as I come to a stop on the front porch. A shiver runs through my body from the cool night air, making goosebumps appear on my skin. While the days are still warm enough, you can start to feel the chill in the air as soon as the sun goes down.

"They just turned the corner," Aunt Mabel says from the step on the porch.

"Dammit," I mutter. I'd really hoped I'd get a chance to see Emmett. Maybe even sneak a kiss or two before he had to leave.

"He left you this, though."

Mabel extends her hand, a plain, middle-sized gift bag in her hand. I suck on my lower lip, looking at the offering. I don't remember when the last time was that I got a present. And this isn't just any present. It's from Emmett.

"Aren't you going to open it?" Mabel asks, pushing the bag closer.

"You know gifts aren't actually free?"

I grit my teeth to hold in my irritated response. I tried my best to ignore Mom's lurking when I descended the stairs, but of course, she had to come out and meddle.

I grab the bag, pulling it to my chest protectively. There is no way I'm going to let her ruin this for me.

"Maybe not in your world." I look over my shoulder at Mabel. "I'm going to go up to my room."

She gives me an apologetic smile. I'm not sure what she has to apologize for. We both know how Mom can get. "Sure thing, hun."

"Hey, I'm not done talking!" Mom protests. I can hear her stomp her foot behind me, but I ignore it.

"Well, I'm not in the mood to talk," I say, hurrying toward the staircase.

"Well, we're going to talk."

Mom catches up to me; her fingers wrap around my wrist and pull me back before I can step a foot on the staircase, spinning me to face her.

"What?" I glare, pulling my hand out of her grip. My wrist stings from the force of her touch, but I don't let her see my discomfort.

"Mary!" Mabel hisses at her sister. The front door closes shut as Mabel moves closer.

"Don't get into this, Mabel, it's none of your business."

"You're in my house, Mary. Let's not forget that," Mabel says coolly. I don't think I've ever heard her use that tone of voice with anybody. She's always so nice. I didn't think she had it in her.

"Only because you stole my girls from me!" Mom yells. Mabel sucks in a breath like she slapped her, but Mom ignores her, turning her attention to me. "But that's done. We're going home."

I blink. Her words echo in my mind, but I can't wrap my mind around them.

Home.

She wants to...

"We are home," I say, my voice in complete contrast to my mind, which keeps screaming one word over and over—no.

"To *our* home, Katherine." She makes a point of accentuating our like there was ever a place that was home. But there is now. It's right here. In Bluebonnet Creek, Texas. "Back to California."

I hate when she uses that tone with me. Like I'm a foolish little girl who doesn't know better.

"Are you crazy?" I pull back, my fingers clenching the bag in my hand. "No."

"Seriously, Katherine. You can't stay here forever. It was

nice of Mabel to take you girls in for a little while, until things cooled off, but it's time to go back home."

"What home? We're enrolled in school here. Penny is finally getting the help she needs, being surrounded by people like her..."

"Mary, please," Aunt Mabel tries to reason, but there is no reasoning with her once she gets this way. I know that better than anybody.

"Don't you *Mary* me, Mabel!" Mom turns her attention back to me. "Penny doesn't need all that." She waves her hand dismissively. "She has us, and she's okay."

"She was not okay, Mom!" I yell, stomping my feet. "She was not okay. She was hurting. She didn't feel like she could belong, and she most certainly didn't have the proper help to deal with her blindness. She has all that now. And we finally found a place to call home."

Mom glares at me, her lips pressed in a tight line. "Is this about that Santiago boy?"

My cheeks heat, but I lift my chin defiantly. "Emmett doesn't have anything to do with it."

"Oh, really?" She shakes her head. "It didn't look like that a moment ago."

"Leave Emmett out of this." I grit my teeth. I don't want her anywhere near Emmett, not even asking around about him. "He doesn't have anything to do with any of this."

She observes me for a moment, as if she's trying to figure me out. Finally, she tsks. "You should know better than that, Katherine. Seriously, do you really think that boy is your forever? Please, like he'd settle for a girl like you."

Her words shouldn't sting, but they do. Oh, how they do.

It's one thing to know you're not good enough for somebody, but to have it thrown in your face, by your mother of all people?

"You don't know anything about him, and you certainly know nothing about us."

"Is there even an *us*? Please, I don't need to know him. I know guys like *him*. They're fine playing with you for a little while, but when the world comes calling, and by the stories I've heard around town it will, he'll leave you without a backward glance. Is that what you want? To stay in this stupid little town, crying over a boy?"

"Mary, you should stop," Mabel protests.

"He loves me."

Mom smiles, a vicious glint in her eyes. "Oh, silly girl. Of course, he does, but fame is a powerful thing." Her gaze rakes over my body. "Do you really think you'll be able to compete? It might not happen tomorrow or next week, but one day something bigger and better will come, and what are you going to do then? Stay in a small-town like Mabel, closed off from the rest of the world?"

Mabel sucks in a breath. My whole body stiffens, the rage boiling inside of me. My hands clench by my sides.

"Better than trying to reach your dreams only to fail over and over again, doncha think?"

She sucks in a breath, her cheeks turning red in anger.

Before she can regain her wits, I turn around and continue climbing the stairs.

"Run all you want, Katherine. You can't run from this. Want it or not, we're leaving."

I choose not to dignify her with an answer. My whole body is tense as I reach the second floor and march to my room, making a point to shut the door behind me.

Stifled yelling continues downstairs as mom and Mabel go at it, now that I'm not present.

I throw myself on the bed face first, burrowing my head into my pillow before I let out a muffled scream.

My fingers clench into a fist, and I pound it against the mattress.

I hate her. I hate her. I hate her.

The door creaks open, paws scratching against the wooden floor.

"Kate?" Penny asks tentatively.

I turn my head to the side. "On the bed."

She walks toward the bed, patting the mattress to check that it's open before sitting down on the edge. She's in her pajamas. Her familiar strawberry shampoo brings me comfort as she settles on the mattress next to me.

"By the noises coming from downstairs, I gather she told you."

Of course, she'd go and tell Penny first. Why am I not even surprised?

"Yeah," I whisper, my voice hoarse.

"I don't want to go," Penny confesses after a moment. "Does that make me a bad person?"

Penny nibbles at the inside of her cheek. She looks so young, too young to be dealing with this shit. I grab her hand, giving it a little squeeze.

"No, of course not. I don't want to leave either."

I move back and pat the open space next to me. "Come here."

Penny gets on the bed and snuggles next to me, and Henry follows after her, curling by our legs.

For a while, we stay silent, just holding onto one another like we did when we were little girls, alone for the night in one of the apartments we were renting at the moment while Mom was partying outside, trying to dazzle some of Hollywood's newest and hottest producers and directors.

"What happens now?" Penny asks, the first one to break the silence. "Will we have to go back with Mom?"

Not if I have anything to do with it.

But no matter how much I want to say it, I just can't voice the words out loud. I can't make a promise I might not be able to keep because a little part of me can't help but wonder... What if Mom is right?

Chapter 26

KATHERINE

Becky screams loudly as soon as she sets eyes on us. "You've been holding out on me!"

"Hey, Becky," Penny greets her as we both slide into the car and close the doors.

"Hey, honey." She turns around to take Penny in. "Look at y'all! Emmett will be so happy!"

We're both wearing Eagles jerseys with Santiago written in bold, gold letters across our backs. Last night, we fell asleep before I managed to open the bag, but Penny found it when she woke up and insisted I open it in front of her. I'm not sure which one of us was more surprised when we opened the bag.

"Well, it was technically Emmett who bought them." I pull on my seatbelt. "He came by last night after practice."

"Oh, did he now?"

"Stop it, he was just being nice."

"Well, I'm his best friend, and he didn't bring me any jerseys."

I look pointedly at her overly big purple jersey that's tied into a knot on her side, showing a strip of her flat belly.

245

"He didn't!" she protests, starting the car. "I had to steal this one from Miguel."

"And that was such a hardship."

"Oh, are you and Miguel friends again?" Penny asks, poking her head forward from between the seats.

"He's her *boyfriend*," I say, making sure to drawl out the last word.

"So, you don't want to kill him any longer for ruining your dress?"

"I wouldn't go that far, honey. It was one nice dress."

The drive to the school is slow since the whole town has decided to come to tonight's game, apparently. We chat for a while until one of Becky's favorite songs comes on the radio, then she cranks it up, and together we sing along to one of Carrie Underwood's hits.

"There!" I say, pointing out an empty space.

"Finally."

Slowly, Becky maneuvers her car into the open space, honking when a group of students passes by without checking for cars first.

"Seriously, those kids drive me crazy. They never look further than their noses." Becky glares at their retreating backs. "C'mon, let's get out, the game's about to start."

I nod my agreement and slide out, waiting for Penny to do the same. She extends her cane, her fingers curling around the handle.

"It's good we left Henry home."

Penny loops her arm through mine and nervously looks around as all the noises assault us at once.

The parking lot is full; people are shouting to one another, the band is playing out on the field, and car engines are rumbling as people keep coming to watch the game.

"Yeah, me too," I agree, trying to take it all in. "It's crazy out here."

"It usually is for a big game like this one. Folks want to support their favorite sons." Becky locks her car and drops the keys into her purse. "Ready to go and find our seats?"

"Sure, let's go."

Hand in hand, Penelope and I follow after Becky, who's practically bouncing with excitement, as she leads us toward the football field. People greet her as we pass by, some simply waving while others ask about her mom and brothers.

"Hey, Mr. Murphy! How's the knee?" Becky asks an older guy who is just taking his seat.

"Becky, my darlin'." His whole face lights up. "It's good. It's good. How are y'all?"

"We're all doing great."

Mr. Murphy nods, his gaze shifting to the field. "Our boys ready to beat some asses today on the field?"

"Let's hope so."

"Well, with cheerleaders as pretty as you girls, they better." He gives me a little wink, and my cheeks heat at the attention.

"Excuse me?"

I look up to see a woman waiting for me to move so she can pass by.

"Sorry." I shift, giving her space. When she's gone, I look down to the sidelines, hoping to catch a glimpse of Emmett, but he's nowhere to be seen.

Rose Hathaway, however, is right there, staring up at me, or more like glaring. Her hair is pulled in a high ponytail, with a purple-gold bow on top that matches her cheerleading uniform. Her makeup is flawless, and she'd look beautiful if it weren't for the scowl on her face. She looks between Penny and me, her gaze zeroing in on the cane clasped in Penny's hands.

"Coming?" Becky places her hand on my forearm, snapping me out of my staring contest.

"Hmm?" I look back, but Rose's back is turned to the bleachers. "Oh, yeah, right. Let's go."

EMMETT

"Fuck, yeah!" Miguel fist-pumps as Vincent, our wide receiver, runs into the end zone and throws the ball on the grass.

People in the stands cheer and clap as the score on the board changes to 21-21 after we score the extra point.

The game has been a mess since the start. We lost the coin toss, and they chose to start with the offense. While we have the advantage of playing on our home turf, those guys are hungry to win. We've been going back and forth the whole game. They'd score a touchdown, and then we'd do the same, but with mere minutes left on the clock, we can't let them score again.

As if he can read my thoughts, Coach stops us before we get out on the field. "Whatever you do, do *not* let them score. Keep an eye on the receivers. That Kelly boy's got fast feet."

"Got it, Coach."

After a slap on my shoulder, I run out onto the field, taking my place on the line.

The quarterback calls out the play, and the center snaps the ball. The first lines collide.

I keep my eyes on the Kelly guy, waiting for the ball to fall into his hands, but it never does. Then I see one of the running backs slipping from the side.

"Fucking hell."

Miguel sees him a second later too, but it's already too late because he's running toward the end zone. Thankfully, Nico manages to tackle him to the ground at thirty yards.

"A perfect time to change the fucking tactic." Miguel spits on the grass.

"Keep your eyes open."

The referee blows the whistle, and we take our places.

"Ready to run off to your momma to cry once the game's over?" one of the opposing players asks with a grin on his face.

"The only one who'll be running off is you once we wipe the grass with you."

His grin is replaced by a scowl, but then the quarterback calls out a play. This time, I don't look for where the ball should go. When the offense and defense crash, I go for the guard, giving Miguel a chance to slip through their line and go for their QB. He tackles him to the ground, but it's too late, because the ball is sailing through the air.

The pass is weak, and before Kelly can change course to catch it, Nico intercepts it and starts running to the end zone.

The chants of the crowd grow louder when they realize we've got possession of the ball.

Getting rid of the asshole guard, I run after the players who're at Nico's heels. He passes the ball to Miguel, two of the Panther players on his tail.

His eyes meet mine, and just before one of them tackles him to the ground, he lets the ball spiral into my hands.

My skin burns when the pigskin slips between my palms. Tucking it to my chest, I run as my teammates do their best to clear my path.

Thirty yards.

Twenty.

Ten.

"The-fucking-end!"

I throw the ball to the ground as soon as I cross into the end zone.

The whistle blows, signaling the end of the game, and the field turns into pandemonium. Miguel sprints toward me, throwing his arms around my shoulders and screaming at the top of his lungs. "We won! Fuck, yeah!"

The rest of our teammates come rushing onto the field and jump all over us until we all land in a mass of limbs on the grass.

I laugh as the last few moments play over in my mind.

Un-fucking-believable.

The next few minutes pass in a daze. Referees cut our celebration so we can kick the extra point, and then it's really done.

As soon as the whistle blows, the field overflows with people. It seems like the whole town has come to the game and is now standing on the field, celebrating our victory.

"Holy shit, that was amazing!" Becky squeals loudly, throwing herself at Miguel and kissing him soundly on the mouth.

Seriously? Gross.

But if Becky is here, that means... I turn around, my eyes falling on Kate and Penny instantly. Kate's arm is wrapped around her sister's shoulder, holding on to her tightly as they try to push their way through to us. Penny's clenching her white cane tightly.

Seeing them on the field, dressed in the purple Bluebonnet Eagles shirts I got them, makes my chest tighten a bit.

Kate's eyes meet mine for a second before one of my teammates gets in the way. I push him out of my way and close the distance between us.

"Hey, there," I say, pulling both of them closer, doing my best to shield them from the people mingling around.

"Hi," Kate breathes, stumbling a little when somebody pushes her from the back. "This is crazy."

"Congrats on the win, Emmett," Penny leans closer and yells over the noises of the crowd.

"Thanks, Little Adams. Whaddya think?"

"Well," she drawls, trying to imitate the southern accent. She's actually pretty decent. "From what I could *see,* you were not too shabby."

I pinch her nose. "You think you're funny, huh?"

Penny giggles, swatting my hand away. "Hey, you asked!" Tentatively, she reaches for me. Her hand pats its way up my chest and over my shoulders until she wraps it around my neck, giving me a hug. "I mean it, though. Becky made a point to explain everything to me, and I do mean *everything,* since Kate is hopeless when it comes to sports. Congrats."

"Thanks, darlin'," I whisper, my throat suddenly dry. I tighten my hold on her, lifting her slightly off the ground. "I'm happy you made it."

Kate and I exchange a look over Penny's shoulder before I put her back down.

"You know I really like you, right?" Penny takes a step back.

"Of course, I do."

"Then don't take this the wrong way." Penny's nose scrunches. "But you stink, Emmett."

"What? You wound me, Little Adams." I turn to Kate, throwing my arm around her. "What do you say, Kitty? Your sister is ruthless. And that's the thanks I get for winning this game?" I tsk. "I'm not that bad, right?"

Kate makes a face. "She might be right."

"What?!"

Her hand slides behind my neck, and she pulls me down for a kiss. "But I like you anyway. Stink and all."

I pull back so I can see her face. Her hair is loose, falling down over her shoulders, her cheeks pink from all the excitement. I skim my knuckles over her cheek. Those blue eyes stare into mine intently, her teeth grazing over her lower lip.

I like you.

Not exactly what I want, but it's a start.

"You better, since you're stuck with me." Brushing my mouth against her cheek, I twine my fingers with hers and throw my other arm around Penny's shoulder. I'm not sure where Miguel and Becky got lost, but right now, I don't want to think about it. "Let's go, and see if we can find my parents in this crowd."

Chapter 27

KATHERINE

"Kate, Emmett's here!" Aunt Mabel yells from downstairs.

I turn around to face Penny and Henry, who are sitting on my bed. "He's here!"

"So, I heard." Penny giggles. "Probably half the town, too."

"Don't be sassy with me, missy," I reprimand her, nervous excitement coursing through my body.

"How can I not? It feels like déjà vu."

She's right, dammit. It's just like that day Emmett took us to our non-date date. The day I kissed him, just like he asked me. Then he kissed me back, and the rest is history.

Was it just a few weeks back? It feels like so much longer.

"Kate?"

"She's coming!" Penny yells, jumping off the bed.

"C'mon, you don't want to keep him waiting."

I give myself one final look in the mirror, smoothing out the hem of my skirt. It's dark purple-blue, the perfect match to my eyes. The lace is delicate, making the simple design look absolutely gorgeous. I still can't believe I've gone ahead and bought this dress.

"You look great, Kate."

I turn around and face my sister. "No offense, Pen, but you can't actually know that."

She places her hand on my chest, right in the middle. "I know your heart, and it's the most beautiful thing you can offer to anybody."

My throat tightens, making it hard to breathe, my eyes turning misty. "You're going to make me cry."

"Then you better hustle." Penny gives me a little push toward the door. "Let's go."

The three of us walk out of the room and down the stairs. The foyer is empty, but I can hear Aunt Mabel laughing at something in the living room. I'm not sure where Mom is, but thankfully, she's not here. She hasn't been since her fight with Aunt Mabel last night. Hopefully, she left and won't be coming back anytime soon. It's highly unlikely, but I don't want to think about her tonight. She won't ruin this for me.

Crossing the hallway, I stop in the doorway of the living room. Emmett is sitting on the couch while Mabel fills a glass of sweet tea on the coffee table in front of him.

Penny lets go of me and enters the room with Henry by her side. "Hey, Emmett," Penny greets him cheerfully.

Emmett turns around at the sound of her voice, and then his eyes land on me. He stands up abruptly, mouth slightly open as his gaze takes me in from head to toe.

I shift my weight from one foot to the other as I drink him in.

Emmett is usually handsome, but the black suit and white dress shirt make him downright, mouthwateringly gorgeous. I can only hope I don't start to drool.

"You look..." He shakes his head. "Beautiful. Stunning."

"You're not so bad yourself."

Emmett takes a step closer, extending his hand toward me.

Slowly, I place my hand in his, our fingers brush, and there is that sizzling feeling that appears every time he touches me.

Aunt Mabel walks around us to stand next to Penny. "Y'all look so sweet! Want to take a few photos before you go?"

Emmett pulls me into his arms, his lips brushing against my neck. "Always."

"You guys sure know how to party," I yell so Emmett can hear me over the sound of the country music playing loudly. I have to give it to the decorating team, or is it a committee? Beats me. Whatever they call themselves, they did a really nice job of transforming the school gym into a dance hall for the party, decorating everything in purples and golds. Balloons are scattered all around the floor, and there are twinkling lights hanging on the walls, giving the whole room a magical feel.

"You sure you don't want to join them?" Emmett wraps his arms around my waist from behind, his chin leaning against my shoulder.

"No chance in hell."

"Never danced a two-step?"

I turn to the side so I can look at him. "You did?"

"You can't be born in Texas and not know how to two-step."

"Well, I wasn't born in Texas. What I *was* born with, however, are two left feet. I'd most likely tangle and fall on my ass."

Emmett laughs, the soft rumble of his chest vibrating against my back. "We'll make a true southerner out of you one of these days. Besides, didn't I already tell you?" Emmett's fingers brush against my cheek. "I'll never let you fall."

My heart thumps rapidly against my ribcage. My stomach

clenching tightly as if there're a dozen butterflies fluttering around.

The song comes to an end, and another one starts almost instantly, this one much slower. Emmett's hands slide down my sides until our fingers intertwine, and he turns me to face him.

"Dance with me."

It's not a question. Not like I'd ever say no to him.

With my hands in his, he pulls me out on the dance floor. I'd be surprised he hasn't crashed into anybody, but then again, this is Emmett we're talking about.

Emmett pulls me back into his arms. Our bodies brush against each other as his hands settle at the small of my back. I wrap my arms around his neck, my fingers playing with the hair at the base of his neck.

"I like it when you don't wear a hat."

"And I like you in this dress."

His hands move lower, brushing the curve of my ass.

"Emmett," I whisper in warning, my fingers tightening in his hair.

He quirks a brow, his hand moving just a bit lower. "Katherine."

"Don't tease."

"I just like to see you blush," he murmurs, his lips brushing against my ear.

My whole body shivers as his hot breath brushes against my skin. With one lingering brush over my extreme lower back, he returns his hands back where they belong.

We slowly sway to the song. Emmett hums the lyrics into my ear, his strong arms enveloping me completely. I lean my head against his chest, feeling his warmth radiating through the layers of clothes between us, and the sound of his strong heartbeat just under my ear.

I love being in his arms like this. It's comforting, safe. Kind of reminds me of how home must feel.

Even as the song draws to an end, Emmett doesn't let go of me. And when another upbeat song comes next, he doesn't pull away.

"Okay, you two love birds, that's enough." Becky loops her hand through mine and tugs me back.

"Back off, Becs." Emmett tries to shoo her away, unsuccessfully. "Go get your own boyfriend."

"Can't bring him where I need to go."

"And where's that?"

"To pee, if you really want to know." She rolls her eyes at Emmett's pouting face. "Don't be a baby, we'll be back in a bit. You two go and grab some punch."

"You heard her, bro. We've been dismissed."

Becky pulls me toward the door. "C'mon, let's go before I burst."

Some of our teachers are standing by the walls and talking between each other, not giving us a backward glance when we pass by. When I look at Becky, she's sporting the biggest smile I've ever seen.

"You seem to be having fun," I comment and take a deep breath as we enter the hallway, enjoying the cool air on my heated skin.

"I am! School dances are always fun, but it's even better because I'm here with Miguel."

The happiness is radiating off of her, and I can't help but smile too. It's infectious.

"You were killing it out on the dance floor. Who'd have thought Miguel has such moves?"

They have been dancing almost since the moment they got here. I hadn't pegged Miguel as the dancing kind, but he looked like he was born to dance. If the football thing doesn't pan out, maybe he should try it.

"Oh, he does," Becky laughs. "He's a showoff and loves to be the center of attention. Kind of goes hand in hand."

"Yeah, now that you said it, I can totally see that." I look at her. "Does this mean you guys are finally done with all the bickering?"

"Oh, I don't know about that. I might be in love with Miguel, but he still drives me batshit crazy. The fighting is messy, but I can't complain about the make-up part. If you know what I mean."

I shake my head, laughing. "You both are cr—"

The words die on my lips as I come to a halt before the bathroom. The door is slightly ajar, and I can hear voices coming from inside.

"What—"

"Shhh." I lift my finger to shush her.

"I don't know, Rose. They seemed like the real deal to me," the first voice says. I don't recognize it, but if she's talking to Rose, and there is only one Rose in Bluebonnet that I know of, it has to be one of her friends.

"Oh, please." Rose comes into my view through the little crack. She rolls her eyes, fluffing her hair a little until she's happy with her reflection. "Emmett just feels sorry for her because her sister is blind. Emmett is a sucker for doing good deeds, and they're a charity case through and through."

My whole body goes rigid at her words, my hands clenching into fists by my sides.

How dare she?

"Kate?" Becky whispers behind me, but I can barely register it from all the buzzing in my ears. What I can feel are her fingers digging into my skin.

How dare she talk about Penny that way?

"I'm telling you, he'll get over it sooner rather than later, and when that happens, who'll be here, waiting? That's right, me."

Like hell you will.

Something in me snaps. I rip my hand out of Becky's grasp —which I'm pretty sure will leave bruises—and push the door open so hard it bangs against the wall. Three heads turn my way, mouths hanging open, eyes wide.

"You say whatever the hell you want about me, but don't you dare bring my sister into this," I hiss, pointing my finger at Rose.

I have to give it to her, she schools her features quickly, turning into a perfect example of serenity and the poise of a southern belle.

What a load of bullshit that is.

"You shouldn't be listening in on other people's conversations, Katherine. It's not nice."

I take a step toward her, but somebody—Becky—grabs my hand and pulls me back. Doesn't stop me from getting in her face, though.

"What's not *nice*, Rose," I spit, "is you talking shit behind other people's backs. Didn't your momma teach you that?"

She crosses her arms across her chest, her chin tilting up a little. "I'm just saying the truth."

"The truth? By talking shit about my sister?"

I want to lunge at her, and Becky must sense it somehow because she puts all her strength into holding me back.

"Don't be a sore loser, Rose." Becky glares at her. "Not that you had anything to lose in the first place. Emmett never gave you a backward glance."

Rose's cheeks turn red. Embarrassment or anger? Probably a little bit of both.

"At least I wasn't pining after my best friend my whole life." Rose flips her hair behind her shoulder and starts walking toward us. Becky stops next to me as we come face to face with Rose.

"No, you haven't. You've been pining all your life after a guy who doesn't want you. That's the difference between the two of us."

Rose huffs angrily and pushes between us, her posse following after her.

The door falls shut as they leave, and only when we can't hear the sound of their footsteps echoing in the hallway does Becky let go of me.

"I seriously hate that girl, she can be such a bitch sometimes, ugh!" Becky turns around to look at me worriedly. "Are you okay?"

"I don't know," I answer truthfully. My whole body is trembling with suppressed anger, and my fingers are clenched so tightly, I can feel my nails dig into the skin of my palms.

"That was some nasty shit she said."

"Yup." Avoiding Becky's stare, I walk around her to the sink, turn on the cold water, and put my hands under the spray. I have to consciously force myself to unclench my hands, and when I do, I see the half-moon marks on my skin.

"You don't believe her, do you?" Becky asks from behind me. "About Emmett? He's crazy about you."

"I'm not worried about Emmett," I whisper, my head hanging low.

"Then?"

"Penny. I—" I gulp, my tongue sliding out to wet my dry lips. "She's been through a lot, and hearing Rose say something like that..."

I shake my head, unable to finish. How do you explain something without saying too much? It's not that I don't trust Becky, I do, but this isn't the time nor the place to unload all my worries on her.

"That was a low blow." Becky wraps her arms around me from behind and places her chin on my shoulder. "I seriously can't believe she'd actually go there."

"I can take anything she's willing to throw at me, but Penny... she's off-limits."

The memories of what happened a few months back come rushing back. If she were to hear just a whisper—just one. Damn. Whisper—I don't think she'd be able to take it. She has just started to heal, and although I can see the improvement in her, I don't want to see it all fall down like a house of cards because of the pettiness of one girl.

Pettiness that's directed at me, no less.

I won't let Penelope become collateral damage.

Becky leans forward and turns off the tap. "After this, Rose'll probably think twice before bringing her up."

Looking up, I meet her reflection in the mirror. "She better because next time nobody will stand in my way."

"I hear ya." She brushes my hair behind my ears. "C'mon, let's get you all dolled up before we get back out there."

I nod my agreement, not really caring one way or the other. Becky hands me some paper towels to wipe my hands while she fusses with my hair. Once she's happy, she takes a couple of towels and runs them under cool water before patting my neck with them.

"You're all flushed."

What I am is angry, but I bite back the words because I know Becky is trying to help me. After she deems that I've cooled off enough, she hands me a tube of lipstick before dashing quickly into one of the stalls. I reapply it carefully while I wait for her to finish her business. She emerges a few minutes later, and after washing her hands and putting on another coat of her own lipstick, we're back out.

"Are you going to tell Emmett what happened?" Becky asks, giving my hand a squeeze.

"No," I say immediately, the word coming out harsher than needed. Forcing myself to take a deep breath, I repeat, this time calmer, "No, I don't want to upset him."

The look Becky shoots my way tells me she doesn't agree, but she doesn't contradict me either. And since we're already back in the gym she doesn't have time to. Becky pushes the door open, and we slide inside the gym just as Mrs. Burke announces: "And homecoming king is..." There is a slight pause to keep the suspense before she finishes, "Emmett Santiago."

The lights find him immediately in the middle of the room. He looks genuinely surprised as his teammates push him toward the stage. A stage where Rose is waiting for him with a plastic crown on her head, and a smug smile on her lips.

Becky curses silently next to me as we watch Emmett get to the stage, accept his own crown, and pose for the photos with the rest of the homecoming court.

"This is such a stupid tradition," Becky mutters, but I'm barely listening; my eyes are glued to the couple on the stage.

Mrs. Burke leans in to tell them something. Emmett pulls back, his eyes scanning the crowd, before Rose demands his attention. He shakes his head at whatever she's saying, but she's insistent. Finally, he sighs, giving in. Emmett takes her hand and leads her to the dance floor, the other couples following after them.

My stomach rolls in revulsion, everything that I've eaten earlier today wanting to make a reappearance.

Rose wraps her hands around him, moving way closer than necessary, and if I thought I wanted to rip her hair out earlier today, it has nothing on this feeling right here, right now.

Becky tugs on my arm. "Maybe we should go—"

I'm shaking my head no before she can even finish. There is

no way I'm leaving. Not when Rose has her claws—quite literally—dug into Emmett.

No, I stand there, watching my boyfriend dance a slow song with another girl.

Rationally, I know it's not his choice. I know if he could, it'd be me in his arms right now. I can see his eyes searching the crowd as they move over the dance floor. Looking for me.

But I keep to the shadows, hoping the darkness will help hide the ache deep in my chest. Knowing doesn't make it hurt any less.

Do you really think that boy is your forever? Please, like he'll settle for a girl like you.

Mom's words ring in my mind, loud and clear, mocking me.

I know guys like him. They're fine with playing with you for a little while, but when the world comes calling, and by the stories I've heard around town, it will, he'll leave you without a backward glance. Is that what you want?

I didn't want to believe her, but looking at Emmett with Rose, messes with my mind. It's so easy to imagine him in a few years in some big hall of a fancy hotel, celebrating a win while playing for some professional team.

Because he's that good. But he's also kind, and caring, and genuinely nice.

He deserves it.

Emmett's eyes catch mine just as the song dies down. He holds my gaze as he steps away from Rose. She tries to get his attention, but he's already moving in my direction, determination written on his face.

He deserves it all.

And no matter how much it hurts, I know I'll never be good enough for him.

Chapter 28

EMMETT

"Why so quiet?" I ask softly, my hand landing on Kate's thigh. She jumps a little, surprised. It's like she's been stuck in her own world ever since she got back from the bathroom, and no matter how much I tried to reach her, I just couldn't. "Is it the dance?" I ask once again. "Because I—"

"It's not the dance. You did what was expected of you. I don't blame you for that."

"It's a dumb tradition. I tried suggesting we each dance with our own dates, but..."

"That's what Becky said." Kate offers me a small smile, so small it's barely noticeable. And just as quickly as it appears, it disappears once again. "It's fine, really." Pushing a strand of her hair behind her ear, she looks out of the window. "Where are we going?"

I take a quick glance in her direction. "Do you want to go home?"

I don't want to take her home just yet, but if that's what she wants, I won't object. I just hope she doesn't ask it because I'm not ready to say goodnight. Not yet.

"No," she says quickly. "Not yet. I'm not ready for this night to end."

There is something in her voice, something that I can't quite pinpoint. But then Kate leans her head against my shoulder and lets out a soft exhale. Her body relaxes against mine. I put my arm around her shoulder, pull her closer, and lean down to brush my lips against the top of her head.

"I'm not ready for that either."

For the rest of the drive we stay quiet, the only sound filling the cab of the truck is the low music coming from the stereo. I take a turn onto the familiar dark road, our only guide the faint moonlight and headlights illuminating the path in front of us.

"I don't know why, but it always surprises me how peaceful it is out here," Kate says as we get out at the pond.

"It really is, especially like this."

I pull out the blanket and pillows, tossing them into the bed of the truck. Then I open the door and set everything up.

Placing my hands on Kate's hips, I hoist her up and then follow after her.

We lie down on the blanket and look out at the sky covered in thousands of shiny stars. The air is chilly but still manageable, and the blanket definitely helps.

"When I need to think, or just want a moment to breathe, I come out here."

Kate turns onto her stomach, propping her head on her palms. "What do you think about?"

"Life. Future. Just..." I shrug. "Stuff."

I place my hand over hers, the tips of my fingers gliding over the soft skin.

"Nobody can bother you here, that's for sure."

I chuckle lightly. "It's not just that, although it definitely helps."

Our fingers intertwine, and I pull her down so she rests her head on my chest.

The silence stretches between us as I run my fingers softly through her loose strands, the only thing you can hear is a lone cricket and the hoot of an owl somewhere in the distance.

"What do you want?" Kate asks softly, breaking the quiet. "You said you think about your future. What do you want? Where do you see yourself?"

"This." My answer is instant. I tuck my free hand behind my head and bring our twined fingers up so I can kiss the back of Kate's hand.

"What this?"

"Just what I said. This. This field, this ranch, this pond, this moment." I let go of her hand and cup her cheek. "I love football, but at the end of the day, football is just a game. A fleeting moment for a chance at glory."

Kate turns her head to the side to look at me. Her teeth are grazing over her lower lip, making it red and plump. My tongue darts out to slide over my lip as I watch hers pop.

"You don't want that? The glory?"

Reluctantly, I lift my gaze to meet hers.

"Why take a chance at glory if you can have the real thing, surrounded by people you love, creating a legacy that will last a lifetime in people you leave behind?" I cup her cheek, pressing my lips to hers. "You, Katherine. I can see my future with you."

Her blue eyes widen, and I can see her slender throat work as she swallows.

"You can't say that."

"Why not?"

"Because." She sighs. "What happens after, when we go off to college?"

"We figure it out." I shrug, because to me, it's as simple as that.

"Just like that?"

"Just like that." I roll over so I'm hovering over her.

"Emmett, you can't know—"

I skim my thumb over her cheekbone, lean down and press my mouth against hers, stopping whatever she wanted to say. The words disappear as she melts in my arms. A soft moan escapes her lips as our mouths mash together.

"We can't know, but I'm not going to waste my time thinking about all the ways things could go south, when I can just love you."

I haven't been raised to overthink or to quit. If you want something you'll work hard, and once you get to a problem, you find a way to solve it. Nothing else is an option.

Kate raises her hand, her finger tracing the outline of my mouth. "You make it sound so simple."

"There hasn't been a simpler thing in my life. You're head-strong, stubborn, and loyal to a fault, but I've known you'd be it for me from the moment I laid eyes on you. I love you, Katherine Adams. I love you, and I don't see that changing."

"It's scary."

Kate runs her fingers through my hair, her nails scratching the back of my neck.

"What is?"

"The way you make me feel." With her free hand, she takes one of mine and presses it against her chest. "My heart is thumping so loudly, like it's about to burst any second now."

"Kate..."

She undoes me, slays me to my very core, and just when I think I can't fall harder, she convinces me I'm wrong.

I wonder if it'll ever stop.

I hope not, because I don't want to know a world in which looking into those big blue eyes doesn't make my heart ache with love.

Kate's fingers tighten at the nape of my neck, pulling me closer. Our mouths brush, sending jolts of electricity through my system.

"I love you too, Emmett." Another soft brush of her mouth. "I know I didn't say it back the other day, but you're not alone in this. I love you."

This time when our mouths lock it's different. Deeper, harder, needier. My tongue slides into her mouth with a vengeance. This need to touch her, taste her, feel her, growing inside of me until I feel like I'll burst.

Kate's body arches off the floor, the lace of her dress brushing against me. The dress that's been driving me insane all night long.

"Kate, I need you so badly."

Her eyelashes flutter, those blues of hers dark with need and passion looking up at me. "Show me," she whispers, her fingers brushing against my cheek. "Make love to me."

I look at her for a moment, not sure if she's for real, but there is nothing but love and faith staring back at me.

So, I kiss her.

Disentangling our fingers, I slide my hand up her bare leg, enjoying the smoothness of her skin as I work my way up.

I press my mouth against her neck, inhaling her sweet scent as I pepper the silky skin with kisses, working my way up until my mouth is pressed against hers in a deep kiss.

"Are you sure about this?" I ask, breaking the kiss.

She nods her head, her fingers working the buttons on my shirt. "I need you."

When she gets to the last one, her fingers graze over my crotch. My cock jumps excitedly at her soft touch.

Down, boy.

Inhaling sharply to get some much-needed air into my lungs and clear my mind, if only a little, I help her push the shirt off.

Kate nibbles at her lower lip as she takes me in, her eyes roaming over every inch of exposed skin.

"I want to touch you," she whispers softly.

"I'm all yours, baby."

I take her hand in mine and place it on my skin. We both inhale sharply at the touch. Kate sucks her lip between her teeth, her fingers exploring my naked chest. Her touch burns my flesh, or maybe that's me. Fuck, if I know.

"You remember that first time I was here?" she asks, her eyes fixed on the path she's tracing.

"Y-yes," I answer comes out as a stutter. With her fingers on my skin, I can barely remember my name, much less think coherently.

"That's the first time I saw you shirtless up close and personal, and oh, boy..."

"Yeah, it did seem like the cat got your tongue there for a little while."

"I remember thinking it was so not fair. Teens shouldn't look like you do. It should be against the law or something. After that, I couldn't get the image of you out of my mind."

"I like that."

Kate playfully rolls her eyes. "I figured you would."

Her finger swirls around my nipple, and it hardens instantly. I don't dare move, or breathe for that matter, as her hands slowly glide over my skin, over my pecs, and down between the hollow of my abs.

"Kitty." My voice is like a rough growl even to my own ears.

She looks up through those long eyelashes, releasing her lip. The color rushes to the plump flesh but before I can claim it, Kate pushes me back. I fall down on the pillows, air rushing out of my lungs.

"What are you—"

But before I can finish, she straddles my lap and kisses me.

Groaning, I slip my hand behind her neck, pulling her closer and deepening our kiss. My free hand slides over the side of her leg. Her skin pebbles at my touch, but I don't stop. My fingers skim up and down her flesh, moving deeper under her skirt with every new pass.

"Emmett," she protests, pulling back.

"Hmm?"

Kate kisses and nibbles her way down my body. Shy and tentative. Her cheeks are flushed, but there is fire burning in her irises. When she reaches my pants, she looks up at me. Her tongue peeks out, wetting her lips.

"I'm not sure if I know how to do this."

"We don't have to do it."

"I want to."

With that, she unbuckles my pants and pulls the zipper down. My dick is painfully hard, and even with my help, it takes us a moment to pull the rest of my clothes off.

"Oh..." she breathes as I lean back against my arms, letting her take her fill. Her eyes are wide, pupils dilated. Once again, her tongue slides over her lower lip, and there is no way I can hold back a groan.

"Are you in pain?" Her gaze darts to my face before it lowers once again at my lap.

"Not that kind of pain." I chuckle. "C'mere." I beckon her closer. "You're awfully overdressed, Kitty."

She sits back on my lap, my dick nestling between her thighs. She gasps, her hips rocking against my hard length, the lace of her panties the only barrier between the two of us.

"Does this thing have a zipper?" I ask, nibbling at her neck.

Kate shakes her head.

I trace my tongue over her pulse, feeling the rapid beat of her heart. "You better help me out here, Kitty, or you'll have nothing to wear home later tonight."

"J-just slide." She shifts, her hips rocking and making us both gasp. "S-slide it o-off."

I kiss her, my hands gripping the hem of her dress and pulling it over her head.

"Fuck, Kitty," I rasp, my hands sliding down her sides. The dress was stunning, but seeing her bare like this, in only a matching lace bra and panties, she's simply breathtaking.

"So fucking beautiful." I skim the underside of her bra, tracing the pattern of lace on the cup. Kate shivers slightly, her fingers digging into my shoulders.

"Emmett..." she sighs.

There is a need in her voice that matches the type coursing through my blood.

"Rock against me." My fingers dig into her hips, guiding her movements. "I want to see you come."

"Fuck," Kate hisses, speeding up her movements. Her head falls down, eyes closing. "I don't think—"

"Don't think." I brush my nose over the column of her neck. "Just feel."

With shaky fingers, I unhook her bra. Her tits are in front of me, and I suck one pert tip into my mouth.

"Emmett," she moans softly, tugging at my hair as she pulls me closer, her movements turning jerky. My dick throbs, and it takes everything in me to hold back as Kate chases her release.

"I'm co—" The words die on her tongue as she bites into her lip, her whole body trembling in my arms as she comes.

I wrap my arms around her, loving the weight of her body draped over mine. I can feel her wetness through her panties, the only layer of clothing there still is between us.

Kate continues to grind against me as she comes down from the high, her forehead pressed in the crook of my neck.

"That's it, baby." I press my mouth against her neck feeling her heated, salty skin.

"That was..."

"Good? Amazing? Earth-shattering?" I offer playfully.

Kate pinches me.

"*Ouch.*" I rub at the sore spot. "What?"

"Don't tease."

I push my hips up so she can feel my hard cock. "Does this feel like teasing to you?"

Her eyes grow wide. "You're still..."

"Hard? Fuck, yeah."

At this point, I think I could cut stones with my dick, that's how hard I am. But I'm not about to blurt that out loud and scare her off.

Instead, I brush my mouth against the corner of her lips. "You see what you do to me?"

Kate's mouth presses against mine, and I get lost in her kiss, intoxicated by her apple scent.

"C'mere."

She slides off of me and lies on her back. I move over her, my hands roaming her body until I get to her lower belly. She quivers under my touch as my fingers trace the edge of her panties.

"Are you sure?" I ask again, needing her to be one-hundred percent on board.

She tugs her fingers under the elastic and pushes her panties off without a trace of hesitation. "Yes."

"Let me."

I help slide them all the way down, leaving her completely bare in front of my eyes. The moonlight touches her pale skin, making her look like a goddess.

My goddess.

Not breaking our stare, I search for my pants, grab my wallet, and pull out a condom.

Kate's eyes are glued to me, watching intently as I open the package and put the condom on before getting between her legs.

"Do you know how beautiful you are?"

Kate shivers. "You said it once or twice."

"And mine."

Her eyes soften. "All yours."

I push her legs further apart, settling between them. "Have you ever…" I gulp, unable to finish the sentence. I want to know because that way I can make sure to take care of her, but I also don't want to know.

She shakes her head. "No."

"Fuck, Kitty." Leaning down, I kiss her hard. "This might hurt," I warn, sliding my hands under her thighs.

"Doesn't matter." She cups my cheeks, pressing her forehead against mine. "I want you. Please."

I brush my nose against hers. "I love you."

"I love y—" She sucks in a breath as I slide into her.

Fuck, she's tight. And so fucking perfect.

I push forward, her body stretching to accommodate me.

"Emmett," she cries out, her eyes closing tightly.

"I'm sorry." I start to pull back, but her legs tighten around me.

"N-no," she gulps. "I need you to finish."

"I don't want to hurt you."

"I can take it, please. I need you inside me."

She arches off the bed, her nipples brushing against my skin as she kisses me. Trying to hold on to my sanity, I slowly push back inside, deeper this time. Then I repeat the process, slowly pulling out and sliding inside, keeping an even tempo, so I don't hurt her more than I have to.

"Faster."

"Kitty," I hiss in warning, not sure how long I can hold back.

Her pussy tightens around me, holding on to me every time I try to pull out of her wet heat.

"I need you to go faster."

I grit my teeth, speeding up my tempo. Kate sucks in a breath with every thrust, but when I look at her there is no pain hiding in her irises, on the contrary.

"I love you, Kitty." Leaning closer, I graze my teeth across her shoulder. "What do you need?"

I need her to come because I don't think I have it in me to hold off much longer.

"I-I..."

"I'm barely holding on here, darlin', but I want you to come with me." I slide one of my hands between our bodies, finding her clit. It quivers under my touch. "This?" I flick my thumb over the bud. "Does this help?"

"Y-yes..."

"Fuck, yeah."

I grind my hips into hers, going deeper and deeper and deeper. The pressure at the base of my spine starts to grow.

Our skin is slick, droplets of sweat coating my brow as I try my best to hold back.

Just a little bit longer.

"Emmett," Kate yells, her fingers digging into the skin of my back as her pussy quivers around me.

I speed up my tempo, chasing my own release.

"Fuck, Ka—"

Kate covers my mouth with hers, her tongue sliding inside and capturing my yell. My body tenses as I shoot my release inside her, and only when I'm completely spent does my limp body fall over hers.

I'm not sure how long we stay like that. I know I'm probably crushing her, but Kate doesn't protest, and I'm not about to move if she doesn't ask me. Her soft body is warm underneath me. The smell of the field, sweat, and something that's all Kate cling all around me.

Kate softly runs her fingers through my hair, sending tingles down my spine.

"That was..."

"Good? Amazing? Earth-shattering?" she asks, giggling.

I sink my teeth in the top of her breast softly.

"Hey!"

"Don't tease."

"I was just repeating your earlier words."

"Once in a lifetime," I whisper.

Kate blinks. "What?"

"This." I cup her cheek, sliding my thumb over her swollen lip. "You're my once in a lifetime. I love you, Kate."

She smiles at me. "I love you too, Emmett."

Chapter 29

KATHERINE

"I don't want to go back home," I protest as Emmett takes the turn onto my street a little while later.

His fingers tighten around mine. "I don't want to let you go either."

His eyes look down at me, filled with so much love it's almost too much to bear.

He loves me.

Emmett Santiago loves me.

And we just made love.

I can feel the heat rise up my neck and spread over my cheeks. The corner of Emmett's mouth lifts as if he can see it somehow, although the cab of his truck is shadowed since it's late at night. I look at the dashboard. Little after two AM. Okay, early morning.

After we made love, we just stayed curled together, watching the stars and talking. And kissing. And touching.

It's been the most beautiful night of my life.

We pushed going back as long as we could, but I didn't want to worry Aunt Mabel. I hope this time around she isn't waiting up because that would be mortifying.

Emmett stops by the curb in front of my house, killing the engine.

I look at the dark windows of the house. At least nobody is waiting for me. I turn to Emmett, pouting. "Do I have to?"

"I'm afraid so," he chuckles, his finger skimming over my cheek. "Come to breakfast tomorrow."

"Like with your family?"

He nods. "Mom asked me to invite you. Well, both you and your family. Mabel, Penny... well, everybody."

"Do we have to be there at the crack of dawn?"

"No." Emmett leans down and kisses me. "I'd come to pick you up later. You know, at a reasonable hour so you city girls aren't grumpy."

I shove him away. "Hey, I'm not grumpy!"

"Just when you don't have your coffee," he laughs. "So what do you say?"

"Fine." It's not even a question. "I'll come."

Anything so I can spend more time with him.

A grin spreads over his lips, and he gives me another quick kiss before pulling back. "Wait here."

Emmett gets out of the truck and walks to the passenger side to open the door for me.

"I could have done this on my own, you know."

I slide out of the truck, and Emmett's hands are instantly on my waist, pulling me closer.

"I like spoiling you."

I rise on my tip-toes and press my mouth against his. "Thank you."

"You're welcome."

Hand in hand, Emmett walks me to the front door, giving me one final kiss before I unlock the door.

"I'll wait for you to lock it," he warns.

I nod and grab the handle. "Good night, Emmett."

His thumb slides over my lower lip before he lets his hand fall to his side. "Sweet dreams, Katherine."

Nibbling at my lip to hold in my smile, I blow him a kiss and slip inside.

Dark and quiet greet me on the other side, but I don't bother turning on the light so as not to disturb anybody. I turn the key locking the door.

For a split second, I press my palm against the cool wood. I swear I can feel Emmett on the other side.

I turn around and maneuver my way through the dark. I climb up the stairs and slide into my room, only sighing in relief when I'm safely inside.

With a smile still on my face, I get out of my dress, slip on the jersey I wore earlier today and get into bed.

The events that happened today are going through my mind.

Emmett's smile.

The way he embraced Penny out in the open.

The look in his eyes when he saw me in the dress.

The way his arms felt around me as we slow-danced.

The way his kiss unraveled me from the inside out.

His hands on my body.

The feeling of being home as we became one.

With those memories and a smile tugging at my lips, I let sleep claim me.

———

The door bangs against the wall, startling me awake. "Get up."

The light turns on, blinding me. I jump upright in the bed, the sheet falling into my lap. I blink a few times sleep still clinging to my mind as I try to grasp what's going on. I look around the room, my eyes landing on Mom's back.

"What are you doing?" I ask, my voice groggy from sleep.

My body feels as if I just fell asleep, and doesn't appreciate the interruption. Emmett would probably point out I'm grumpy, but it can't have been that long since I got home. I look at my phone. A little past six? What the hell? I didn't even think Mom had it in her to be up before ten.

"I said, get up." Mom storms toward the wardrobe and starts throwing things out onto the bed.

"Are you crazy? What the fuck?" I jump out of bed, looking at the pile of clothes that just keeps growing.

Mom grabs my bag and shoves it into my hands. "Pack, we're leaving."

"What?" An icy chill enters my bones as her words sink in. "No!"

What the hell is she doing? She can't be serious.

I look at her more closely. She still has on the clothes she wore yesterday, and her hair is a mess, eyes wild.

Unease creeps up my spine, my stomach clenching uncomfortably.

What is going on here?

"I've already booked us the tickets. The plane leaves at eleven so you better get your ass going."

"We can't leave!" I protest, my fingers gripping the bag tighter, when in reality, I want to throw it across the room. "We have school, and—" I try to reason with her because she can't be serious about it, but she's not even listening.

"You'll re-enroll into your old school. I already talked to your principal, and it's all settled."

She what?

"No." I stomp my foot. I feel like a petulant child, but ask me if I care. This is not happening. Not now, not ever.

"You don't get a choice." Mom gets in my face, jabbing her finger in my chest. "Now pack your shit because if you don't I'm going to pack it for you."

I lift my chin. "You can't make me. If you want to go, then leave."

I'm not leaving. Not after everything that happened last night. I can't...

"Fine," Mom grits through clenched teeth, but the look in her eyes stops me from celebrating just yet. "You stay, but Penny and I are leaving."

"What?" My blood turns cold. "You can't take her!"

No. No. No.

This can't be happening.

Mom gives me a smug smile. "If I remember correctly, she's still my daughter. My *underage* daughter. If I say she leaves with me, she leaves."

I grab her hand, pulling her toward me. "You can't do that."

"I can, and I am." She gets in my face, her brows rising. "So what's it going to be, Katherine?"

EMMETT

"You're up early." Mom gives me a quizzical look as I enter the kitchen through the back door.

"Couldn't sleep." I shrug. When I snuck home last night, after leaving Kate at her aunt's house, I couldn't relax enough to fall asleep. I kept tossing and turning. You'd think that everything that happened would leave me exhausted, but nope. There was this suppressed energy that was boiling inside of me, wanting to get out.

"You came home late last night," Mom comments, stirring something on the stove. "Y'all had fun?"

It's amusing seeing her pretend she's all chill, when I know she's dying to get an answer.

"Homecoming was good." I lean against the doorway and tilt my head to the side. "How do you know when I got home? You were asleep."

Mom rolls her eyes. "A mother always knows." There is a slight pause, and then, "Kate coming?"

I look at the clock on the wall. "Yeah, I'll go up to shower and change before I go and pick her up."

"Sounds good. I'll let Dad know."

Pushing off the wall, I cross the room and stop behind her to press a kiss on her cheek. "Thanks, Mom."

"Anytime, darlin'."

I rush up the stairs, taking two at a time, and start unbuttoning my flannel shirt as I cross the hallway to my room.

The bed is still unmade like I left it when I got up earlier to go out and help on the ranch. Ignoring it, I go straight for the dresser and start pulling some fresh clothes out when I see the notification on my phone. I pick it up and check the message.

Kitty: I'm sorry, but maybe this is for the best.

"What the hell?"

I stare at the text, frowning for what feels like forever, trying to comprehend what she's saying, but come up empty.

What is for the best? The hairs at the back of my neck prickle. *What the hell, Kitty?*

"Fuck this."

I press the call button and wait as the phone rings.

And rings.

And fucking rings.

"Goddammit, Kate!"

I try two more times but both end the same.

What the fuck is happening? Where is she? She didn't actually think she could send a cryptic message like that and leave me hanging?

Pulling out my contacts, I dial Becky who thankfully answers almost instantly.

Ignoring the pleasantries, I get right down to it. "Do you know where Kate is?"

"What? Hello, to you too, E—"

"I don't have time for this, Becs." I pound my clenched fist against the dresser. "Do you know where Kate is? Yes or no?"

There is a slight pause. Part of me feels guilty for yelling at her, but I can't help but feel like the time is running out. "No, I don't."

"Shit."

"What's going on, Emmett?"

I run my hand through my hair. "She sent me this weird message, and now she's not answering."

"Weird? Weird how?"

"I don't know, just weird."

Becky groans. "What did it say, Emmett?"

"'I'm sorry, but maybe this is for the best.'"

What is for the best? And best for whom?

Those two questions keep rolling on repeat in my mind.

"What? Why?"

Apparently, I'm not the only one blindsided by all of this. Not that it makes me feel any better.

"If I knew I wouldn't be talking to you now," I snap.

"Did something happen last night?"

The events of last night flash in front of my eyes. Kate looking stunning in that dress. Dancing together at homecoming. Undressing her in the bed of my truck. Making love under the stars.

"No," I croak, my throat tight. "Last night was perfect." So fucking perfect that this makes even less sense. *Fuck this.* I turn around and go for the door. "I'm going over there."

"I'm coming with you," Becky says immediately, and I can hear some rustling in the background.

"No."

"Ha, try to stop me." With that, she hangs up.

Cursing, I shove my phone into my pocket and rebutton my shirt as I descend the stairs.

Mom peeks out of the kitchen. "Are you already done?" She frowns when she sees my face. "Did something happen?"

"I have to go, sorry, Mom."

"But what about the—"

I don't hear the rest because the front door shuts behind me before she can finish, and, in the process, I almost crash into Bradley.

"Whoa, there." He puts his hands on my shoulders to steady me. "What's the rush?"

"Sorry, something's going on with Kate..." I shake my head, walking around him. "I've got to go."

"What—"

Done with listening to questions to which I don't have an answer, I hurry to my truck, which is thankfully parked just in front of the house, and get out of there.

What the hell is going on, Kate?

"Hold your horses. I'm coming!" Kate's aunt yells from the other side of the door. She pulls the door open just as I'm about to knock again. "Emmett? What are you doing here?"

"Where is she?" I ask, my breathing labored as I push my way inside. "Where is Kate?"

I look around, hoping, praying really, that Kate will come down the stairs or out of one of the rooms and tell me I've got it all wrong, but it doesn't happen, so I turn my attention to Mabel Adams.

Realization dawns on her, and her face falls.

"What? What happened?"

I want to put my hands on her shoulders and shake her until she tells me what the fuck is happening here.

"She's gone."

"What?" I take a step back. "What do you mean, she's gone?"

She can't be gone. That's not how it works. Besides, she'd have told me. Wouldn't she?

After everything that happened last night, she would have told me if she was planning to leave.

Mabel sighs. "They left a little while ago. Mary decided it's best for them to go back home."

"And you just let them leave?" I yell at her, unable to hold in the rage that's been accumulating since I saw the message any longer.

Best for them? What's that? A phrase of the day? Un-fucking-believable. In what fucking universe is that what's best for them?

If Kate told me what happened with Penelope back in California, her aunt must know something, too. She can't actually believe that shit. It's not best for them to go back to the place that hurt them both so badly in different ways.

"What was I supposed to do?" She crosses her arms over her chest defensively, but I can see her lips wobble a bit. "She's their mother."

Un-fucking-believable.

"Where did they go?"

"What..."

"Where did they go?" I repeat, not in the mood to mess around. God only knows how much time they have on me. Can I even catch up? Maybe they took the bus, and they're already on their way to California.

No. I shake my head, trying to clear my mind. *No, I'm not going there.*

She can't be gone. She can't leave. I won't let her.

Not without a fight.

"To the airport, but—"

"Thank you," I mutter and turn on the balls of my feet. There is an hour-long drive ahead of me. Maybe I could make it in forty. Depending on the road I take. But maybe...

"Where are you going?" Miss Adams calls after me.

Is she for real?

"To get them."

"You don't really think you can stop them?"

"I can do my best to try." I look over my shoulder. "Kate and Penny... they belong here."

In this little town. With us. With *me.*

"I know, and as much as it pains me to watch them go..."

"Then you should have stopped them!" Miss Adams flinches at my harsh tone. *Dammit.* "I'm sorry for yelling, ma'am, but I can't waste any more time. And I can't let her go without doing my best to try and get her to stay."

"It's not up to her."

Her words feel cryptic somehow, like there is more hiding behind them than the plain obvious, but I push it back because there isn't much time. And even if there were, it wouldn't change the outcome.

"I don't care. I have to try."

At least I have to let her know that whatever happens, nothing between us changes.

Nothing.

"Emmett."

"I don't have ti—"

This time when I turn around, I find her grabbing her bag.

"I'm coming with you."

Chapter 30

KATHERINE

"I'm sorry, ma'am, but you should have given us notice that you'd be traveling with a guide dog," the clerk behind the counter says evenly, keeping his professional face on the whole time.

Mom clenches her teeth, her face turning red, which is a sure sign that she's losing it. But I have to give it to him; he doesn't even flinch.

"Well, I didn't know that! Shouldn't those things be allowed everywhere?"

"They are, ma'am." The clerk nods. "But there are procedures that need to be followed when we have an animal onboard."

Mom clenches her fingers into a fist and pounds it against the counter. Penny jumps a little at the sound that echoes, even in the busy airport. Her fingers dig into the skin of my upper arm. "What's going on?" she whispers softly. Not that Mom's paying us any attention, she's too busy yelling at the clerk, demanding her rights.

"Mom's just being Mom," I reply dryly.

People start turning around, looking at us like we're crazy. Or maybe just unstable. Probably a little bit of both.

"We should have stayed home. I don't want to go back."

Penny turns to look at me, her unseeing eyes wide, every line of her face filled with worry.

I tuck a runaway strand behind her ear. "It's going to be okay. We're going to be okay."

"But what about you and Emmett?"

Just hearing his name is like a punch to my gut. I hate myself for sending him that message, but I didn't know what else to say. And I didn't have time to think it through, not with Mom's threat hanging around my neck.

"Where's his passport?" Mom turns around to glare at us.

"W-what?"

I've completely tuned out her part of the conversation with the guy behind the counter.

"Where's the little shit's passport?" Mom hisses. "ID? Or whatever the fuck he needs." Henry starts growling. "For fuck's sake, control the beast." She shakes her head. "I knew we should have left him at your aunt's."

I step in front of Penny and still-growling Henry. "Don't talk to her like that." I move closer, keeping my voice quiet. "And for all that's holy, please keep your voice down. You're making a scene."

"I. Don't. Care," Mom mutters slowly, glaring at me. "Papers, Penelope."

"I-I d-don't have them."

"What?!" Her head snaps up abruptly, and she looks over my shoulder at Penny. "What do you mean you don't have them?"

"Ma'am, I'm sorry, but if you don't have all the documents required to check-in, I have to ask you to step aside," the clerk chips in.

Mom turns around and glares at the man. "I have the tickets, and you *will* check us in."

"I'm sorry, but if you don't have the documents required for the guide dog, we can't let you on that plane."

Mom turns her ire on the poor man, giving me a moment to figure out what's going on. My heart is already thumping rapidly at the hope that maybe, just *maybe*, we might get out of this.

I turn to Penny, putting my hands on her shoulders as I whisper. "You didn't bring Henry's papers?"

"No." Penny shakes her head, tears gathering in her eyes as she keeps fumbling with her bag. "I thought I did, but they're not in my bag. I think I left them with Aunt Mabel the last time we took Henry to the vet? I don't know."

"It's okay. It's not your fault."

Mom's yelling becomes louder, making Penelope more agitated.

"Katherine!" I hear my name being called, but Mom and her tantrums can wait.

"I didn't mean to forget..." Penny hiccups, and I wrap my arms around her.

"Hey, it's okay." Pulling back so I can see her face, I brush away her tears. "Things like that happen. We'll go back and get it. No biggie."

"But Mom's mad. I told her when she woke me up that I don't want to go, now she'll think I did it on purpose."

"Of course, she won't." If Mom was going to do this, she shouldn't have put us on the spot, Penny especially, and think this would end up well for anybody. If there's somebody to blame, it's definitely her. "Come on now, no crying."

"Kate!"

There it is, once again.

I'm about to turn around and tell her to chill when my mind registers the voice.

My whole body stops.

It can't be.

My heart starts racing so fast I think it'll beat out of my chest. This time I do turn around, looking for the person calling out my name.

Don't be stupid, Kate. It can't be. Whoever it is, is probably calling out to somebody else.

"Katherine!"

My eyes land on his, finding him among the hundreds of people surrounding us. I suck in a breath as the world underneath my feet shifts.

"Kate."

This time his voice is gentler. He stops in his tracks like he too can't believe he's seeing me.

But it's him.

It's him.

"Emmett," I breathe, not wanting to hope this is real.

He's here.

He came.

As if the sound of my voice snaps something inside of him, Emmett starts moving again, determination written in every line of his face, every stride he takes in my direction.

There are people between us, but he moves as if they're not there, not stopping once until his hands are on me.

He pulls me into his arms, lifting me off the ground. I wrap my arms around his neck and bury my head in the crook of his shoulder.

"Emmett."

"I'm here," he whispers, his grip tightening to the point it hurts. Not that I care one bit. *He's here.* "You're here. I thought I'd be too late."

"What—"

I don't get to finish because the next thing I know, he's kissing me. His mouth is pressed against mine, and there is nothing gentle about his touch. It's hard and bruising, marking me. His hands dig into my hair as he holds me still, his mouth sweeping over mine.

"Kate!" A hand falls on my shoulder, pulling me back. "What the hell do you think you're doing?" She turns to Emmett, her eyes narrowing even further. "What do *you* think you're doing? We're leaving!"

"No," Emmett says almost instantly. He pushes Mom's hand away and pulls me into his side.

"No? Who do you think you are?"

"Kate's boyfriend, and I'm not going to let you take her." Emmett's grip on me tightens.

"*Let me?* What makes you think you have a say? I'm their mother."

By now, we've moved out of line, but people still stare and grumble in our direction.

"Kate?"

My head snaps up at the sound of Penny's voice. She's holding tightly onto Henry's harness, looking around in complete confusion. Slipping out of Emmett's embrace, I go straight to her.

"I'm here."

"What's going on? I swear I heard Emmett—"

"You heard right, Little Adams," Emmett says, giving her hand a squeeze. But when he turns his attention back to our mother, the reassuring and loving man is gone. "A mother who doesn't give two shits about them, yeah, we all got that part."

Mom flinches back like he slapped her, red coloring her cheeks.

"Listen to me you..."

"What's the deal with leaving so suddenly anyway?" I ask the question that's been bugging me since she barged into my room. "Why let us come here in the first place if you planned to drag us back home in a few weeks?"

Something must have happened to make her snap like this. I just don't see what.

Mom glares at me. "Things have changed. But we're leaving. I'll call Mabel and tell her to get the stupid documents for the dog, and then get that imbecile at the counter to find us the first flight out. But we're leaving this godforsaken town today. Penny, let's go." Mom tries to grab for her, but Emmett pushes Penny behind his back.

"I don't think so."

"I swear to you, boy, if you don't get out of my way..."

"Mary!"

I turn around at the sound of Aunt Mabel's voice. She's breathing hard, her hair is a complete mess, and her cheeks are red like she ran all the way here. That's because she probably did.

"Of course, this is your doing!" Mom hisses. "Seriously, Mabel?"

"Let the girls stay," she pants, pressing her hand against her chest to control her erratic breathing. "They want to be here."

"They're my daughters, you have no right..."

"They're happy here."

"They were happy at home, too!"

"No, we weren't." I look at my mom. Really look at her. Can't she see what she's doing? "We weren't happy there. Penny wasn't *safe* there. She needed help, and she got it. *Here*, she got it here."

Mom shakes her head, her eyes wandering around the airport. "You can't stay here."

"Why not? You let us come. What changed?" I ask softly,

hoping my tone helps her relax and maybe see things from our perspective.

"It doesn't—"

"Tell her, Mary," Mabel says, moving closer to our group. We probably seem like a bunch of weirdos to people, but nobody's tried to kick us out. Yet.

Mom glares at her sister. "Don't tell me what to do, Mabel. And don't get between my daughters and me."

"You need to tell her. You should have done it ages ago."

"Tell who what?"

I look between the two of them, completely confused by this turn of events. I knew there had to be a reason why we never visited, why Mom was so opposed to us coming in the beginning, but what?

Mabel ignores me, her attention completely on Mom. "If you don't do it, I will."

"What is going on?" Penny whispers, clinging to Emmett, who looks equally confused.

"You don't have a right!" Mom points her finger at Mabel. "No right."

"No, *you* don't have the right to keep doing what you did."

Icy chills run down my spine. "What did you do, Mom?"

"It's none of your business."

I turn to Mabel. "What did she do?"

Mabel's face softens, and I can see her fighting whatever she needs to say.

"Your mom." Her throat bobs as she swallows. "She lied."

"Mabel, don't you dare..."

"Your dad, he lives here." The words come out in a rush. "In Bluebonnet."

"W-what?"

I pull back, looking between the two of them, Aunt Mabel's words echoing in my mind.

This isn't true. I shake my head, looking between the two of them. *It can't be.*

"Dammit, Mabel!" Mom stomps her foot. "You had no right!"

"You should have thought about it before. You can't just take her from here. From *him*. Not after all these years. He should damn well sue your ass."

I can hear them fighting, but all my mind can think about is what Mabel said.

I have a dad.

In Bluebonnet.

He's been here all this time.

Have I met him?

Who is he?

Does he know?

If he does, why didn't he say anything?

So many questions and not one answer.

"Kate?" Emmett crouches down in front of me so we're eye to eye. "Breathe, darlin'. Just breathe."

He looks worriedly at me. His big hands are placed on my shoulders, steadying me.

I suck in a breath, trying to concentrate on his eyes, the warmth of his touch, letting the familiar feeling of him ground me when it feels like the world is shattering under my feet.

"I'm okay." I'm not sure who I am trying to reassure, him or myself. "I'm okay."

Mom and Mabel are still fighting. How can they fight after the bomb they just dropped on me?

"Who is he?" I croak out the question, but neither of them hears me.

Irritated, I get between the two of them and face my mother. "Who is he?" I yell at her, done with the secrets, done with being ignored, just done. I need some answers, and I need them *now*.

"Kate, I—"

"Who is he?" I repeat for the third time, shaking her. "You owe me that much."

She must see the determination in my eyes because she finally gives in. "Bradley Jones."

"Bradley Jones?" I whisper, more to myself than to anybody else. I can hear Emmett mutter something behind me, but I can't concentrate on what he's saying.

Bradley Jones is my father?

The charming, Stetson-wearing, handyman Bradley Jones? My gut tightens, and it feels like I'm going to puke.

I've met the man. Talked to him. Joked with him. Not once knowing...

"Why?"

Why didn't you tell me?

Why now?

Why him?

Why?

Why?

Why?

Mom shrugs her shoulders, not an ounce of regret registering on her face. "It never seemed to matter."

"Never seemed to matter?" I yell at her, finally losing it. "Never seemed to matter? It's my life we're talking about! My father!"

"It was just the two of us, and then Penny came, so it was just the three of us against the world."

"It was never the three of us!" I scream at her, hot tears burning my eyes. "It was Penny and I scraping for bits and pieces and trying to hold it together while you were out there chasing your dreams. So don't tell me it was ever the three of us."

"Kate..." She tries to reach for me, but I get away from her touch, not wanting her anywhere near me.

"Go to California, Mary."

"But..." She tries to reach for me, but I pull back before she can touch me. I don't think I'd be able to stand her touch right now. It's all too much as it is.

"Go to California, but we're staying here."

She presses her lips in a tight line. "Fine. Penny, come."

"No."

Penny comes to me, wrapping her arms around my middle. It feels good to have her close. Familiar. The one person who's been there all this time. The one person, one family member who hasn't kept secrets nor lied.

"Your sister can stay, but you're coming with me."

"No, I'm not. I want to stay with Kate. Besides, Henry doesn't have his documents so we can't go anyway."

Mom glares at the two of us. "Fine, suit yourself. But don't come crying to me when this is all done."

With those parting words, she turns around and forces her way to the front of the line where our bags have been pushed to the side, not once looking back.

"That was..." Emmett shakes his head, at a loss for words. Not that I can blame him. I'm still too dumbfounded myself.

"Yeah," I agree.

He opens his arms, and I go willingly, needing him to hold me.

"It's just all messed up."

"But you're here. That's all that matters."

"I'm here."

Staying in the town where my father lives.

Emmett brushes his lips against my forehead. "Let me grab your bags, and then we're getting out of here."

"Okay."

Emmett starts to pull away, but I tighten my hold on him. "Emmett?"

"Kitty?"

"Thank you for coming for me."

His face softens, the love showing in his eyes. "You're my once in a lifetime, Kitty. I'll always come for you."

Chapter 31

KATHERINE

"Well, that was an eventful day," I mutter as we get out of the truck once Emmett parks it in front of Aunt Mabel's house.

Our house.

"Kate!"

I turn around at the sound of my name just in time for Becky to crash into me, wrapping me into a hug.

"Becs, give her some space to breathe," Emmett chuckles, his hand brushing against the small of my back.

"I was so worried when I got here, and I didn't find anybody. Well, anybody except..." she looks over her shoulder, and I follow her line of sight.

"And apparently, it's not done just yet," Emmett mutters quietly, but my gaze is glued to Bradley Jones, who's just getting up on his feet. He brushes his palms against the sides of his legs as he watches us.

Bradley Jones.

My father.

I still can't wrap my mind around it. It feels surreal. But he's standing *right there*.

"Do you want me to stay with you?" Emmett leans down to whisper in my ear.

"I—" I suck in a breath and then shake my head. "No, I'm good."

"What's going on here?" Becky asks, looking completely confused. Who could blame her? It's hard for me to wrap my head around it, too.

Emmett just shakes his head, and Becky closes her mouth.

"Let's give them a moment, okay?" Emmett gives me a reassuring smile. Kissing the top of my head, he locks his hand with Penny's. "C'mon, Little Adams. I hear there is some unpacking that needs to be done."

Aunt Mabel offers me a smile before following the other three toward the house. I stand, glued to the spot like a statue. There is a soft *click* when the front door closes, leaving me alone with Bradley.

"Hey," he says, the first to break the ice.

I watch him, not knowing what to say. What to do? There are so many things that are going through my mind, but above all, I'm not ready. I didn't expect to find him standing on our front porch, waiting for me.

I figured there'd be time. Time for me to process everything, come to terms with the fact that Mom has been lying to me, and I've been living in the same town as my father for the past few weeks, talked to him, and not once did I suspect...

"Did you know?" My voice is rough from crying, sounding harsh even to my own ears. "Did you know that first day?"

He shakes his head, a small, sad smile playing on his lips. "That attitude, it's all Mary."

I press my lips together, not amused in the slightest at the comparison. I still don't know what to do with the fact that Mom lied to me. All my life, she lied to me.

"But to answer your question. Yes, I had my suspicions."

"Then why—" I swallow, trying to get the words out. "How—"

God, I'm such a mess I don't even know what to ask. Where to start.

Bradley must feel it somehow because he takes pity on me.

"It was the lines of your face." His eyes look at my face intently, and I can't help but wonder, what does he see when he looks at me? His throat works as he swallows. "And your smile. Your smile is all Abbie."

"Abbie?"

I don't remember hearing that name.

"My sister."

"Oh."

"She died in an accident," he explains. There is a faraway look in his eyes that speaks of sadness and heartache that feels familiar. "Little after I moved to California with Mary. My family needed me so I came back, but Mary, well..."

"I'm sorry, I didn't—"

"It's okay," he interrupts me. "It was a long time ago."

A heavy silence falls over us. Uncomfortable, I shift my weight from one leg to the other, but when even that doesn't help, I finally give in, walking to the porch and sitting down on the step. Bradley sits down next to me on the other side of the step.

"Why didn't you say anything?" I ask once I can't take the quiet any longer.

He shrugs. "I didn't know for sure. I wasn't about to say something just based on a suspicion. Who does that?"

Who indeed?

"Then Mary came and..."

"You confronted her," I finished. That was the reason why she never came back home. Why she never let us come here to visit. Why she wanted us to leave so quickly.

To keep up her *lie.*

"She wasn't really forthcoming. There's been a lot of bad blood between us."

I could only imagine. Mom has never been forthcoming about anything that didn't benefit her.

"So I've heard. Still, it doesn't give her the right to lie to me. All my life I thought…" I shake my head. "It doesn't even matter any longer, does it?"

Bradley lifts his hand, as if he's going to reach for me, but then thinks better of it.

"If I knew…"

"But you didn't. Neither of us did."

I look at Bradley. His dark eyes, sun-kissed skin, crinkles in the corner of his eyes, his square jaw. I try to find myself in the lines of his face but come up empty-handed, so instead, I observe him intently, hoping to memorize his face, as though if I close my eyes only for a moment, he'll disappear for good.

"What happens now?" I ask quietly. So quietly that I'm not sure he can hear the question. But he does.

"Whatever you want to happen. I'm not going to force you into anything, but…" Once again, he brushes his palms against the sides of his worn Levi's. Probably his nervous tic. For some reason, that makes me feel slightly better. Less alone in the mess of Mary Adams's creation. "But I'd like to get to know you. I know it won't make up for all the lost time, but it's a start."

I look down at my lap, my fingers fidgeting. There is a slight sliver of hope that blooms in my chest.

"I don't know… Penny…"

"She could come, too." I look up instantly, surprised by his words and the sincerity in his voice. "We could have breakfast one day. When you're ready."

"I— That sounds nice."

"You—" He seems surprised for a moment, but then the corners of his lips lift in a half-smile. "It does."

EMMETT

"So, how did it go?" I wrap my arms around Kate from behind, leaning my head on her shoulder.

I had this need to touch her from the moment I laid eyes on her at the airport, just to make sure she's real.

She's here.

And she's not going anywhere.

Kate puts the last of her things in her closet before leaning against me. "It went... Okay? I guess." She pushes a strand of her hair behind her ear. "I mean, I'm no expert on meeting a father you never thought existed and trying to figure out where to go from there."

I chuckle. "No, I guess not."

"I always thought he was some nameless guy. Just one of the many that passed through our house when I was little. Just like Penny's dad. I never thought..." She shakes her head, at a loss for words.

I tighten my hold on her, brushing my lips against her temple. "Nobody can blame you; it all just seems surreal."

"Right?" Kate turns in my arms, her fingers skimming over my cheekbone. "I wanted to stay," she says quietly. "I wanted to stay so badly, but she..."

"Shhh..." I tighten my grip on her, swaying us from side to side. "I know, baby. It's okay."

"She threatened to take Penny, Emmett. Back to that place that drove her to darkness, and I couldn't..." She chokes on the words, all the emotions finally crashing down. "I had to pick her."

"I know, baby. I know."

God, I hate that woman. How can she be so selfish? So self-centered?

Kate pulls back. Her eyes are red-rimmed and filled with tears. Still, she's the most beautiful person I've ever met.

"I'll always have to pick her, Emmett. Always."

One tear slips down, followed by another.

I cup her cheek, brushing away her tears. "And that's why I love you. And I'll always come for you. Both of you."

"You can't." Kate shakes her head. "You shouldn't—"

I press my mouth against hers, kissing the protest away.

"Don't tell me what to do, Kitty. It won't make any difference. I love you, and there is nothing that will stand in my way. Not now, not tomorrow, or in a year. You're my endgame. My once in a lifetime."

"I don't want to stand in your way or drag you down."

"There is no chance of that ever happening."

"How do you know? How can you..."

I press my finger against her lips, shushing her. "Because I just know you. And that's enough. I meant what I told you. There is nothing that could ever compare to a future with you. And I'm going to try my damnedest to make that future a reality. You and me, Kitty."

"You and me." She lifts on the tips of her toes and presses her lips against mine. I can taste the saltiness of her tears on her mouth, her tongue. "I love you, Emmett."

I press my forehead against hers. "I love you too, Katherine."

"Hey, Emmett?"

"Hmmm?" I nuzzle my nose against the side of her neck, smelling her sweet scent.

"I kissed you first."

"I guess I better kiss you back." I brush my nose against hers, making her chuckle.

"Yeah, you better."

So, that's what I do.

Over and over and over again.

Epilogue

KATHERINE

SENIOR YEAR

"Hey there."

I look to the side to see Bradley coming toward me. He leans against the wooden railing next to me, his trusty black Stetson sitting on top of his head, shielding his eyes from the late afternoon sun.

"Hey, I didn't think I'd see you today. Emmett said you guys were working out in the fields."

"We are, but I had to come back to grab some tools to fix one of the fences, and I saw you guys, so I figured I might stop by quickly to say hi."

I nod, turning my attention forward once again at the sound of my sister's laugh.

I can't believe it's been a year. A year since we moved here. A year since I found out that I have a dad. An actual *dad*. Not some good for nothing, wanna-be actor Mom hooked up with, but a dad who wants me and embraces both my half-sister and me with open arms.

It has been far from easy. In the beginning, it was downright awkward trying to navigate this new normal, but after this year, I can actually say we've made progress in the right direction.

We're keeping our Sunday breakfast, and two times a week Bradley joins us at our house for dinner, or we go out to eat together.

"She's doing really great out there," Bradley comments.

"She is, isn't she?"

Together we watch Emmett and Penny ride across the field on Thunder. Penny is sitting in front of Emmett, holding onto the reins as Emmett guides her and the horse.

After months of getting two pairs of puppy-dog eyes, I finally gave in and let Penny ride with Emmett. He's one of the rare few I'd ever trust with my sister's safety, so it's not like I had too much ground to stand on to protest. But seeing her out there, a beaming smile on her lips, her laughter carried by the wind, I'm happy that she has this moment. That she has Emmett, period.

"He's so good to her. I don't think I could have asked for a better boyfriend even if I tried."

"You guys doing okay?"

"We are." I nod, a small smile curling my lips. Thinking about Emmett always brings a smile to my face. We've been inseparable since we got together, but I couldn't imagine it being any other way. "The school year has barely started, but it's going to be a busy one, between turning in our applications for college, my job, and Emmett's football."

Last year, shortly after Mom left for California, this time for good, it seems, I was sitting at the diner talking to Mrs. Letty when she asked me if I'd like to work for her part-time. Since then, I've been working there a few afternoons a week.

Mom, well, she's been in California since last fall. We talk occasionally, although it's been far from easy. A little part of me still hates her for keeping Bradley a secret, but the rational part of me understands that it's just the way she is. I can either accept it and move on or remove her from my life. And I can't do that, because I can see that Penny, although happy here, misses her. The last time we heard from her, she actually seemed happy since she got a supporting role in some sitcom.

"Any idea where you want to go yet?" Bradley asks casually.

I know he's been wondering about it but had tried not to ask too many questions because I didn't want to look too far in the future.

No matter how much I tried, a small part of me is still afraid of people leaving. And the idea of going to college terrifies me.

What if Emmett and I don't get into the same school? What if we end up thousands of miles apart? I don't think I'd be able to take it.

Emmett and I have become inseparable, and I can't imagine not seeing him every single day.

The familiar fear rises in my throat, asphyxiating me. Inhaling through my nose, I force my lips to part, my tongue sliding out to wet the dry flesh.

"I have a few ideas."

"Really? I didn't..."

The sound of a steady trot grows louder, and Emmett pulls Thunder to a stop by the fence.

"Hey there, Bradley! What brings you here?"

I shield my eyes and slowly work my way up to meet Emmett's eyes. Between helping his dad on the ranch and keeping up with his football conditioning, he's added some muscle over the summer, but he looks even bigger sitting on top of the horse, his strong arm wrapped protectively around my sister's middle.

"Just came here to say hi. Looking good out there, Penny."

"Thank you, Bradley. I'm really enjoying it, and Thunder is

a good boy, aren't you?" she coos, nuzzling her face into the horse's mane.

"Penny's been an amazing student." Emmett grins proudly. "You wanna give it a try, Kitty?"

I look at the beast of an animal standing in front of me. "Yeah, I think not."

"It's not that scary." Penny rolls her eyes. Now that she's gotten on the horse, she's determined I do the same. I, however, don't share her obsession with the animals since I don't have any desire to break my neck anytime soon. "Besides, Emmett will take good care of you."

"You hear, Kitty? I'm going to take very good care of you."

"I'm good, really. But you two enjoy."

"Party pooper." Emmett pouts. "What do you say, Penny? Wanna go try jumping next?"

"What?" I shriek. He can't be serious, can he? Because that most definitely was *not* part of our deal.

"Yes!" Penny claps excitedly. "Let's do it."

Like hell.

"Emmett Santiago, you better not—"

Bradley chuckles, reminding me we're not alone. "I guess I'll leave you to it."

I sigh and turn to face him. "Talk later?"

"Tomorrow morning?"

"Same time, same place."

"Sounds like a plan."

I look over my shoulder at Penny and Emmett galloping away. From the corner of my eye, I see Bradley move. He places his hand on my shoulder and gives me a quick squeeze. "Don't be too hard on him, okay?"

"We'll see about that."

EMMETT

"Are you cold?" I look down at Kate as a shiver runs through her body.

"Nah, it's oka—" she starts to protest, but before she can finish, I'm already taking off my plaid shirt and draping it over her shoulders.

"What about you?"

"I figured you'd know by now that I'm running hot."

I throw my hand over her shoulder and pull her into my side. She snuggles tightly against me, her arms wrapping around my middle. "True. Every time you hug me, I get all toasty. Do you think I could request it as a standard room temperature?"

I chuckle. "I don't think it works that way, darlin'."

"Well." She pouts. "Talk about a bummer."

This time I can't help but laugh. She's so cute when she gets this way.

In silence, we walk the rest of the way to the pond. Mom offered to drive Penny home after dinner so Kate and I could have a moment alone together.

I love that my parents embraced both Kate and Penny like they're their own daughters. They both come to the ranch often, and sometimes even their aunt and Bradley join us all for dinner. Just last week, Kate and Penny helped Mom bake cookies for the ranch hands for our annual end of the summer party.

When we get to the pond, we get down on the dock, scooting our legs over the edge. I open the blanket I've been carrying to wrap it around us, and Kate snuggles into my side, resting her head on my shoulder.

I lean down, placing my lips on top of her head in a gentle kiss, and inhale her sweet apple scent that's become as familiar as my own.

"What are you thinking about?"

She's been quiet since early this afternoon, but I didn't want to ask her about it in front of my parents and her sister.

"Things."

"What kind of things?"

"Future."

Her voice is so soft it's barely a whisper.

"What about the future?" I ask softly. My finger slides under her chin, and I turn her head toward me so I can look into her eyes. I don't like the distant tone I can hear in her voice. The one she used in the beginning, just after she got here.

"What's going to happen next year." Those blue eyes of hers are distant and unfocused as she says the words. Her tongue darts out, sliding over her lip. "When we go to college."

Everything in me stills. We haven't talked much about the future. I know thinking too far in advance unsettles her, and I... well, there is nothing for me to think about. I know what's in my future. What's in *our* future.

"I want you to go with me."

Kate blinks, her eyes focusing on me. "W-what?"

"Hear me out, okay?" I let my hand fall down, so I can take her hands in mine. "I know it's selfish, and I know it's not fair of me to ask, but I want you to go with me. You and Penny, you guys are my future."

"You want us to apply to the same college?" she asks, as if the thought hasn't even crossed her mind.

"Yeah, we can sit down, check everything out, find places that we'll both like."

"But you have colleges scouting you. We're talking about Ivy League schools here, Emmett, and I don't think..."

I lean down and kiss her, stopping any protest from passing her lips. As always, she melts into me, her fingers digging into my shirt, holding on to me, as my tongue slides into her mouth and tangles with hers. My fingers dig into her hair, tilting her head just slightly to get better access. A soft moan rips from her throat.

Sighing, I break the kiss, slowly pulling away.

"I don't care about the Ivy League schools. I don't care about football. The only thing I care about is you, Kate."

Kate slowly pries her eyes open, her blue irises dark with need.

"You can't mean that."

"But I do. You're the most important person in my life, darlin'. My once in a lifetime, and nothing, and I really mean *nothing*, will ever get in the way of that."

"Oh, Emmett..." Kate cups my cheek and presses her forehead against mine.

"Once in a lifetime, Katherine Adams." I brush her hair off her face. "Say you'll go with me."

"I'll go with you." She kisses me. "You're my once in a lifetime too, Emmett Santiago."

"Good, because if you said no, I'd have to take you with me the old-fashioned way."

"And how's that?" Kate chuckles.

I get to my feet quickly and pull her up. Bending down, I throw her over my shoulder.

"Emmett!" Kate yells in protest, but I can hear the laughter in her voice.

"Caveman style, of course."

"Put me down!"

"I don't think I will. Not before you pay up, at least."

"And how should I pay up? Because I think I feel dizzy hanging like this."

I pull her upright but don't let her down. She throws her head back to get her hair out of her face. Tightening my hold on her with my right arm, I push the strand that got stuck out of the way.

"Why, you've gotta kiss me first, darlin'."

Thank you so much for reading! Want more of Kate and Emmett? Grab your bonus epilogue here! Or you can continue with Blairwood University series with Kiss To Conquer, an enemies-to-lovers sports romance where you'll see more of Emmett and Kate as supporting characters.

Want to stay in touch with Anna? Join her newsletter or reader's group for the latest updates.

Bloggers, bookstagrammers and reader's: join Anna's master list to be first to know about all Anna's upcoming book news!

ACKNOWLEDGMENTS

You didn't see this one coming, now did you? I feel like, at this point, I keep repeating myself. But it's true, not all my stories are planned. When I first created Emmett and Katherine, they were these characters in the background, an already formed couple that help move the storyline along. Not all the jocks have to be manwhores; some are genuinely nice guys. And this guy already got his girl.

I never thought too much about how it happened until I got to that one part of Zane's story in which Emmett is talking about Kate and mentioning their relationship. And my brain instantly started to wonder, but how did they get together? And once I started thinking about it, my heart wasn't content with summing it up in just a few sentences; no, the whole story had to come out.

If you follow me on social media, I did talk a little bit about how I had a hard time sticking to one book after finishing *Kiss To Forget*—not because I didn't like the characters or because I wasn't inspired. Sometimes my mind just needs to process things, and that process is different depending on the characters and storyline. While I had to mull over Zane and Jackson, I was ready to dive right into *Kiss Me First*.

I hope that you enjoyed this unexpected surprise and glimpse into the world of Emmett and Katherine. We'll be seeing more of them as they go off to college and make new friends. And who knows, maybe one day, I'll take you back to Bluebonnet Creek, Texas!

A big thank you to my beta team, both old and new members. I can't tell you how much you girls help me when it comes to working through my ideas on how to make this story perfect. And also, thank you for helping this little foreigner bring some southern charm to the pages of *Kiss Me First*.

Thank you to Lindee for creating a stunning photo that just screamed Kate and Emmett, and to my lovely designer, Najla, who always knows how to make the most beautiful covers.

Thank you to all the bloggers and bookstagrammers who helped me share the news about this release.

And, as always, thank you to you, my readers. Thank you for reading and loving the stories I give you, even though they're sometimes a bit unexpected.

If you have a moment, please consider leaving a short review online.

Until the next book...

xo,
Anna

PLAYLIST

Shawn Mendes - There's Nothing Holdin' Me Back
Calum Scott - You're The Reason
Parachute - Kiss Me Slowly
Ed Sheehan - Perfect
Gabby Barrett - The Good Ones
Morgan Evans - Kiss Somebody
William Michael Morgan - I Met a Girl
Brad Paisley - She's Everything
Brett Young - In Case You Didn't Know
Taylor Swift - Love Story (Taylor's Version)

ABOUT THE AUTHOR

Anna B. Doe is a *USA Today* and international bestselling author of young adult and new adult sports romance. She writes real-life romance that is equal parts sweet and sexy. She's a coffee and chocolate addict. Like her characters, she loves those two things dark, sweet and with a little extra spice.

When she's not working for a living or writing her newest book you can find her reading books, binge-watching TV shows or listening to music while she walks her shi tsu puppy Tina. Originally from Croatia, she is always planning her next trip because wanderlust is in her blood.

She is currently working on various projects. Some more secret than others.

Find more about Anna on her website: www.annabdoe.com

Join Anna's Reader's Group Anna's Bookmantics on Facebook.

Printed in Great Britain
by Amazon

11871460R00187